DIAMOND EDELWEISS

Published by The Cabotte Press 2020

UK edition ISBN 978-1-5272-6485-4

Book cover design by Stefan Proudfoot of Spiffing Covers.

DIAMOND EDELWEISS

ANN KRONBERGS

The Cabotte Press

For ZGK

On turning a rough diamond into a smoother one

PROSPERO ...this thing of darkness I
Acknowledge mine.

William Shakespeare, *The Tempest* (Act V scene i)

The new abbey at Cîteaux was governed according to the fundamental teachings of St.Benedict. The monks' religious enthusiasm and work ethic were renowned. They believed in spartan lifestyle and physically exhausting hard labour. This philosophy apparently led to the Cistercians' decision to cultivate the poor, infertile soil of what today is known as the Côte d'Or. This stretch of limestone hillsides had long proved unsuitable for crops, but the Cistercians, with their commitment to back-breaking labour, believed the vine could be cultivated and quality wine produced. While it may have been just good fortune, it seems more likely that the shrewd monks realized all too well that the production of quality wine, and its presence on the finest tables of Europe, was of greater influence than their most articulate and persuasive diplomat.

Robert M. Parker, JR., *BURGUNDY: A Comprehensive Guide to the Producers, Appellations and Wines.*

Part One

Vera

Prologue: A Homecoming

Home. Always a loaded word.

The taxi driver dropped me at the top end of the street, near the high-rise council flats where the landscaping was softened by horse-chestnut trees. May. Too early for conkers. Here was the best view of Charlton Hill as it descends towards the river. '*Sweete Themmes! runne softly, till I end my Song*'. The rhythm of my footsteps brought back that line from Spenser. I thought of my swotty schoolgirl self, feasting on poetry in a vain attempt to ease an aching heart.

No 73 Albert Way was on the bend in the road, a Victorian end-of-terrace property. Warily I climbed the steps up to the front door with its flaking green paint, but as I pushed my key into the Yale lock it refused to budge. Instinctively I tried the old trick of pulling the brass door handle, whilst twisting the key again. This worked. I stepped into the hallway with its stale smell of cigarettes mingling with undertones of damp. It was a year since I last came back, for my father's funeral. Now I was here to arrange my mother's.

As I closed the front door behind me, the click of my heels on the tiled floor was deafening in the silence. The clock on the hall table had stopped. I was too late. Too sodding late.

I had promised to visit my mother on her birthday at the end of April, but decided to cancel at the last minute.

'Mum, I'm terribly sorry. Another story's come up, would you believe?'

Impossible to mention the real reason for cancelling the visit, which was Hermann's surprise booking of a weekend in Rome whilst his wife was away on a cookery course.

'I've agreed to cover it, so I've re-booked a flight for a fortnight's time.'

There was a pause at the end of the line. She was thinking before she spoke. Always her way.

'Mum, are you O.K.?'

More silence, then she said 'You mustn't worry, Vera. We'll see each other soon. When you have time. Goodbye.'

With that, the line went dead. Her last words to me. Ever.

The unopened milk bottles on the front step were the tell-tale signals. My mother was slumped over the dining table, head resting on her right arm, when the police and Joan, her neighbour from across the road, found her on 6th May. They called me at the Bonn office with the news of her sudden death and a couple of days later the postmortem results confirmed she had had a stroke, followed by a major heart attack.

They told me they had deliberately left the living room as they had found it, for me to sort through. It looked like the scene of a crime. The table was strewn with bundles of papers and letters, an old album. There was a blue fountain pen with its lid off, lying where my mother had been using it, alongside a letter she must have been writing when she died.

73 Albert Way, London, SE7.
4th May 1985

Dear Vera,

I wish I had your talent for putting thoughts into words: I've struggled to find a way of telling my story. There were many times when you came close to guessing the truth about me. But I could never bring myself to tell you what it was.

I learned how to let the sleeping dogs keep lying, that was it I suppose. Marrying your father helped me turn my back on what had happened and from the moment you were born, you made me live in the present with a new kind of hope.

It was only after he died last year that I knew I must put in writing my dark history. Knowing time is not on my side, I have tried to recover what I can and pass it on to you. The memories came in fits and starts. I have kept going to the bitter end in the belief that you will want to read it even if no-one else does. I know you will have the determination to wade through the pages of these notebooks, though the handwriting is very difficult to read.

If I'm no longer around to answer your questions, you will, knowing you, want to find others who can. In the first instance I would suggest you take my papers and documents (which you will find in the lid of the writing case) to …

I had not expected this. I had hoped to make one visit and draw a line forever between the past and the future. What would be the point of trying to breathe life into this litter from the past? Was I obliged to follow my mother's unfinished instruction?

Now, at any rate, there was no time. I had her funeral to organise, I must speak to an estate agent about selling the house. Perhaps I'd leaf through these documents later on, back at the hotel. Perhaps not.

As I was packing all the items into the case, including a pile of notebooks, a small metallic object fell out from one of them and rolled onto the floor. From a distance it looked like an old sixpence, but close up I could see it was an elegant ring made to look like a flower with rows of seed diamonds forming petal shapes around a large sapphire. It was completely at odds with the damp, musty papers, but obviously belonged in a small ring box close to where my mother had been writing. This I slipped into the corner of the case before clicking shut the catches. Then I read the name 'Liliane Lemoine' stamped in the leather of the lid.

But who was she?

Untold secrets. Mysteries to unravel. But not now.

*

In the few days before the funeral I put the house in the hands of an agent and left instructions for the clearance of most of the furniture and effects. I went back a few times to pack up books, records and photographs and to arrange for them to go into store.

The funeral was a small affair at the local crematorium; my mother had had few friends and no family apart from me. Over the years the close relatives on my father's side had died. I had had virtually no contact with cousins and so, in the end, I invited Joan to the short service.

After the brief words of respect and comfort from the minister in charge, we heard the soft rumble of the motor that propelled the coffin into the incinerator. The two of us filed out to the Garden of Remembrance, a place in which the dead would be almost instantly forgotten after the flowers had withered in the small space allotted them. I felt a deep emptiness.

Joan hugged me, tears in her eyes:

'I never really knew your mother, Vera. She never told me much about herself. But I'll miss her.'

Before we parted, I gave her the collection of my mother's Walt Disney figurines, each one wrapped in tissue paper. As she unwrapped the Snow White ornament, her eyes lit up.

'Ahh! You darling girl! She'll always remind me of your mother!'

I suppose it was the jet-black hair, the bob cut and the life of homebound domesticity that made Joan match my mother to her Walt Disney counterpart. My mind travelled back to my last visit a year ago, seeing her come bustling into the living room from the kitchen carrying a tray set with the best bone china cups and saucers, a newly baked cake. She was a small woman wearing a Chanel-style suit she'd made herself, cut from her own patterns.

My school friends used to say 'Your Mum's weird, Vera. Why's she so smart? Why does she wear so much make-up? She's like an actress. Like a mannequin.'

'She's French, that's why.'

That seemed to shut them up.

Though I refused to admit it to them, I knew they were right. Every morning she put on a heavy layer of face powder and rouge to conceal the wrinkles, eye-liner to enhance her sharp, blue eyes. There was always an aura of French perfume about her. *Je Reviens.* Worth. That was it. I pictured her bending down to set the tray on the little coffee table, passing me a cup of strong coffee, held awkwardly in her well-manicured hands, joints swollen with arthritis. She would speak softly, her speech a peculiar blend of estuary English in a stylish French accent.

I couldn't quite believe I'd never see her again.

Meantime I had a holiday booked in Thailand later in

July: Hermann had planned it for us. He'd said I'd love the beaches, the temples, the little restaurants, the anonymity and if he booked it, I couldn't back out.

But I no longer had any interest in this plan. There was a stony silence when I called him to tell him my change of mind. He said, sharply: '*Zum Teufel*!' and slammed the phone down.

What now? *Let sleeping dogs keep lying*, as my mother used to say?

Part Two

Lily

Chapter One:
The Photographs

I never told Sid when I married him that I'd killed a man. Of course, I'd shared some facts with him about my life, given him the edited highlights, as you might say. So he made up a cover story, which he used in his wedding speech.

'Liz fled France during the war. The Jerries took over her small town. Village really. Made life hell for her and her family. She escaped in the nick of time, otherwise she wouldn't be here now, would you, love?'

I tried to smile as I shook my head, putting my arms round him as he went on.

'There's not much I'd thank 'itler for, but let's face it. Liz would not be here if it wasn't for 'im!'

The joke made everyone laugh, me included. And he was almost right.

He had a way of blocking out the past, living only for the present. He hated old keepsakes of any kind. One of the first stories he told me when we met at a dance, early in 1946, was how he had set fire to all the photographs of him in uniform which his mother had put on her mantelpiece.

'I dumped them all in the backyard and set fire to them. That's what I did. Bloody marvellous it was.' Little bits of black confetti, blown away. Gone.

Sid liked to do all the talking and I didn't mind listening, trying to laugh in the right places. Back then, it was easier for me to stay silent. To frown when people spoke too quickly or shrug my shoulders and appear not to understand if they raised tricky questions.

He asked me out a few times. There were kisses in the back row in the Odeon cinema on Saturday nights, holding hands on a country walk in Kent in early spring.

'This is England at its best, Liz. A green and pleasant land. It beats France any day, I bet?'

He paused a bit to see my reaction, but I didn't reply. Then he put his arms round me and said: 'Let's get married, Liz. Right away.' So that's what we did.

I look at the photograph here on the sideboard, taken that day outside the Woolwich Registry Office, 8th May 1946, Sid grinning broadly, dapper in his demob suit, with me on his arm, austere and unsmiling, in a grey woollen dress with a big wide belt and over it a cream swag coat, carrying a bouquet of tulips. Black hair tied back in a bun, eyes looking sideways away from the camera. Evasive. Troubled.

They say opposites attract, don't they? Sid was happy to turn his back on the past and make a new life with me. I found that impossible. At first. I had a daily ritual of opening the writing case to leaf through this album. The photographs showing the faces of people and places I had known paralysed me with grief.

Finally, one day, Sid snatched the album from me: 'Not this again, Liz. For God's sake!'

Without glancing at any of the pictures, he slammed the covers shut.

'Don't sob like that, girl. What good will it do? Watch this.'

Putting the album back in the case, he pressed the lid down and left the room. I listened to his footsteps echoing down the wooden staircase into the cellar. When he came back, he said to me:

'The past is dead and gone, Liz. Believe you me. I've put that old rubbish away. No need to look at it again. Out of sight, out of mind. You remember that, will you?'

There was a frown on his face as he spoke, and he paused awkwardly before giving me his order. 'What about a nice cup of tea, girl? And a slice of that cake!'

Obediently, I went through to the kitchen to fill the kettle and set it on the stove.

Sid's wife. That's who I was now. Elizabeth Walters. The shrill sound of the whistling kettle cut in and I reached out for the brown teapot, warming it first with boiling water the way Sid had taught me to do. Then emptying it down the sink before adding two scoops of tea from the caddy and one for the pot. English tea, the way Sid liked it. Served in china teacups with a triangle of Victoria sponge on a matching plate.

'Ooh! Very posh this is, Liz.'

I tried to avoid his eyes looking at me when he spoke, in case he guessed what I'd been thinking.

Later that evening, Sid poured himself a beer and I made a few beef sandwiches from the leftovers of the Sunday joint.

'Let's head up early tonight, Liz. Another crack-of-dawn start tomorrow.'

I knew what that meant. Afterwards in bed, he said:

'You know how to keep a man happy, girl. Where did you learn all that then? You're a dark little horse, you are!' Soon his snores broke the silence between us.

Now. This moment. This hour. This day of the week in this month of the year: Sid helped me live my life with the past locked away, mouldering somewhere in the dark, cold cellar.

Chapter Two: Vera

When I hold my pen still for a moment and glance to my right, I see the rest of the Walters family photo gallery on the sideboard. There's one of me with Vera the toddler, sitting on my lap. I'm smiling as the photographer, a friend of Sid's, tells us to 'Say cheese!' as he focuses the lens and clicks the shutter. Vera is wearing her smocked and belted frock with matching knickers. I made the outfit from a pattern in *Woman's Weekly* magazine using a remnant of Liberty print fabric. I taught myself how to gather the material for the smocking and to embroider the pleats with Coates embroidery silks. Always the Best of British from the start. For her.

Her name was Sid's choice, after Vera Lynn.

We'll meet again, don't know where, don't know when…

I hated that song and the wheedling voice reminding me of something I knew was never going to happen. 'We' would never, ever meet again. That summer meeting, up above the vineyards, could never, ever be repeated. Knowing this made me hate Sid and this place where I'd ended up.

I agreed to the name Vera, though. To please Sid. A few months after she was born, he said to me in bed one night:

'What about a Max, Liz? A brother for little Vera?'

I turned my back on him. Vera's birth had been enough for me. With every contraction, it had brought back that other time in France. Hours and hours of labour, dipping in and out of consciousness with the wrenching pains, believing for a moment in my delirium that I was back in the old farmhouse near Dijon, the farmer's wife holding my hand. As I shouted and cried, writhing in agony, I could distantly hear her soft voice saying '*doucement, doucement, chérie*' But when I came to, there was Joy the midwife leaning over me, smiling and saying:

'You have a beautiful baby daughter, Mrs Walters!' She helped me sit up and cradle the baby in my arms as my tears fell onto her tiny face.

Vera, the speaker of truth. Our bright spark. She loved reading right from the very beginning. She would sit in her cot turning the pages of little rag books in primary colours, one object and one word per page. Every word she learned, I learned too: dog, cat, mouse, house, bucket, spade. I wrote in the French words so that she would know both: *le chien, le chat, la souris, la maison, le seau, la pelle.*

She picked up from Sid the English nursery rhymes; he used to sit her on his lap and play the same games over and over again:

'*This little pig went to market. This little pig stayed at home and...'* he'd run his fingers up her arm and tickle her under her chin, making her giggle and laugh and shout: 'Again Daddy! Again!'

From me came the French songs and stories. Repeatedly I'd sing the lullaby my mother had taught me almost before I could remember:

Frère Jacques, Frère Jacques,
Dormez-vous, dormez-vous?
Sonnez les matines, sonnez les matines,
Ding ding dong, ding ding dong.

The verse brought back the sound of the morning bells in our little village and my brother Auguste, singing that last line in time to the chimes of Saint Vincent. It was easy to get distracted. To look at the photographs he'd taken, to remind myself of his eyes, his face that last summer, before the coming of war changed everything. But Sid had hidden them away. There was no going back.

Elizabeth Walters, that's who I was now, wife of a craftsman builder, mother of 'clever little Vera'. I grew older and changed. I learned the names of new people and places, streets and houses, and all the time a kind of numbness slowly froze the feeling of terrible grief. Perhaps none of it had ever happened. And if it had, nobody knew or cared. Except Vera, that is. Later on.

She was my *raison d'être* in those days, my hope for the future. It was as if I were seeing the world for the first time through her eyes. Whilst some children are greedy for toys and sweets, all Vera wanted was books and more books. Visits to our local library and bookshops were her passion. In the early days we read together the safe books with happy endings: *Treasure Island*, *The Secret Garden*, *The Sword in the Stone*. We went on long walks through Greenwich Park, to the Cutty Sark, the Maritime Museum, Greenwich Observatory.

When she was about nine, she started to wage war on my 'funny accent,' mocking and teasing me whenever I struggled with 'th' sounds and English diphthongs. 'Come on, Mum. Say it right. Listen: keep on saying it until you get it properly: Seth at Sainsbury's sells thick socks… Seth at Sainsbury's sells thick socks…' She would go on repeating it, beating out the syllables with the nod of her head, making me do the same until I, too, could speak the Queen's English. She wanted me to be like other Mums. "Normal", whatever that meant.

One evening at supper, after she had come back from a school trip to Boulogne, she said:

'The three of us could book a trip to France, Mum. It's so easy: ferry across to Calais, then train to Paris. See the sights first, then head south to Burgundy.' I felt her blue eyes fixed on me. I didn't know what to say. I shook my head, cleared away the dishes, went into the kitchen. I couldn't tell her why it was impossible. Another voice was drowning out hers.

'Leave now, I tell you, and never come back.'

The start of a lifetime in exile. No going back. Ever.

Sid used to call Vera his "little tomboy", taking her to

the park with him by the time she was old enough to kick a football about or play cricket with him in the summer. She picked up the rules of games quickly and seemed to enjoy going with him to football matches at the Valley. For birthdays and Christmas, he bought her the large box sets of Meccano and Lego and even built a railway track in the spare room upstairs for Hornby model-railway engines. It was as if Vera was the son he'd never had. He taught her basic joinery. 'You won't get any woodwork lessons at that snobby girls' school!' One summer holiday when she was twelve, they designed and built a tall bookcase for her bedroom and he taught her how to use the saw and fix the joints herself.

Eleven-plus, the Grammar-School years, drove a wedge between us: gradually we saw less and less of her. She stayed late for Debating Club and hockey matches. She did her homework in the local library rather than at home. On Saturdays she went off in the school minibus to fixtures at other schools in London or the Home Counties. On Sundays she stayed in her room, reading.

She started to look down on Sid. He wasn't like her friends' dads, who went to work in suits with briefcases, whereas he set off in the morning in navy overalls and returned home covered in concrete dust, with dirty hands. Eventually she refused to go to the rec. with him to kick a ball and the last time he ever offered her a ticket for a match, she said

'Why don't you get it, Dad? I'm a girl. Not a boy. How

many girls do you see in the Valley stands? Hardly any.'

I saw him shrink at her sharp words. Bitter conflicts grew between them. 'She's too bloody clever by half!' he used to say after a row. As a Sixth Former and chairman of the school Politics Society, she started to question what she called the "paternalistic assumptions" of our household.

'How can you put up with it, Mum? You're not a servant. You shouldn't have to wait on him like this. Tell him to make his own damn tea for a change, and yours! See how he'd like to be bossed about!'

Sid retaliated by tipping his tray onto the floor, smashing the china and spilling tea over the carpet. Vera left the house, slamming the front door, breaking a pane of the stained glass.

It never crossed her mind that I had learned to like things the way they were.

Vera excelled in everything at school, except relationships with the other students. In the early years I tried to encourage her to bring her friends home for tea, or supper or to stay the night. 'They're all thick bitches, Mum. I can't stand any of them.' There was not much I could do.

Her lack of popularity did not stand in her way, though. Form prizes for Outstanding Achievement every year, ten O-levels at grade A, winner of the Jules Verne travel prize. The list went on and on.

'Your daughter is a very gifted linguist, Mrs Walters. I'm not sure if you are aware of this?'

I buttoned my lip at her French teacher's condescension at a Sixth Form parents' evening and said nothing.

'I have taught her since she joined my O-level class and I can truly say her French is flawless.'

I didn't mention to her that Vera was bilingual, a fact which was surely obvious.

'She is way ahead of her peers. She has an outstanding grasp of the French language and an extraordinary and rich vocabulary. What is more she has a wealth of reading behind her which I have never seen before in a girl of her age. I feel confident she should apply to Oxbridge next year. I believe that she will find her match at university.'

Out of the corner of my eye, I can see the graduation photograph, taken at the front of Senate House, June 1971. Vera Walters BA (Cantab.) in mortar board and ermine-trimmed robes. Our daughter. Our bright spark. Our star.

Chapter Three: Sid

For thirty-eight years I kept house for him, shopping, cooking, washing up, like Snow White for the Seven Dwarfs. I made it my business to keep him sweet in return for his security, affection, ritualised love. 'You never stop, Liz. Come and sit down,' he'd call out from his chair next to the settee, a tone of irritation in his voice.

Without giving it much thought, I indulged his vices: buying cigarettes for him at the shops, then emptying the ashtrays filled with cigarette stubs at the end of every day; preparing chips with everything, not the oven-ready sort you get nowadays that leave no mess, no. They had to be made the hard way: potatoes peeled and chopped into fat little chunks then fried in deep fat in a huge, oil-blackened pan fitted with its special wire basket. Fish and chips, sausage and chips, steak and chips. He loved nothing better on a Saturday night than to sit with his supper on a tray, Heinz Ketchup ready to dollop straight over each chip, pint-sized beer mug to hand and football on the radio. Later it was *Match of the Day* on television.

In the end the chips and cigarettes were the death of him. Cholesterol clogged up his veins. Despite a minor heart attack, he refused to take medical advice and change the bad habits of a lifetime:

'They can't teach this old dog new tricks, Liz. Pop and get me twenty Players. Let's have a nice steak for supper.'

Then came the lung-cancer diagnosis in April this year, and after being taken into Greenwich Hospital for intensive-care treatment, he died on the day of our wedding anniversary.

Back at home I found Vera's business card on the mantelpiece and quickly dialled the code for Germany and the number for Vera's direct line. Seconds later, I heard a male voice speak in German. I replied in English, stating Vera's name and in a moment I was relieved to hear her say:

'Hello Mum? Is this about Dad?'

I told her. After a slight pause she replied:

'I know this must be terrible for you, but we did expect it was going to happen any day, didn't we? After the diagnosis?' Not a flicker of emotion.

Her voice distant and echoey, she was talking about dates, the funeral arrangements. I'd stopped listening. There was a pause. Vera was waiting for my reply. I said: 'I'll call you about the arrangements, Vera.' And replaced the receiver.

Vera arrived late for Sid's funeral. The small congregation of his work colleagues and I were kneeling in silence as the minister read from the Book of Common Prayer. Suddenly the door at the back of the chapel opened and the tap-tap-tap of her stilettoes on the parquet floor caused me to suddenly turn and look. I hadn't seen her for some time. She was wearing mostly black: black hair in a bob cut and a black double-breasted leather jacket over a dark print dress. Black tights. She saw me, nodded and forced a smile, joining me on the front row. As she sat down, I caught the strong musky scent of her perfume.

I was glad she had come. I was dreading going back to the house alone. The smell of Sid's cigarettes hanging in the air made me think he was somewhere around, about to appear any moment. He and I had spent all that life together. But what now? I didn't know what to do with myself without him to give me orders. Vera would have a plan.

'Now's the time to get out of this place, Mum. Put it on the market: these houses are selling like hot cakes. Use your "Get Out of Jail Free" card now!'

We had returned together after the funeral party I'd arranged at a local hotel. She went on:

'Come to Bonn and stay with me. See something of the world. You can afford it! You don't need to worry about money.'

She was right. Sid had earned a good pension. I had no money worries.

'Buy a nice cottage in the country, Mum. Down in Kent. Find a small town with all the amenities. Escape the urban jungle while you can!'

The thought of moving had never occurred to me. Did I want to get out of London? To start a new life somewhere else?

Vera, on the other hand, was a rolling stone, forever restless and on the move: after Cambridge she took a job as a cub reporter on an East Anglian local newspaper. Her coverage of a scandal involving prostitutes and men in high places quickly won her the attention of the BBC and in no time, it seemed, when I switched on the radio, there was Vera Walters reporting hard news stories across the country. In the seventies, she worked for Reuters in West Berlin, and then she went back to the BBC to work as a foreign correspondent in Bonn.

She had agreed to stay one night in her old room, before catching a return flight from Heathrow.

'This place gives me the spooks, Mum. Especially now Dad has died. Get rid of all this old junk. Buy some new stuff from Habitat! It'll give the place a breath of fresh air. It certainly needs it!'

Over supper, I tried to get her to tell me about her life.

'So what do you do with yourself at the weekends, Vera?'

She looked at me with raised eyebrows and said:

'I think I know what you're getting at there. The answer is: yes, I do have a lover, but I don't want to talk about him.'

Our conversation petered out and she switched on

the television to watch the news programmes.

In the morning before she left, she phoned a local estate agent on my behalf to set up a viewing and valuation of the house. I raised no objection to this although I had made up my mind that I would not sell up.

Later that day, a ridiculously over-dressed young man arrived from Wright's the Estate Agents, to make notes and take measurements of all the rooms. He seemed delighted by Sidney's craftsmanship in the sixties. His loud after-shave reminded me of Vera's perfume.

'That's what people want nowadays: this is a DIY enthusiast's dream house, Mrs Walters. No problem finding you a buyer: is there an attic or a cellar? Mind if I have a look?'

After a trip up to the loft, I led him down into the darkness of the small, damp cellar, shining a torch over old, and some new, beer kegs Sid used to keep down there.

'Not much headroom, but it's surprising what people are doing with cellar space these days: wine clubs are all the rage, did you or your husband ever think of fitting wine racks down here, Mrs Walters?'

'My husband only drank beer,' I said, pointing the torch at the rows of real-ale kegs (Sid had been a founder member of Camra), an old table covered with neat rows of beer mugs and German 'steins' with quaint silhouettes of cities such as Munich, Frankfurt and Hamburg, each one given to Sid by Vera after trips to her pen-pal in Germany. In the early days at the Grammar School Vera had still tolerated him. She was a budding linguist, already fluent in French, razor sharp and keen to learn and speak the German language. She astonished her teachers, never mind Sid and me. It was later on in her teens when she turned against him. She started to think and speak like her English teacher, Miss Otterway, the one who lent her copies of Simone de Beauvoir in translation and suggested she should try for Cambridge. A real Miss Jean Brodie!

The coal dust down there made me cough and cough and my eyes had filled with tears when through this blurred vision I caught sight of the small case on a low shelf. It was partially hidden by unused beer bottles.

The agent stood staring silently at the dusty muddle in front of us. Shrugging his shoulders, he said:

'Are you alright Mrs Walters? It's the dust that's doing that to you.' Nodding in agreement I led the way back upstairs.

'I bet you've got a few old skeletons hidden away in this old cellar, Mrs Walters!'

I quickly showed him out after that.

'I'll give you a bell, Mrs Walters, as soon as I've completed my valuation. If you're happy with it, I'll pop back with a sale board. Have a good day!'

I murmured a polite goodbye and closed the front door quickly. Then I went straight back down to the cellar.

CHAPTER FOUR:
THE WRITING CASE

Clutching the handle of my old writing case, I made my way back upstairs one more time, surprised how the climb had made me quite so breathless. The dining room table was the place for it, and I could sit down, try to breathe deeply, stop my head spinning.

After a minute or two of staring at the familiar object, I found myself distracted by the long-forgotten details: the corners stitched in thick cotton twine, reinforced with strips of thick leather. I fetched a damp cloth to wipe away the thin film of white dust covering the lid. Seconds later an elaborate monogram appeared in faded gold letters, two Ls intertwined by complex gothic script: 'Liliane Lemoine', my lost name. It rolls so easily off the tongue, the liquid 'l's and long vowels of the French language stirring up an avalanche of memories like heavy rocks or stones, bombarding me again just as they used to do before Sid helped put a stop to them. I hesitated to open this Pandora's box. Safer, surely, to leave the lid tight shut?

The surface of the case was scratched and in places

the leather was raw and worn, especially on the handle, which was made from a thin section of leather folded back on itself through hinged loops. On either side of it were two hasp spring locks, reddened with age. I tried to trigger the spring, pulling sideways on the little discs, with no result. Then, after I twisted the locking discs inwards towards the handle and pulled sideways, the hasps flew open with a loud click; with little effort, I pulled back the lid. A smell of must wafted up from the contents. The photograph album rested on the top, where Sid had placed it that last time. I lifted it out and put it to one side: I'd look at it later, when I'd sifted through the confusion of letters and objects heaped together. No rush.

Pulling up the lid further, I saw the neat, leatherette compartments, and in a flash remembered the desperate hurry I was in on that last day when I emptied out the sheets of notepaper and in their place slipped all my travel documents. I looked behind the panel of leather reserved for stamps and saw two stamps protruding. They slid out easily and with a shock I recognised the small profile image of Adolf Hitler on stamps the colour of blood.

The events of the day in January 1943 when I'd packed the case in a frightened panic, hardly knowing what I was doing, came back to me. I heard my father's words and saw his solemn face saying 'Now leave and never come back.'

So I did what he told me. And never went back.

What had appeared at first to be a chaos of random objects started to make sense as I sifted through them, putting them in some kind of order on the table here in front of me. This deep blue fountain pen, a lady's size; the lid unscrewed with some persuasion and revealed a nib clotted with brown ink, the filler mechanism now transparent and empty. There were a few fragments of paper covered in brown handwriting – mine from that other time – letters begun and never finished. Other letters and postcards, also, which felt familiar, but I didn't want to read them, not yet.

At the bottom of the case I found a roll of wine-bottle labels held together by a fraying elastic band. Then I noticed a large buff envelope covering the whole base making it easy to overlook. I had to tug hard at the corners to pull it out. It weighed very little. There wasn't much in there. I upended the envelope, shaking it slightly to dislodge a few letters and postcards which fell with a clatter onto the table. A small leather ring box and a silver hexagonal compact had slipped out, hitting the level surface. I could hear his voice once more as he handed it to me: '*Spieglein, Spieglein…*' and clapped my hands over my ears to try to stop myself hearing any more words. I picked up the black and white postcards of Bavaria, of the sights of Munich and views of the Alps. One was made of thick card showing a large chalet in the foreground with snow-capped Alps behind; a sprig of edelweiss, its furry petals now brown and withered and its thin leaves shrivelled, had been taped to the postcard with red tape. On the back was the simple, undated message: 'For Lily from K.F.'

I took the pen into the kitchen to clean the nib with soapy water. I watched fascinated as the water turned brown and the nib suddenly changed to a shining gold. I found a bottle of blue Quink on Vera's desk in her room and pumped the small mechanism to fill the pen. When I tried it on a clean sheet of paper, it worked. I made a trip to W.H. Smith's to buy several hardback A4 lined notebooks and a new bottle of brown ink.

Chapter Five:
Saultmur

Vera was right that I should make a journey. But how to begin? I pick up the album first. Auguste, my older brother, gave it to me for my eighteenth birthday: here on the cover, gold lettering on black, I read the stencilled message: '*Bon anniversaire, Lily. 8 avril 1939*'.

He'd taken most of the photographs himself with his Leica camera given to him by our parents on his twenty-first birthday. Later, after he'd gone, I took a few more during the war years and added them to the pages: the Mercedes-Benz convertible, the *Kommandantur* at the Hôtel de la Chasse in Beaune, a billing poster for Charles Trenet hanging on a Paris railing.

No pictures of him, though. My lover. K.F. I was stupid in those days, yes, but not that stupid. As I pore over the pictures I find, an old map of Saultmur starts to unfold in my head. Although I have not lifted a pencil to draw for over four decades, I try my best to sketch a street map of our village here at the front of the notebook. It's easy to start with the main landmarks: our family home, the *mairie*, the church, the war memorial and the cemetery, and as I draw the lines on the page in front of me I feel like a ghost wandering the streets, trying to find my way back.

I open the album and it's as if Auguste were here with me now, using his camera to tell the facts, in case one day I might forget them. On the first page of the album is a close-up of the imposing gateway which closed off the Domaine Lemoine from the street. The tall stone posts stood either side of two ornate wrought-iron gates decorated with my mother's family crest and the initials RV. My mother Jeanne, only daughter of René and Ursule Vallet, became the sole inheritor of their estate after their deaths.

I imagine opening these gates – dark green I think they were – and stepping from the rue de Genevrières into the courtyard. In this next picture, my parents are posing at the top of the double staircase at the front of their beautiful *maison de vin*. This is where they began their married life, back in 1916, living in a small apartment in this wing here on the left of the courtyard. My father, Antoine Lemoine, had had a narrow escape. In 1915, when he was taking part in the Tenth Army attack at Vimy Ridge, a piece of flying shrapnel had hit his right leg.

'Best thing that ever happened to me', he used to say. I suppose he meant that he was the lucky survivor, injured so badly that he could not fight again. Unlike his brother and so many of his friends whose names are carved on the War Memorial in the place de la République.

There they are, my parents, smiling and waving still,

as Auguste takes the picture, standing near the gates. I note the elegant glass *marquise* over the doorway behind them and remember the night it was smashed by hailstones in a terrible storm in the summer of 1941. As I stare at this photograph, I remember what you can't see: the series of vaulted cellars and the orderly rows of barrels and racks filled with wine bottles. This was where customers came to taste our wine and place their orders.

There were two ways to reach the garden at the back of the house. Either through the workshop to the left of the staircase, or through the kitchen, which was on the right. Auguste had only included one picture of the garden, showing seven white Easter lilies planted by my mother. I can remember reaching up and pulling one of these cream cone-shaped flowers towards me when I was very small, pushing my nose into it and getting the tip smudged brown by the stamens. A sickly, heavy scent. My mother always said it was the fragrance of the lilies filling the church of Saint Vincent on Easter Sunday, 1921, that triggered my arrival whilst she knelt at prayer in a front pew. The picture shows the tall wall behind the flowers with a rose scrambling up it. This wall encircled the kitchen garden, where we grew vegetables and fruit for the household, and I remember it supported a vine and several trained fig trees. It was noisy with chickens that were allowed to roam free, pecking at the gravel on the paths. The photograph doesn't show the low gate in the back wall, which led out into a vineyard giving easy access to our vines on the other side of the rue des Charrons. Only a short walk from there, up the hill, is the Saint Denis monument and sweeping views for miles around. A place for a chance meeting. A first kiss.

Chapter Six: Then and Now

What I've always liked about our street in this part of London is the way people leave you alone: perhaps a wave when you pick up the milk bottles in the morning or brief chat when you're unlocking the front door. No looking after their children if they'll look after yours. No visits to their houses for coffees and teas. None of that. Thank God.

It was different in the village where I grew up: everybody knew everybody else, and if you wanted to keep a secret, you were in the wrong place. I look at this picture of *l'église de Saint Vincent*, only six minutes' walk from our house and its tall spire visible for miles around.

'Look at the peepholes up there, Lily. Father Benoît watches us at all times of the day and night. Remember that!'

Two eye-slits in the bell tower keeping watch, never letting us out of sight.

The loud tolling of the Angelus bell shaped our days, morning, noon and night. There was no escape. It was my mother who drilled Auguste and me in obedience to the teachings of the Catholic Church. She saw herself as a kind of Mother Superior and me, her daughter, as a young novice. When the early evening bell sounded, we had to cross ourselves and recite three Hail Marys. On Sunday mornings when the bells tolled continuously, we would walk behind our parents, stopping at the west door of the church near the marketplace to greet our special friends: a kiss on each cheek – what were their names now? Florence, Charlotte and Marthe. Marthe Cordier, that was her full name. Little girls in frilly dresses with satin sashes and big bows. My bosom pals, my soul mates. Until things changed, that is.

Sid had no time for religion.

'It's all a load of nonsense, Liz. That's what I say. Look at what's happening in Northern Ireland: Protestants killing Catholics and vice versa. That's Christianity for you. I've got better things to do on a Sunday than go to church. Church-goers are a bunch of hypocrites.'

So the Walters family kept away from any organised religion: no Christenings or confirmation classes. None of that clap-trap, as he called it.

Deep down I thought he was wrong, but I never took him to task or challenged his views.

'Do you think Vera's missing anything, Liz? No. More time for a Sunday lie-in. Time to get her homework done. Do some reading. None of those Sunday School distractions.'

Vera would ask the tough questions.

'Mum, why don't you do what Joan opposite does with her kids? They go to Mass every Sunday. Liam told me he knows his catechism and he's going to dress up in white trousers and a shirt and have a first Communion service or something. Then his mum's going to do a special party and he'll get to eat ice cream.'

I didn't have an answer for her. Kept quiet.

'Are we atheists, Mum?' she asked me once and I supposed we were.

'Does it matter, one way or the other?'

'Not to us anyway. But Liam says I'll probably go to hell since I'm not christened, never mind confirmed!'

What could I say?

Sometimes when I heard the peal of church bells on a Sunday in London, I'd feel again the chill air of Saint Vincent as you stepped inside the main entrance, along with a faint smell of damp. People speaking in whispers, genuflecting and making the sign of the cross, taking their places in view of the altar. The seats of the pews hard and uncomfortable. When he was eight or so, Auguste became an altar boy and I can still see him carrying the censer, wafting it from side to side, leaving a trail of grey aromatic smoke. 'Father Benoît has bad breath: Pierre told me it can kill you.' He had other tales, which he said were not for my ears.

It was good while it lasted, I suppose. To belong. To believe.

We were young innocents, Auguste and I, back then.

I find a note dashed off on a scrap of white paper:

'Spot the birthday clues, Lily!' The birthday clues? Where? Once again, I'm searching the pictures, counting the details: eighteen bottles lined up in the dog-cart in the courtyard. All with the *Lemoine et Fils* labels, though you can't read them from here. And I find I still get the visual jokes. Five ducks in this picture wandering towards the ruisseau des Cloux, near the old stone mill; ten chickens strutting across the little green near rue de Martrey, disturbing the men playing pétanque. Fifteen cows grazing in the flat pastureland at the end of the rue des Charmes: Auguste counting my years with the farm animals in his photographic tour of our village.

'You wait, Lily.' Yes, I can remember him speaking like a prophet.

'When we're old we'll look back and this extended farmyard – our village – will have disappeared. You'll see. The cattle, the horses, the stinking back yards full of clucking hens: they'll go once mechanisation comes. The little barns. They'll be useless in a few years. We'll all be selling them off so people can turn them into houses. My photos are for posterity to show it as it is now, Lily, not as people will pretend it was.'

Posterity is here and now, Auguste, but it's not how you or I imagined it back then. You chafed at your role in the family wine business, wanting instead to be a photographer with a studio in Paris, to have your photographs published in glossy magazines. The album has a magnetic force and I can't put it down. And I, Lily? What did I want back then? To have a corner in your studio in Montmartre for my easel and paints, my sketchbooks. To get away from that primitive village life, domestic responsibilities and above all, my mother's rules governing whom I should marry.

Youthful rebels we were, or wanted to be. Early summer 1939, it must have been. 'Zazous'? Was that the right word for us? Me wearing your old tweed jacket, sloping off to meet you and Jacques Boissart without telling anyone. Dusk up in the Lemoine vineyard, and the three of us swigging from one of the dusty old wine bottles Jacques had pinched from his father's cellars. Vintage Burgundy! And you, Auguste? Another broken thread.

Then and now. The past melting into the present, disappearing and reappearing in words that turn into stories about a different time and a far-off place: fairy tales or nightmares?

Chapter Seven: 1938

I took this picture with the Leica: Auguste with Papa. *Antoine Lemoine et Fils*, as it says here on these wine labels, the unused ones I kept. The two of them standing together under the *Clos Lemoine* archway. The beginning of a new era. Not quite the one we all had in mind.

'Come on, Lily: you take this one,' he'd said.

'Stand over there. Make sure you click the shutter only when you've got us properly lined up.'

It was early evening. That's right: you can tell from the length of their shadows. The perfect picture. Papa is slightly squinting into the sun as it hangs low in the sky. He's beaming with pride as Auguste, his son and heir, towers above him, his hand resting affectionately on his shoulder. Their eyes are fixed on me and I feel their affection as if I were just seventeen, a girl again.

Behind them, through the archway, you can make out the rows of vines just now coming into leaf. A couple of crows, squawking loudly, are circling overhead. Another one has landed on the arch.

The crows. The arch. The vines and two pairs of eyes looking at me. 'Click', and I passed the camera back to

Auguste. The three of us hurried back to the house for the party. I was wearing a thin, cotton dress. That one. With rosebud sprigs on a pure white background. It was new, fresh. Suddenly I was shivering with cold and as we looked back towards the town the sun was hidden by slate-grey clouds. We could hear thunder in the distance. Any minute it would rain.

'To hell with blessing the vines,' my father finally said. 'If we wait any longer for the priest, we'll all be soaked to the skin.'

He led the way with his rocking gait down the stony pathway, across the rue des Charrons and then a short climb up the rue des Charmes to No 1, rue des Genevrières, at the top of the street. Stopping for a moment he said: 'You two run on ahead. I'll get there in the end.'

So Auguste and I raced each other up the road, leaving Papa limping behind us. At the gates he said 'You go in, Lily. I better wait here for the poor old sod. Might as well open the gates for the guests.'

Auguste spread over two pages the rest of the photographs of this family celebration in May 1938: some were taken indoors using a flashgun, causing a sensation with the guests. Others were taken outside in the courtyard. It was a two-in-one event that had been months in the planning by my mother: his birthday and the launch of the new Lemoine wine.

This one shows the two trestle tables set up for the event in the dining room: the well-starched white linen cloths, twelve settings per table, each arranged with the best silver cutlery. Those napkins ('Mitre the napkins, Lily,' Maman had ordered) an exercise in folding twenty-four stiff linen serviettes as though it would take just a minute. It took hours: folding and pressing the tough cotton damask.

I remember stopping my work to gaze out of the window, standing there alone in the dining room. It was lofty and spacious, with its two large dormer windows opening onto the balcony. In the middle distance were the vineyards stretching across the hillside, dotted with the quaint stone huts, the *cabottes*. The small figure of our father just about visible, working his way along the vines with a horse-drawn plough. My glance shifted back onto the collection of silver serving dishes now lined up in rows on the sideboard, each piece shining like glass. The walls were hung with Vannet family portraits and, between the windows, were two paintings by contemporary artists given recently to my father by his best friend, Charles Santot, in exchange for a few cases of *Lemoine et Fils* wine.

'Charles says now is the time to buy art, Lily. He says he'd like to introduce you to a dealer he knows in Paris. You could take some of your work, get her opinion on it. He also says that he thinks you'd have a good eye for a bargain, better than mine I think!' Painting and pottery, they were my passion in those days, and so was Paris. Had Charles really meant what he'd said to Papa? Did he really have a plan to take me to Paris by myself?

In this photograph you can see the guests all seated. Fellow winegrowers from the village and their wives. The Lemoines were unusual: no uncles or aunts, no elderly relatives. In the picture Papa is standing, looking at the camera and about to give his speech at the head of the table, Maman on his right, Auguste's empty seat on his left. Here I am, just seventeen, smiling and looking up as Auguste cracks a joke to make us all smile. Opposite me is Charles Santot. He seems to have taken his eye off the camera and he's looking straight at me. Always the dandy, sporting a neat bow tie – red with white polka dots - and a lounge suit tailored for him in Paris.

Despite the years that have separated us, I can still hear Papa's proud voice giving the opening speech.

'This is a landmark day in the history of the Lemoine family: this little vineyard you can see up there on the hillside represents the promise of our future years and the years for all of us here who commit their lives to the production of the finest wines in France; some would say, in the whole world.'

There were cries of '*Vive la Bourgogne!*' and '*Vive la France!*' with widespread nodding and murmured agreement.

'On this day twenty–one years ago, my son Auguste was born: today he is a fine young man, strong and hard-working and already the master of many of my skills. Where are you, my boy?'

There was applause and glasses were raised as my

brother stood up, smiling awkwardly, to acknowledge the toast.

'Congratulations, my son. One day, who knows, you may be prepared to give your old man a bit of a rest. Now, though, *tout le monde*, please sample the new Lemoine *appellation*. Beware, it is still very young and should be at its best a few years from now; I'd say, by 1944.'

He paused briefly and raised his glass, saying in a theatrical way, 'Here's to *Antoine Lemoine et Fils*', and voices echoed these words around the room.

Auguste rested the camera and flash gun on the sideboard and sat down with everyone else and surprised me by saying in lowered tones 'Papa certainly knows how to impress his listeners.'

Quickly he began eating the plate of hors d'oeuvres in front of him. I picked at mine without enthusiasm: *jambon persillé* was a local delicacy. It had been made from one of our own pigs. I found the thought disgusting as I looked at the neat slice of chopped cold pork bound together with shiny aspic. No-one noticed: people were exchanging comments on the new wine and cracking jokes. At some point my mother came over to ask for my help in bringing up the trays of food from the kitchen for the main course.

When I sat down in my place again, Auguste said 'Promise me something, Lily. Don't let them turn you into another Josephine.'

How could he say that to me? Josephine was the family servant, paid with her board and lodging and a few francs in pocket money. His resentment surprised me that night.

'What I'm trying to say is, don't let Maman and Papa use you as an unpaid servant. That's all. You're just seventeen. You've got your life ahead of you. Let them pay for another pair of hands.'

His words cut deep, and it must be why they come back to me now, so clearly. I felt the tears welling up. I don't remember what I said, scared in case the other guests might overhear us, although other conversations were continuing rowdily on either side, and no-one was listening to us.

'Lily, it's up to you to get what you want.'

His discontent was catching. At my age then I still did what was expected of me: genteel domestic tasks, each of them trivial in their own way. Josephine did the hard graft for us all. Her finger-nails were chipped and uneven, the skin roughened by work, whilst my nails were manicured, my hands softened daily with a lavender cream.

I looked at Auguste as he was speaking: his expression was hard, even bitter.

'So what do *you* want, Auguste, never mind me?'

He didn't look at me when he answered, saying 'I can tell you what I don't want, for a start. I don't want to be tied to all this here, a slave to the vines, just like Papa, and to the Lemoine name. Of course, I'm proud that I now have a bigger share in the business, that Papa has made me a kind of partner. But you know, Lily, I'd much rather people knew me for the photographs I can take.'

Naturally, I sympathised with his frustrations, but I hadn't expected what came next.

'Lily, it's time for you to work in the Lemoine business. Papa needs all the help he can get. He's talking about doubling production in the next few years. When I ask him if he will be taking on more staff, he says only for the *vendanges*. He's like a machine and he thinks I'm machine No 2. Well, I'm not!'

I saw him clench his fist and thought he would thump the table, but then he continued trying to win me over.

'Why don't you tell him you'll do the bookkeeping and the secretarial work, Lily? You're intelligent. Of course, we have our dreams, you and I. Who doesn't? Photography! Painting! Paris! But what would happen here?'

Domaine Lemoine had to come first. Regardless of everything else, I knew he was right.

'Do a stenographer's course in Dijon. Get to understand the trade. You and I, we can take it on together eventually: *Lemoine Frère et Soeur*!' Subversively he chinked my glass.

Brother and sister. Business partners. Plans and possibilities; new departures; change. Like the deep red wine Auguste kept pouring into my glass that evening, the vision of the future I tasted made me feel light-headed, excited. Drunk on the dreams of a future that never came.

Chapter Eight: Gifts

I'm trying to get hold of a couple of other moments from that evening: one at the dinner and the other in the courtyard, later on.

I remember Auguste's saying provocatively to Charles Santot 'So, Charles, when are you going to invent a machine that will replace the horse and plough and start to make light work of the vines for us all?'

'I have a few ideas in my head and a few sketches somewhere. But no time to do anything with them at the moment, Auguste. Work has been very hectic: it was touch and go whether I'd make it down here for tonight.'

They moved on to a heated discussion about how to mechanise the wine industry, whilst I helped my mother and Josephine serve up the *boeuf bourguignon*. When I returned to my seat the two of them had moved on to a discussion of the Maginot Line and Auguste was singing its praises.

'It's a brilliant fortification and a superb example of the best in French engineering – surely you agree, Charles?'

I thought he sounded just like a government spokesman.

'In one underground fort alone, over one thousand soldiers can be housed, ready for any attack from German forces.'

Charles was not impressed with this view, however.

'But everyone seems to have forgotten about the Belgian border, as though the Ardennes could never be crossed by the enemy. Can't they remember that the Germans made their way through Belgium in the last war?'

His voice was drowned out as Papa made a further toast to Auguste and the *Domaine Lemoine.* Again, we chinked our glasses and I noticed a look of irritation in Charles's eyes as he dropped what he was saying to raise his glass once again. Together we all swallowed more of the deep red wine and for a moment the tension in the air was dispelled. Gently Charles touched Auguste's glass, then mine, saying in lowered tones:

'To great Lemoine achievements, past, present and to come. Knock this back, the two of you, and let's go outside for some fun!'

He downed the contents of his glass in one gulp, shook Papa's hand and patted him forcefully on the back.

'Another good feast, Antoine. But I think we should give this wine another five years before we open another bottle. Meanwhile I'm stealing these two from the table.'

He gave a conspiratorial wink as he strolled over to the door, his steps slightly unsteady.

Outside in the courtyard were two parcels set out on

a table.

'Give me that camera, let me try the flash. Not quite enough light here now. Go on both of you: open up these gifts. The big one's for you, Auguste, the smaller one is yours, Lily. They've come with me all the way from Paris and you should check they're still in one piece!'

The photograph shows us both grinning broadly, holding our up our gifts from him like sporting trophies: Auguste's a new portable Decca gramophone and mine a 100cl bottle of Worth perfume – '*Je Reviens*'.

'I missed your birthday last month, Lily. This is for you tonight: why should Auguste have all the fun?'

Placing the camera carefully on the table and taking the bottle out of my hands to put next to it, he took me by my shoulders and kissed me on the lips. What could I say? I caught the whiff of red wine on his breath and, embarrassed, I remember turning my attention to the large, droplet-shaped bottle, my cheeks burning red. I unscrewed the lid and held the bottle to my nose, smelling the sweet scent and dabbing a little on my wrists. I saw him watching me, and could only mutter

'You're too generous, Charles.'

He turned his back whilst he helped Auguste set up the gramophone on a table outside in the courtyard with a long electrical lead trailing into the kitchen.

'This is a brilliant piece of Anglo-Swiss engineering, you know. Engine and body parts from Switzerland, assembled in London. Latest model, of course!'

They both grinned broadly, delighted by this new toy. I sat on the stone staircase, watching Auguste slip the first record from its brown paper sleeve and set it on the rotating turntable, lowering the needle on to the first track. There was a loud crackle as the needle reached the opening bars of the song.

Charles said 'Listen to those loud trumpets and bass saxophones, Auguste. They're all the rage in Paris right now. When will the two of you come and stay with me in Paris then? You're no fun stuck here in Burgundy, my friends!'

The Big Band music started to boom and echo round the walls of the house and the voice of Cab Calloway drawled lyrics I later learned by heart. Forgotten now.

Shortly afterwards Charles left us to return to the house: 'I must speak to Antoine,' he explained. We watched him hold carefully onto the handrail to steady himself as he mounted the staircase to the front door. Auguste raised his eyebrows at me as we remained together outside.

'Poor old Charles! When shall we go to Paris then, Lily? You'd better learn to jive before he takes us to all those jazz clubs.'

He tried to teach me how to jive to Cab Calloway as he placed the needle back at the start of the record.

Moments later, we heard my father's voice raised in a heated discussion.

'No, Charles, I can't let that happen. Are you mad?'

There was a pause and we could hear Charles speaking

very quickly, but at a whisper so that neither of us could make out what he was saying.

Auguste and I shrugged at each other, not knowing or much caring what the conflict was about. A friendly tiff. Moments later, Charles came out through the front door, stony-faced. He marched down the stairs straight past both of us, muttering '*Bonsoir!*' under his breath. He opened the gate himself and pulled it shut, the clanking sound of the metal echoing loudly round the walls of the courtyard.

'Do you think we should go after him?' I asked, feeling awkward and uneasy at Charles's sudden departure.

'No. Let him go. Whatever it is, they'll sort it out. It can't have anything to do with us.'

I supposed he was right and the two of us stayed watching the record revolving on the turntable time and again, with Auguste slow-stepping and jiving to jazz rhythms in the moonlight whilst I sat on the steps watching him from the shadows in the courtyard on the night of his twenty-first birthday.

Chapter Nine: The Cellar

If I close my eyes, I can let myself feel again the cold rush of air chilling the hands and face when stepping through the door from the kitchen scullery into the cellars. The arched stone walls, blackened with algae, gave off a musty smell that caught in the throat and mingled with the scent of wine spills left from the testing and tasting of the fermenting reds and whites. By the click of a Bakelite switch, a string of light bulbs dimly lit up twin rows of wine barrels ranked either side of a dusty aisle stretching far ahead along the length of the footprint of the house.

Beyond the barrels and the racks of dusty bottles of Lemoine vintages, you reached a workspace at the far end of the cellars near an exit. Here, one evening in early June that year, my father gave me my first lesson on how to cap and label the bottles. On a small table-top was the special device for clenching onto the neck of the bottle the coloured metallic cap and, next to it, a pile of *Antoine Lemoine et Fils* wine labels.

'Think of each bottle as if it were a fine woman: make her look her best, Lily. No crooked labels or lopsided caps. Each of these must be fit to grace the table of a king.

Remember my 1929 and the Prince of Wales!'

The sale of a case of Lemoine wine in 1935 to the English Prince had made headlines in the local paper. It had been the talk of our village for months after.

'He knows quality when he tastes it, that one. This was the wine closest to perfection at that time. In my view it still is. We haven't produced another one like it.'

My father glowed with pride as he poured a small quantity of the wine from a half-empty bottle into a wine glass and handed it to me. 'Smell it first, Lily. So.'

He pushed his nose towards the bowl of the glass, which he was swilling around.

'Perfect, I would say. Now you try.'

I took the glass and smelt the dark red liquid as it swirled around. It smelt like Communion wine when it's handed round in a heavy chalice, a reminder of the blood of Christ. This was Lemoine blood.

'Now taste it', my father ordered, and I savoured the rich, woody flavour of the wine.

'Not only did this beauty win the favour of a future king, but it also won the *médaille d'or* in a Paris trade fair that year. Not many bottles left of it now. It's all the more of a rarity for that. Customers pay handsomely for the privilege of laying it down in their cellars.'

In his office my father had a noticeboard with the yellowing newspaper article pinned up. It showed him holding a bottle of the prized wine and an image of the celebrated royal customer alongside it. There were other newspaper cuttings. I'd entered my father's office a thousand times and seen them from the corner of my eye, but it was from this time that the recognition and success of Lemoine wine started to matter for me.

And now? Here in the dining room at Number 73, surrounded by Walters family clutter, I rummage through the contents of this old case to find that roll of unused wine labels. Tightly coiled and held together with an elastic band, which snaps as I pull it; the labels loosen in my hand. I flatten out this little stack so that I can read again the name: *Antoine Lemoine et Fils.*

'Throw the rest of these labels away, Lily.' I can hear my father speaking with bitterness some two years later, adding: 'We won't be using them again.'

Devastating hailstorms in early June bruised and tore at the vines that year. Mildew and rot threatened the crop. The night-time silence of the house broken by the six o'clock chimes of the church bells calling Auguste and my father to work at the crack of dawn. Then sounds from the different bedrooms: floorboards creaking, doors opening, the toilet flushing and water running in the bathroom along the corridor. Auguste's large bare feet making dull thudding noises in the room next to mine then continuing onto the landing and down the wooden stairs to the kitchen, joined shortly by my father and mother.

I fall asleep again. Then wake up a while later to the clatter of Josephine's metal bucket, as she works her way round the bedrooms, cleaning and clearing, mopping the floor. The bright shafts of daylight strike the furniture and objects in my room: the grey marble-topped washstand with the wide-necked jug and large washbowl. The matching bedside table, narrow with a stiff clasp, which made it difficult to open the door.

There's another memory of that room that jumps the queue and dislodges any other. Of the very last day I was there. But I can't face it and I can't face him for the last time. The man I loved. Then hated. Not yet.

Please. Give me back some more of that time. Before all that.

*

'I want to capture on camera those bloody vines just as they are. Rotten. Nearly every one of them. The leaves are turning yellow. The grapes are decaying. Papa knows we are wasting our time every day, but still we troop up and down the rows pruning and trimming.'

Auguste spoke with bitterness. He was short-tempered and taciturn most of the time. It was early July 1938, I guess. The photographs show what he saw: darkening clouds hovering low over the vineyards seen from a distance. Then black-and-white close-up images of misshapen bunches of grapes where some of the fruit had rotted or been cut away. A view of the hillside covered in grey early morning mist blurring the lines of walls and pathways.

People, too. One of Henri Bizot, dragging a big sack of grain alongside the others on the pavement already cluttered with household objects, outside his general store. Then there's another of the blacksmith (what was his name?) holding a horseshoe with a pair of tongs in one hand, a hammer in the other.

There are a few more of me, also, with my friends near the church door on a Sunday morning, after Mass. The congregation is leaving the church, the men in smart suits and the women in their best clothes, it's a rare sunny day in a wet summer. There I am, dressed very plainly once again, wearing that cotton shirt-waister, and a cardigan, there's a slight breeze blowing my hair over my face, it is glinting in the summer sun. Golden hair it was in those days. Before I went and dyed it black. I'm squinting and holding my hand up to shield my eyes, the sun is so bright that morning. Marthe Cordier is looking at me, she's the one talking and I'm listening to her. Neither of us realises that Auguste has strolled into the square to capture this moment.

I want to go back there. One last time. To be that pretty girl again in the cotton dress when it was starched and new. Stainless. The bells. I want to hear their deafening clang as I step out of the cold church and to look up and see the swallows swooping to their nests under the eaves of the church porch.

I hear the bells now and they lull me to sleep. Their sound fades and it's as though there's a loud trumpet playing near me, here in this room. The notes long and drawn out. I smell smoke, not Sid's cigarettes, but Gitanes. The air is hazy with it. It's dark and I'm seated at a small table. Who's that man with the clownish smile, the trilby hat? It's Charles Trenet. He's performing on a small stage. I can't believe I'm here in Montmartre. But I'm uneasy. Frightened. The lyrics conjure up my village, the spire of the church, the countryside around. I see it all vividly in my mind's eye and it makes me want to cry to go back there:

Un petit village,
Un vieux clocher

But as I clap my hands at the end of the song, the diamond edelweiss spins round on my finger. Too big for me. Far too big for my skinny finger. I know I should take it to a jeweller, but the thought makes me panic. This is my secret treasure. I daren't show it to anyone.

Then, for the first time, I look at the people sitting around the table and my stomach lurches: Wehrmacht officers, complete strangers to me, each of them wearing braided grey uniforms cut to fit trimly and belted at the waist. They are all looking at me with their cold, grey eyes, exchanging jokes in German. They laugh loudly and I feel angry that I don't understand. That I can't share the joke. Suddenly I feel two firm hands on my shoulders, close to my neck. Is someone trying to strangle me, for Christ's sake? Then I feel the stubble of his cheek scratch my face. He kisses me. Sits down next to me, holds my hand. I look at him closely: those eyes the colour of summer sky, blond hair glinting in the candlelight. There's a trickle of blood on his cheek and I scream. Scream and scream.

CHAPTER TEN: THE LETTER

It has come back again. That nightmare. The same nightmare that kept haunting me in the early days until Sid made me box up the memories and bury them.

Now I dread going upstairs to sleep at night. I've taken to staying down here where I feel safe and secure. When I'm too tired to write any more, I just lie down on the sofa, with my head on a cushion. I cover myself up with Vera's bedcover. The one I made for her to take to university: dozens of crocheted squares, multi-coloured. Cheerful. She never used it though: not trendy enough for her. Something like that anyway.

It was Sophie, Sophie Edelman, who showed me how to make them that summer. One wet afternoon, sometime in July 1938 it was, when she had nothing better to do. I let my thoughts linger on the words until the whole scene comes back like an old film.

It was pouring with rain and when I looked out from the kitchen window, the pane blurred with raindrops, I saw her waving to me, so I ran across the cobbles to open the big gate. She stood there with her dark, thick wavy hair soaking wet, laughing.

Difficult to remember what she said, but I can see her sitting down at the kitchen table and pulling out skeins of wool, chattering about her aunt, about Paris, whilst she pushed and pulled her crochet hook to create a chain of stitches. 'Now you try, Lily!' She had the hands of a pianist – long, slender fingers.

She was like the swallows that nested in the eaves of our house, coming unannounced for a few weeks every summer, staying with her aunt Mme Bèze-Conti, wife of one of the richest *vignerons* in the town. She would dart around from house to house and place to place in our village. She knew everyone and they knew her, but she was not one of us. She never would be.

'Have you noticed, Lily, we never see Sophie or her aunt at mass on Sundays?' Marthe Cordier's words echo back to me here and now from over forty years ago.

Here today and gone tomorrow, sending me postcards from her fashionable destinations: Biarritz. Cannes. Nice. That was how it was for her back then.

Then she was gone as suddenly as she had arrived.

I have all Sophie's correspondence. In date order, ending abruptly in early 1941. Here with me now, this thin bundle of yellowing papers and cards I tied up back then with a piece of string. It is too painful to untie it now.

*

We were all expecting the news, though none of us dared

talk about it; we'd listened to the broadcasts on the radio, knew the seriousness of the Sudetenland crisis. Then the French government started to call up reservists and to mobilise a million men: Auguste was one of them. First, he had to go to Dijon for special training, then to join an army regiment. This happened just after the grapes had been gathered in September.

I can still see him now, in my mind's eye, leaving our house with me following behind him:

'You take my place here now, Lily. I'll be back soon.'

I remember him saying that as he hugged me. He was wearing civilian clothes, the tweed jacket he'd worn on the occasion of his twenty-first.

Again I sat down at the top of the stone staircase, watching him march across the cobbles, the sound of his footsteps bouncing off the surrounding walls. He turned and waved to me as he climbed into the back of the car where my parents were sitting in the front, waiting for him.

Unsmiling. Resolute.

*

A bulky wireless set dominated the sideboard in the dining room. It was dark brown Bakelite and on turning the knob, it uttered a crackling sound and behind a brown wire mesh a dim light would appear. Then, by adjusting the tuning knob carefully, you would eventually stumble on the right wavelength for Radio Paris. In the warm September evenings we listened avidly to radio broadcasts, the three of us sat at the dining-room table, hoping for brief titbits of information to assure us about the welfare of Auguste and the million other soldiers now stationed along the border between France and Germany.

In the mornings, early, I went with my mother to St Vincent to light a candle and say a prayer for Auguste. Odd, but true, that lighting the flame of a thin vanilla candle and placing it on the candle rest created the illusion that we were both doing something for him. In my naïveté this solitary ritual bolstered my faith in the church at this time, particularly when in late September we heard the crackly news announcement on a radio broadcast: the Sudetenland crisis had been resolved. The threat of war had been lifted by the signing of the Munich Agreement.

Auguste and the other soldiers were on their way home!

In early October, I stood with my father on the platform in Beaune on a dull afternoon ready to meet Auguste from the Dijon train. Both of us stood solemnly looking up the line, anxious to see it loom into view. I remember the excitement that ran through the crowd of other people waiting when the train drew up. There was a loud clatter of doors opening and the disappointment overwhelmed me when none of the men stepping down appeared to be Auguste.

Then I heard my father say:

'Look. There he is, Lily! You run and meet him. I'll stay here.'

He gestured towards the end of the platform and I saw my brother stepping down from a carriage and felt a sudden rush of happiness as he lifted his hand to wave as soon as he saw me. He looked thin, his face was gaunt and haggard, but he was back. I looped my arm through his and we walked towards our father standing among the thinning crowd. He hugged Auguste and when he stood back his eyes were filled with tears.

Auguste's homecoming marked the onset of autumn that year. I remember it well. Now I, too, was expected to work alongside the men in the vineyards. Together we saw the vines turn from green to gold, then to brown, their leaves shrivelling and turning to brush. As winter came on, my father and Auguste pruned them back, and it was my job to pick up the waste trimmings and burn them. Sometimes in the biting cold wind we stood like three vagabonds in our rough, thick cotton jackets stained with soil and grime, warming our hands as the fire blazed in the rusty old brazier, sending up plumes of grey smoke, smelling the rich odour of burning vegetation.

In the spring the woody stumps once again put out new stems that came into bud and flowered momentarily before storms tore off the petals and sprinkled them on the soil. Auguste and my father drove the horse-drawn plough along the furrows between the vines to keep the roots clear of grass and weeds. Hailstones the size of golf balls came later, just when the neat bunches of grapes were forming, and the mildew and leaf rot forced the heavy use of sulphates on the vines. This was going to be another terrible year, worse even than the one before.

Good humour. Good food. Good wine in that order. Look forward, but don't look back. Think about tomorrow and forget yesterday. Leave politics to the politicians. Just take care of the vines, the cellars, the bottles, the orders.

Chapter Eleven: 1939

Upstairs or downstairs, I can't hide from the bad dreams. The writing case keeps churning them out. They follow me.

Here's another: I'm in the walled vineyard with Auguste. It's a beautiful sunny morning and we can see the new archway ahead of us, the *clos* behind. He is working his way along the vines beside my row, a bit ahead of me. We are both pruning stems and tying them in. At first, I'm happy, clipping and twining the tendrils, and I feel glad to be there, working alongside my brother. Gradually I stop being able to think straight or concentrate on what I am supposed to be doing: the heat is so intense, the light dazzling. As I look across at him, his blond hair suddenly explodes into a huge yellow sun and its rays seem to be burning me up. At the same moment I look down because I can't step forward any further, my ankles are caught: thick huge tendrils from the vines are clutching at my legs, pulling and dragging me down. I fall, but in my panic, I call out to Auguste 'Auguste! Help me! I'm trapped. I can't get out!'

He comes over and looks down at me as I lie on the

soil between the vines.

'Where's the trap, Lily? I just don't see it.'

He glides away and I can hear the distant and regular snip, snip of the secateurs as he carries on with his work.

Bathed in sweat, I wake up in the darkness and remember Auguste is long since gone. But I'm still caught in a trap from which I cannot break free. That's when I switch on the light, pick up my pen, sit down at the table here, check there's ink still flowing. I try to tell a bit more of the story. It helps to deaden the agony.

In early September 1939, France and Britain declared war on Germany. Auguste and his generation were mobilised once more. Again in Dijon he was kitted out with his uniform, his gun and ammunition. This time, in October 1939, he was deployed in the Saar offensive, after which his battalion was ordered to withdraw to the Maginot line. We were never to see him again.

So our house became a place of silence. Waking early in the morning, I could hear the loud tick of the grandfather clock in the hallway echo in the shadowy space, and every hour and half hour the bells of St Vincent rang out loud and solemn, reminding us how time was slipping by. Every day was an agony of loss which my parents never mentioned. Daily rituals for Papa continued the same as before: from daybreak, he would work in the vines, then after a change of clothes he would spend several hours working in his office in the *mairie*. He had been elected mayor earlier that year. In the late afternoon and evening, he would devote his time to the Lemoine cellars and wine business. He never said to me: 'Now Auguste has gone, you must take his place, Lily.' But it was the way things worked out.

My mother had a daily dusting ritual, which started with the photograph of Auguste and Papa taken at Clos Lemoine. She joined with my father in a pretence of certainty that their son would return. Daily I heard her putting on a show of optimism that I just couldn't share. She had a stock of phrases that I hated listening to: 'When Auguste gets back, he can do that for me…' or she would say: 'I'm saving that job for Auguste when he gets home on leave.' Oh yes, and when would that be?

Our family avoided talking about the realities, but every night the three of us, with Josephine, sat down at the dining-room table and Papa would tune in the wireless, adjusting the needle to the correct station. During this period of *la drôle de guerre* – the 'phoney war' as the English called it – we could still listen to the facts reported by the French on Radio Paris. It was frustrating to hear confirmation, night in and night out, that our mobilised troops were sitting in underground bunkers on the Maginot Line.

My mother said 'I don't understand why they leave the troops sitting there: the men would be more use back where they all came from. Auguste could be working in the cellars here instead of sitting cooped up in brick tunnels. He must hate it…'

Her eyes filled with tears at this thought, but somehow, she managed to get a grip on her emotions.

'Mme Dumont has posted off all her invoices with a cheque book to her husband on the Line. She reckons he's got more time there than she has here to sort the payments out.'

'It's just her way of getting rid of her unpaid bills', Papa replied with cynicism.

Josephine and I sat and listened: inert and passive. What could she or I say or do to change what was happening? I felt angry. It was dull and monotonous without Auguste around at home, and I detested the domestic drudgery, which seemed unavoidable.

One evening the three of us were listening to a news broadcast when I decided I could not put up with my parents' mood of sorrow and Josephine's silence any longer. I stood up and left the room. There was some relief to be alone in my room, able to lie on my bed staring out of the window as the light faded in the sky and the darkness fell. Inertia was what I hated most. The feeling of helplessness increased as we all played this ghastly waiting game.

Next door to my bedroom was Auguste's. I felt guilty as I turned the handle and switched on the light: no-one ever came into this room any more. The furniture and objects were just as he had left them on that last morning. On his desk were his three most prized objects: his Leica hanging on the back of the chair by its leather strap, his own wireless set and his gramophone. There was a record still on the turntable and out of curiosity I turned on the switch. Immediately the large 78 rpm record started spinning round and round, slowly accelerating to its full speed. I lifted the needle arm to place it on the opening track and suddenly the familiar Big Band sound of loud trumpets and bass saxophones boomed into the empty room. In a panic in case my parents heard, I lowered the volume to listen once more to Cab Calloway. The lyrics and the swing rhythms brought back the memory of Auguste slow-stepping and jiving to this track in the moonlight, out in the courtyard on the night of his twenty-first. I thought of him stuck underground in a cramped tunnel packed with other soldiers; then the song finished and the needle clicked in the groove. I lifted the needle arm, replaced it on its stand, and left the room.

Chapter Twelve: The Warning

One evening in May 1940, there was a tug on the gate bell by an unexpected caller. When I pulled open the tall gate, I was surprised to see Charles Santot standing in front of me with two wrapped parcels tucked under each arm.

'*Enchanté*, Lily,' he said, greeting me with the customary *deux bises*. 'Still as lovely as ever, I see. But you and your brother have let me down badly, you know. You never came to visit me in Paris despite my offer of hospitality! So do you know what? I thought if you won't come to Paris then Paris must come to you. Here. Take a look at these! One is for Auguste, and I'm sure he gives his permission for you to open it. The other is for you.'

He handed both of the parcels to me and I was surprised by their weight and guessed what they contained: paintings.

'Bring them inside and open them upstairs. Now. Where's that old rogue, your father?'

We went indoors and found Papa on the veranda at the back of the house, reading a newspaper. '*Mon vieux*.'

He shook hands warmly with Papa.' I'm down from Paris for a flying visit. Thought I'd call over to see you and your lovely daughter here. Come on, Lily. Open them up!'

I rested the packages on the table and opened the one addressed to me first.

'Charles. This is amazing!' I lifted up the picture and held it at arm's length. It showed a young woman with a sketchbook in one hand and pencil in the other, seated next to an open window with a view of rooftops and gardens beyond.

'Painted in Montmartre and bought in Jeanne Bucher's gallery on the boulevard du Montparnasse. Little known painter, but he has a wonderful eye for detail. And for the ladies, so I understand!' he added, winking at me. We all looked at the other parcel intended for Auguste and there was silence.

Picking up the painting Charles had given me, I took it to my room, propping it up on the dressing table. From a distance the woman appeared even more lifelike. The artist had caught her at the moment when she was looking up, taking in the scene, then sketching it. How did Charles know this was the image of my dream come true?

When I rejoined the two men, their discussion was becoming quite heated about the work Charles had ordered to be done on his Saultmur house. I knew that Papa took a dim view of his friend's extravagance at this time.

'Well, Charles. Not finished yet, I think? With the

manpower shortage at the moment I'm afraid you may have to wait a while before it is completed.'

'Not far off, Antoine. I know what you're going to say: "You must be a lunatic to run to all that expense for a staircase. What was wrong with the old one?" – that's the kind of thing, isn't it?'

My father said nothing in reply.

'You know why I had to make that change? Simply to let the world see that that house is owned by an *ingénieur*, not a *viticulteur*. That staircase is a sort of drill-bit running down to my cellars, and at the top is my little room for inspiration. I don't need this splendid double staircase to impress my visitors. Unlike you, Antoine. I'm hoping Bernard will finish it any day.'

My father was shaking his head.

'Be realistic, Charles. He's lost all his workforce for now. How can your little folly be of any importance at this time?'

Charles just shrugged, and his expression changed, becoming serious all of a sudden as he changed the subject.

'Antoine, you know what's coming, don't you? After this time of inertia since the declaration of war, there will be some terrible times. Make no mistake. Under Hitler's command, Germany will get its revenge for the defeat of 14-18. And France is going to be caught napping: what has anyone done to improve the army since that time? Meanwhile, the Germans have spent the past few years modernising and re-equipping theirs. They have thousands of tanks and aircraft. They will be ready to thrash us. You mark my words. And it will be any day now!'

My father was rarely lost for a reply, but tonight he said nothing except 'Will you have a glass of Chardonnay, Charles? Lily?'

I knew this was another cue for me to leave, so I went downstairs to fetch a bottle from the cellars and a couple of glasses from the kitchen. What was the reason for the secrecy between them? What were they not telling me? Charles's grim predictions rang true. We were all sitting on a time bomb that could explode in our faces at any moment.

Charles was handling a set of our house keys when I returned with the wine.

'Your father has just handed these to me you know, Lily. He tells me I am welcome to come and help myself to the wine in his cellars whenever I like! Is that correct, Antoine?'

No more was said, and Papa quickly changed the subject.

'So how is Paris, Charles? And business?'

'Magnificent. When is it not? Business is booming. Hard to keep up. Just signed a contract with Renault, supplying small parts, you know.' He paused a moment, changing subject quickly: 'Had a wonderful meal with clients at Maxim's last week and insisted that they try your Pinot Noir 1929. They thought it was *parfait* and said they would order a case from their vintner.'

'And who would that be, I wonder?'

'Haven't a clue, *mon vieux*.'

Their conversation shifted onto the question of business and sales and I retreated to my room to study the painting more closely. I took out my sketchpad and made a sketch of the seated artist, wishing it could be me.

CHAPTER THIRTEEN: THE SECRET CELLAR

A few days after Charles's visit my father returned very agitated from a meeting in Beaune. He was short of breath after rushing from the car into the house. There were beads of sweat on his forehead. He held tightly onto the wooden chair-back, taking his weight off his weak ankle.

'How long will supper take?' he said with a tone of impatience. He looked at the pots steaming on the old range, Josephine in front of them stirring the soup.

'As long as you'd like it to, Antoine!' my mother replied, sensing his urgency.

'We'll eat the soup with some bread quickly now, and we'll save the rest for tomorrow. We have to start work in the cellars tonight and there is no time to lose. Josephine, please leave us.'

Without a word, wiping her hands and taking off her apron, she left the room. We listened carefully to the sound of the door closing and her footsteps crossing the courtyard as she headed to the servants' quarters opposite the main house.

'Why this secrecy, Papa?' I asked.

'Lily, only you and your mother must hear what I have to say, and I mean it. Neither of you must breathe a word of it to anybody else. That means not today, not tomorrow, not next week, not ever. I wasn't surprised by what I learned this afternoon. Mentioning no names, I must tell you that people are frightened a German invasion will happen any day now; their war machine is frankly unstoppable. Charles was absolutely right about this. At this very moment, their tanks are crushing any Belgian or Dutch defensive opposition. Any day now they could cross into France. We can expect Hitler to seize Paris; then he will surely grab every city, town or village which has either valuable industry or agriculture.' My mother interrupted him.

'But you exaggerate, Antoine! You know that will never happen to France! Why are you trying to frighten us? What about Auguste in all of this? Have you forgotten him?'

'Look, Jeanne. Let's hope you are right. But suppose it is only a matter of time before his forces reach Burgundy. We have a duty to protect our stocks of wine above all else.'

He paused while he let the news sink in, waiting for our reaction. My mother shook her head.

'But Antoine, what about the Vannet silverware? The Sèvres dinner service? Those paintings Charles has given to the children? Have you forgotten all that?'

Papa raised his eyes to the ceiling and threw up his

arms in a gesture of frustration. Wine was all that mattered to him at this moment.

'This is an emergency, Jeanne. Our wine is our wealth. Our livelihood and my life's work are on the line and you care more about china and silver and a few paintings?'

She did not reply, but the anger she felt was clear in her look of tight-lipped resignation.

'If those things matter to you, then you must pack them up and I suppose we will try to see if there's space for them.'

To me the plan to "hide" Lemoine wine was useless in the circumstances and I found it difficult to believe that my father was recommending such a naïve strategy.

'But Papa, where on earth are we going to hide it all? The old attics? Surely the Boches will come and pull our house apart until they find what they're after? How can we be a match for them?'

My father gave a confident nod of his head as he listened to me.

'Where?' He gestured with his thumb towards the cellar wall and lowered his voice to a whisper. My mother and I had to lean towards him to hear what he was saying.

'We have room for a secret cellar in the basement if we do some shifting and a bit of brickwork. It shouldn't take long.'

'*C'est impossible, Antoine! Tu es fou!* If Auguste were here, then maybe…'

My mother looked worn and weary, her voice

sounded a note of hopelessness, which fired my father's passion and he raised his voice.

'So, Jeanne, do you want the Boches to seize our finest vintages when they come rolling into town? Shall we just invite them in and say: "Have what you want, boys! It only took my lifetime to stock a cellar like this. Drink it all away!"'

Speechless now, my mother and I followed Papa's disappearing figure through the kitchen door into the cellar. He beckoned us to follow.

He led the way between the rows of barrels which ran under the main part of the house, turning left at the far end as if to head towards our workspace. Instead we saw him pick his way between two barrels that stood in front of a small door leading down to a basement cellar that he never used because it had a tendency to flood in winter. With some coaxing my father opened the door and switched on a light showing four steps leading down to a lower level.

'I cleared the racks down here after your father died, Jeanne. Remember that? I've never needed to use them since. That door is the only way in. It should be easy to make this space totally secure. Granted it's a big job, and you two will have to help me. This is where we will move a quantity of our best wines. Then,' and he tapped his nose and winked at us, 'I have a plan to close it off.'

We started that night shifting Lemoine vintages dating from the twenties through the thirties, bottles thick with dust that flew up, choking us with its cloudy haze.

'Move those!' I can hear my father issuing orders to us as he gestured towards the racks of bottles that had made the Lemoine name famous.

'Take care to leave a few bottles of each vintage behind. We don't want it to look as if there's already been a raid!'

It took about a fortnight for Papa to complete the construction work and meanwhile my mother and I packed up the family silver in wooden wine cases. We stacked the precious china, wrapped in old family linen, in panniers used during wine harvests.

'We'll have to order some more from Henri Bichot, Lily, that's all.'

Finally, we covered the special paintings in a pair of old curtains and a sheet of tarpaulin and fitted them into a drawer from an old dresser used in the office. I begrudged giving up the painting Charles had so recently given to me. I wanted to keep it in my room.

'If the Boches come I can hide it in a cupboard so they'll never find it. What's the point of owning a beautiful painting if it has to be locked away in a damp cellar?'

Their silence told me I would not prevail, and I gave in. As I wrapped it up and packed it away, I felt as if I were burying a dream.

Eventually the basement cellar was filled with the racks of finest Lemoine vintages along with a motley range of baskets and wooden cases holding the most cherished valuables from the house.

'I never thought we'd fit so much into the small space, but we have. It should be safe as houses down here by the time I've finished the walling-up, you'll see,' my father said, looking pleased with his work, although it was a mystery to me how he was going to conceal the door into the cellar. When I asked him he tapped his nose and said 'I have a plan. Don't you worry.'

His confidence had returned now that he felt his wine stock was more secure. Changing the subject, he turned to me and said 'And by the way, I was speaking to Henri Boissart the other day. He says he hasn't got a hope of putting away even a quarter of his stocks. With both his sons in active service, same as Auguste, and his wife not used to hard graft, he says he is falling badly behind in the cellars and the office. He can't do it all himself.'

Then he stopped, his blue eyes fixed carefully on me.

'He took me by surprise when he referred to you as 'Jacques's sweetheart', Lily.'

I could feel my cheeks blushing and didn't know what to say in reply. I had only met Jacques a few times, with Auguste.

'I said: "Now you know more than I do on that subject, Henri!" Sharp as a razor, that one. Already looking out for a good match for his sons, no doubt.'

He paused to let me say something, but I stayed silent, avoiding eye contact.

'So, I hope you don't mind, but I've offered your

assistance, Lily. Boissart said he will pay you a bit for your time. There might be accommodation, too, if you ever have to work late. He needs all the help he can get!'

He stopped and looked relieved to see my reaction.

'The money's not important. What matters is you'll learn all you ever need to know at Boissart's. Biggest cellars in Beaune, you can't go wrong there, Lily. Henri Boissart and I go back a good many years. He and I have fought a few battles in our time with the other wine growers in the area. He trusts me, so he will trust you, but for God's sake keep his business there to yourself. Don't go chatting to Josephine or your village friends like Marthe.'

I could take the hint. It seemed that the two men had already set up an arrangement for me to work in Beaune two days each week. Despite the grim news of Hitler's advance towards France and Auguste's long absence, this change in my working life would be a new start and an escape from the daily rituals of the Lemoine household.

CHAPTER FOURTEEN: CHEZ BOISSART

As I cycled through the vineyards on my way to the Boissart family home, I asked myself why my father was so wary of Josephine and Marthe. Josephine prepared and cooked our meals, she cleaned the house and washed and ironed our clothes and all the household linen. She was the mainstay of the home and we all relied on her. She lived in the wing facing the main house where she had her own room, sitting room and bathroom with fresh running water. Time had made her a kind of honorary member of our family, but one who lacked intelligent discretion. Small as her world was, she did not stint in sharing minor household details with anyone and everyone in the village: Lemoine business was everyone's business.

Marthe Cordier saw her as a kind of mother-substitute. After her mother's death Josephine had helped and supported Marthe's family, assuming the role of surrogate mother at times. Occasionally this exasperated my parents, who felt Josephine's kindness to the Cordiers got in the way of her duties to our family.

The Boissart family home was more of a château than a house. It had a magnificent slate roof with corner turrets positioned close to the rampart walls of Beaune. On that bright May morning, Henri Boissart himself met me at the gate and led me down a path towards the house. He was tall and aristocratic in his manner with white hair, at least a decade older than my father.

'Visitors here always think it's our wine cellars they've come for, but I make sure they appreciate these horticultural works of art first.' He gestured towards two parallel rows of topiary yew trees, clipped in strange and unrecognisable shapes.

'These bushes tell more about Boissart family history than our wine.' He came to a standstill next to the topiary figure we were passing at that moment.

'What do you take this to be, *mademoiselle*?'

I looked carefully at the rounded shape in front of me. It was neither an animal nor a human figure, but I couldn't say what it was. Seeing my embarrassment, he told me himself.

'That is a crown, as is that one over there'. Pointing to its matching pair at the end of the other row, he continued 'And this is an orb.' We had moved on at this point to the next figure.

'Why so much royal paraphernalia? Simple. The Boissarts are royalists. We support the Bourbon line. My ancestors were tenants in the old days of the Dukes of Burgundy. They worked vineyards here in Beaune and also on the hillside between Pommard and Volnay and made wine for the tables of the Dukes of Burgundy and later for the Kings of France. This line of topiary tells our story, but it's the devil's own job to keep up the trimming. Manpower is scarce so I do it myself these days. Look how ragged that sheep is.'

My eye followed where he was pointing, and I recognised there was a sheep form within some straddling branches of yew.

We walked on in silence. I was too tongue-tied to ask further questions.

Eventually he led me through an entrance on the left-hand side of the building and we continued along a tiled corridor. Soon he opened a door into an office which appeared to be in complete chaos. Papers in unruly piles, huge ledgers stacked untidily on top of each other, no horizontal desk surface visible anywhere.

'I hear from your father that you are a demon for hard work and that you enjoy running his office like clockwork?' I suppose I must have smiled or shrugged at his flattering words. 'So he says I can borrow you for one-and-a-half, even two days each week.'

I told him that I understood this arrangement and was very happy to be starting the work.

'You can see how we need your help', he said, thumping his right hand down on the tallest pile of paper.

'The hours will be long, I can't pretend otherwise, but my wife will make a fuss of you and I will pay you for your pains. Office only for now. Cellar may come later. Let's see how it goes.'

I felt some relief that the role I was taking on only extended as far as the room we were in. The challenge was overwhelming, and I had no idea how or where to make a start.

'Take a seat at this desk, *mademoiselle*.'

Pulling out an upholstered chair which looked as if it belonged more in a drawing room than an office, I sat down as he indicated.

'Antoine tells me you are painstaking and methodical, which is what I need here. You will need to spend some time reading these papers and seeing how the ledgers work. Come to me if you need answers to your questions and don't be too particular. We need these records updating. I'll leave you to it, if you don't mind.'

He left me seated behind the desk, daunted by the task in front of me.

*

'Did Henri give you a tour of his cellars? Did he trust you with the secret of his hiding places?' asked my father, when I returned home that evening.

As soon as I arrived, I was faced with a barrage of questions from him. I shook my head and reported to him how the piles of filing and sorting of papers had confined me to the office.

'Ah. Yes. I see. He's no fool. I should have known that's the way it would be. He will have a few friends in the *Action Française*, no doubt, to help him out with his wine reserves. You may depend.'

I guessed he was right. Everyone knew how the leading members of the oldest families belonged to this royalist, right-wing group. The privileged, wealthy set.

'Did you meet Mme B.? Did she look after you properly?'

Yes, I had met her. Mme Boissart was a tall, willowy woman many years younger than her husband. I explained that she had brought me my meals on a tray and talked to me about clothes, promising to pass on to me any items she was no longer wearing. Blouses and skirts, even a suit. She'd said to me: 'You'll know how to make them fit you. You're a clever girl, Henri tells me.' She didn't mention her sons or the war and seemed untouched by the worries that consumed my mother at this time.

My father cut in on my thoughts: 'You can't go wrong now, Lily. You have a golden opportunity there!'

Chapter Fifteen: The Occupation

Daily the vice tightened, not just on me. It tightened on us all in Europe during that May of 1940, when the Germans spurred west and south across the border into France and in thirty-eight days effectively annihilated the armies of France, Belgium and Holland; the British barely escaped back to Britain. The newspapers and radio broadcasts showed the nightmare becoming real: Germany had invaded half of France and taken captive over a million and a half soldiers, Auguste included. Jacques and André Boissart had gone missing. That was all anyone knew.

Another waiting game.

Suddenly our village was at the crossroads of history, with refugees from Northern and Eastern France passing through. At first it was the privileged few in their cars with tanks filled with petrol. Then came people with their goods and chattels loaded onto horse-drawn carts. Others followed on bicycles, some trooped on foot.

They weren't stopping. They were all heading for the South of France where they hoped to find safety.

Working up in our vineyard one afternoon in late May, we looked across and saw an astonishing sight: lorries packed with French soldiers travelling along the route to central France. When we saw them I and some of the young boys from the town ran down to the roadside. Perhaps Auguste would be with them? Perhaps he would come home? We stood and watched the ramshackle convoy led by the motorised vehicles carrying armaments and men; then plodded the horses, pulling cannons and other weapons of war. At the back were soldiers on bicycles and others, exhausted, on foot. Asked where they were going, they pointed out they were heading to Moulins under orders to establish some sort of new line of defence to stop the advance of German troops. They told us they had been abandoned by their leaders. That they'd had enough of this bloody war. Some of them discarded their rifles and guns in the ditches alongside the main road, discarding their army caps and items of uniform also. The local boys swooped down on these new toys, claiming them as their own. One or two of the soldiers stopped and asked us if we could give them plain clothes.

'If not, the Germans will make us prisoners of war when they catch up with us' said one soldier, looking straight at me with his dark eyes sunk into their sockets, face dirty, unshaven. I could smell his sweat. I didn't know what to say, but I was asking myself the question 'Why aren't you Auguste, my brother?'

I ran home and grabbed some old gardening overalls

from the scullery, but the soldier had moved on by the time I reached the road. What could I do?

Our family atlas had a permanent place on the dining-room table. It was the same size as a wine ledger and when open it covered over a third of the polished wood surface. After Belgium capitulated to Germany, I can still see my father stabbing with his finger on the green-coloured contours of the map, angrily showing the southward advance of Hitler's forces towards Paris. 'Burgundy next, you may depend!' We had seen the French army was in no shape to put up any worthwhile resistance.

As the mayor, he ordered the preparation and equipping of some cellars as air-raid shelters in case of enemy bombardment. He set up teams to manage each shelter in the case of an alert. But local support for him and his plans melted away: anyone who owned a car was making preparations to leave, strapping suitcases onto the rooftop. Many homeowners had relatives in the South of France and like the millions of other nomads moving from the north to the south along crowded roads, they believed this was the escape to safety. Less privileged families followed their lead and we saw horse-drawn carts being loaded up with mattresses, pots and pans and even livestock like chickens, hens and rabbits, as they too left the town.

Shops were boarded up and Papa only had one assistant left to help with the administration in the *mairie*. There in his office he hoarded sets of house keys that families in flight had entrusted to him.

'We are going nowhere. I'll do what I can to help the people who remain in this village. You and I, Lily, and your mother, must do what we can to keep our vineyards running and to maintain the production of Lemoine wine. I can keep people's keys, but they can't expect me to harvest their grapes.'

I remember his saying this as we walked home together down the main street towards our house; it was the middle of June, late afternoon, it felt like a ghost town. Large townhouses shuttered up and gates onto courtyards locked. Parents still in the village were keeping their children indoors. It was silent everywhere. As we approached our own house, we could see my mother standing anxiously looking out for us; seeing Papa she came rushing towards him on the pavement, shouting and gesticulating.

'We've just heard it on the radio: Paris has fallen! Hitler has seized the Elysée palace. France is defeated.'

Next day our local paper, *Le Bien Public*, filled its front page with the picture of Hitler and his entourage ranged in an arrowhead formation dwarfing the Eiffel tower behind them.

'They'll be here any day,' Papa announced solemnly. 'Be in no doubt: they will want every bottle they can lay their hands on in every cellar in this part of Burgundy and they will want our women. We must humour them; if we don't, they will kill us, and they will destroy our vines.'

*

In the three days that followed, we heard the rumble of enemy aircraft in the skies and the deafening sound of bombs exploding, as Le Creusot and Chalon became further targets for another German offensive. We could see from our hillside, the smoke rising as silence fell on another scene of devastation. It felt as though our part of the Garden of Eden had turned into a living hell.

Late in the afternoon on the third day, when I had agreed to help my father with administrative work in the *mairie*, we heard the church bells ring five times and caught another sound: this time, of loud engine noise.

In the Middle Ages, the *mairie* had been constructed as a defensive stronghold for the *seigneur* and by climbing the stairs to the top of the building we could look out from the high windows across the whole of the surrounding countryside. There was a thin drizzle of rain falling on a convoy of military vehicles making its way towards the town centre like a long, green caterpillar: armoured tanks followed by Mercedes cars and trucks, and at the back of the procession, motorbikes, some with sidecars and some without, the men with their eyes covered by goggles. Straggling behind were the horse-drawn guns and, finally, a few soldiers on bicycles and on foot.

'We must greet them, even when we'd rather spit in their faces.'

His tone was venomous, but I could hear a slight

tremor in his voice. Together we heard groan of engines, at first remote but then getting louder as they came towards the square at the centre of the village.

'Don't let them flatter you, Lily. Be on your guard,' my father warned me as we walked down the stairs and towards the foyer of the building. 'Stupid girls will hop on those bicycles and be on their backs in no time. Keep your distance. Go home now. We will get the better of them, you and I. Together we can outwit even Adolf Hitler!'

He hugged me with his strong arms and led me out of the entrance, pushing me towards the gate in the railings which gave onto the rue du Château. I knew when I turned around briefly to see him standing alone on the steps of the *mairie* that June afternoon that our world was about to change and that there was no going back. He seemed to have visibly shrunken; there he was dressed in his best Sunday suit, in a white starched shirt and black tie but dwarfed by the building behind him and railings on either side. The suit usually reserved for funerals. His sharp blue eyes watching, hawk-like.

Chapter Sixteen: Newcomers

When in my mind I try to reassemble the events of that time – like piecing together the shards of a smashed mirror – I see myself standing in our dusty road at the end of a day of work, peering through the dark green gates closing off the courtyard in front of our house. It is late June 1940 and that time of day when the sun prints the lines of the barred gates onto the cobbled courtyard on the other side. But it doesn't matter which side of these gates I'm on. I'm just a prisoner. We're all prisoners here now.

A tug on the metal bell-pull set off a gentle tolling sound from the small cavity in the gatepost. In earlier times this sound would always have been followed by a shout from one of the family, the sound of feet striking cobbles, the grating of the gate lock and hinges as they were pulled open. I tugged and pulled on the metal handle impatiently, setting the bell swinging erratically in its niche. Then there was the slosh of water in a bucket and the noise of its metal base grating, then footsteps hurrying across the courtyard. The latch was pulled back and in front of me stood Franz Schmidt, a uniformed German soldier, the buttons of his jacket undone and a sponge in his right hand. Behind him our courtyard was filled with military vehicles and motorbikes. Between the gate and the kitchen door was Major Schiffler's car. Obviously, today Franz had been under orders to wash it down and clean off the thick layers of encrusted mud from its long road run. Now it stood gleaming in the sunshine like a chunk of jetstone.

I glanced into the interior of the black saloon car and saw the shiny leather upholstery and walnut dashboard. Thinking of my father's small car, a Rosengart Cabriolet, it was easy to see at a glance that the Germans seemed to know more about luxury and comfort than the French.

'*Fräulein* Lily' he said in greeting, nodding as I swept passed him, trying to avoid eye contact. My name always sounded strange when he said it, and I couldn't answer because I didn't know a word of German. Not at this time, anyway. Josephine and I were under strict orders from my father never to use the men's Christian names, only their surnames.

'*Bonjour*, Herr Schmidt,' I muttered and scuttled passed him, glad to put a distance between us, to join Josephine in the cool interior of the kitchen.

*

Two wings of our house were now providing

accommodation for the officer-in-charge of the unit of soldiers, Major Schiffler, along with ten of his men. Since the Germans had taken over the servants' quarters opposite the main part of the house, my parents granted Josephine the use of Auguste's room next to mine. This was a major concession for my mother, as though letting Josephine use his room was the first step in recognising he might never return.

'Of course,' she said to me when we were preparing the room together, 'I don't know where Josephine will sleep when Auguste comes back, Lily. We may have to put another bed in your room. Meanwhile I think you had better look after his things. Move what you can into your room: you can use the gramophone and wireless now. Radio Paris or Radio Vichy only. You know that, of course? Do you know how this camera works?' she asked, passing it to me. 'Josephine will be better here; it will lift her morale and make her feel one of us. Less isolated.'

I had never thought of Josephine as isolated in any way: from morning through to night she was with the family in the kitchen, included in all our meals, one of us. But when she moved into the main house and brought over her tiny stock of worldly belongings, I realised how alone in the world she was and how dependent on the Lemoine household for her existence. Her history slips my memory – I believe her parents had both been old retainers in the days of my grandparents, but by this stage her parents had died, and we were her family. Throughout our childhood and adolescent years Josephine had been a noisy chattering presence in the kitchen, always giving a constant running commentary on the minutiae of domestic life. She was a walking encyclopaedia of the contents of the larder and every cupboard in the house. She reigned supreme over Lemoine household affairs.

*

Major Schiffler spoke rudimentary French with a strong accent, while most of his subordinates knew no French at all. Yet he held such power and control over the rest of us. Of course, Papa had taken an instant dislike to his German counterpart at their meeting at the *mairie* on the first day of the Occupation. He had reported to us back home that Herr Schiffler had been most insistent 'With such false sincerity', my father said, that he wished my father to understand how this takeover was intended to be peaceful: 'with respect on both sides.' Of course, it was their duty to use posters and public notices to make sure that the citizens of the town understood any new rules and regulations. His men would also instigate patrols of the town and vineyards and establish checkpoints on the outskirts of the town.

'Be wary of him and any others like him, Lily!'

Overnight, Major Schiffler had become my father's new superior, imposing the German command over the *mairie* with a brief preliminary ceremony: the hanging of a portrait of Hitler on the high wall of the main office in the building.

The first order he imposed, with my father's bureaucratic support, was an arms amnesty. Most households kept a gun – for the purposes of killing livestock, or for *la chasse*. Game-hunting and boar-hunting in the woods of Mont des Mélèzes were popular with the men of the town.

At home my father grumbled as he rounded up his best shotguns to take up to the stockpile at the *mairie*. 'You're not going to tell me that all that game and all that boar will run wild after this? The Boches will shoot the lot of them. You'll see.'

I watched Papa from the office window as he crossed the courtyard carrying his two registered hunting guns. He was in full view of a group of soldiers standing near the gate. I remembered a third shotgun Auguste had used for target practice, which had belonged to our grandfather, René Vallet. That was still in the house. Also, there was the matter of a small Browning handgun with its cache of bullets. 'He keeps it "just in case", Lily.' I remembered Auguste's words when, one rainy day in the school holidays our parents had gone out and he had taken me into the office, unlocked the drawers and located the gun. It frightened me. 'In case of what?' I had asked, looking at this lethal weapon in his hand. Auguste shrugged and stowed the gun away in its secret compartment in the office desk, putting his finger up to his lips, warning me to keep quiet.

Later in the afternoon I walked up to the place de l'Hôtel de Ville to see for myself the mountain of guns and ammunition collected there. There was a small queue of local men waiting in sullen silence for a junior officer to check off names and numbers from the list my father had prepared from the records at the *mairie*. I recognised Marthe's father, Charles Cordier, as he stood awkwardly waiting his turn.

From now on, we felt the iron grip of German control in the Lemoine wine business also. All orders except to German customers had to be cancelled. The transportation of barrels or cases of wine would be under German control, but the individual *vignerons* would be trusted to continue every stage of the winemaking process according to time-honoured tradition. The vineyards, cellars and offices would be subject to scrutiny by Major Schiffler and his men, but generally due notice for this would be given. Major Schiffler took his orders in turn from his commanding officer in Beaune.

Meanwhile, the man everyone was talking about, although nobody had met, was the non-military administrator, Herr Futtermann, who had been placed in charge of wine production in the whole of the Burgundy region. Everyone knew that his office was in the Hôtel de la Chasse, now the *Kommandantur*, in Beaune. People had dubbed him the '*Weinführer*'.

'The *Weinführer's* not going to care about the likes

of us here when he has all of the cellars of Beaune at his disposal.' Papa, like other wine-growers in our village, was trying to make a calculated guess as to whether the Lemoine cellars would come under scrutiny.

'I think I can safely say that we won't see much of him in Saultmur. Boissart should be the one to worry, with the scale of his operation. He needs your help more than ever before, Lily.'

Since the occupation of our village and the imposition of roadblocks, I had not been able to continue to work for the Boissarts. My father had spoken to Henri on the phone and learned that the Germans had also occupied a wing of his house and were using the driveway to park their military vehicles. I could picture his anger at this intrusion. Apparently, he had sent a letter to the *Weinführer* requesting a travel pass (a *laissez-passer*) for me to be able to resume work in his office. Even a simple bicycle ride was now subject to the *Weinführer's* permission.

Chapter Seventeen: First Meeting

Lately at night, or early in the morning: tap, tap-tap, tap, tap-tap – I hear again his quick footsteps on stone paving and glimpse the shiny leather boots; the officer's uniform with a wisp of fair hair ravelled around the top right button. I feel again that tightening in the stomach, the excitement of seeing him. First love. Close to me in the dark sometimes I feel his lips on my lips and the mingled whiff of eau de cologne, soap and sweat. The pressure of his body over mine.

The edelweiss. The diamond edelweiss.

And those German words. His words. His very last words, which I don't want to hear. But no matter how much I clench my hands over my ears I still hear them: '*Doch Lili, mein Liebling, ich liebe dich!*' the German words spoken softly and tenderly, 'But Lily, my darling, I love you' and I can even feel his breath on my face. Here and now.

*

Keep to the story, Lily… One morning before the September *vendange* of 1940, I was taking some documents for signing to my father in his office. He was holding a letter, which he handed across his desk for me to read.

'Take a look at this, Lily. It's from Herr Futtermann himself. Address: Hôtel de la Chasse, Boulevard Molière, Beaune. I hope he and his staff are sufficiently comfortable in their new suite of offices and that the wine cellars of my old friend Jules Lacomte come up to their expectations! The gist of it is that he and his staff would now be "giving extra support to the wine growers of the Côte d'Or in the preparation and execution of the coming wine harvest." What do you think that is supposed to mean?'

I took the letter and read it for myself. The tone was very polite but the message loud and clear: there would be German soldiers on duty in the vineyards during the *vendange*. Watching us rather than working. I handed the letter back to my father.

'As you know, I don't think we can expect to see much of him here, Lily. Remember: he has to oversee Chalon, Chablis and the Mâcon and Beaujolais wine producers, so I understand. He knows he's got Schiffler over here to bark out the orders. He himself will keep a safe distance. I'm sure of it.'

I wanted to believe he was right. It was enough to have our house occupied by Schiffler and his men and the village swarming with German soldiers on patrol. I couldn't face having to be humble and polite to the *Weinführer*, who already seemed to have too much control over our lives, even before we had met him.

*

Later that afternoon, I was typing a letter at my desk at the *mairie*, my father in the adjacent office, when we both heard the sound of a car drawing up outside and a metallic door slamming suddenly.

'Stay calm, my girl! The *Weinführer's* here!'

It seemed Papa had completely misjudged the matter. Saultmur was not as insignificant as he had tried to make out.

When I looked through the window, I saw an open-top black car with a tall uniformed German officer walking towards the building, the heels of his boots making a brisk tapping noise across the cobbles. I was standing in readiness for his entry like a rebellious schoolgirl trying to appear obedient as a new teacher enters the classroom.

'*Heil Hitler!*' he announced, as he stepped through the doorway, making an exaggerated gesture in the direction of the portrait of the Führer which hung on the wall close to my desk. He seemed faintly comic.

'Good Morning to you also, *mademoiselle.* Where is the mayor, please?'

He spoke with a deep voice, using our language with complete fluency, but with a strong German intonation. What surprised me was how young he looked: only a year or two older than Auguste. No more than that.

'He's in his office, Herr Futtermann.'

He nodded as I spoke and his piercing gaze made me feel uneasy, as though he expected me to say something more.

'Please tell him that Herr Futtermann is here to speak with him, if he has a moment to spare.'

He stood and waited whilst I turned my back to knock and enter my father's office. I felt acutely conscious of his eyes on me. When I returned a moment later with my father, his limp seemed more pronounced than usual. He stepped forward and shook my father's hand warmly. Seeing the two together I noted how tall and athletic he looked beside my father, who now spoke with starchy formality.

'Let me say that I and my daughter Liliane here,' and he gestured towards me, 'are ready to welcome you to Saultmur.' He gestured towards his office.

Herr Futtermann smiled and nodded approvingly.

'The feeling is mutual, Monsieur Lemoine. It is an honour for me to visit this village of such great international renown.' Making a little polite bow, he followed my father into his office and the door closed behind them.

He was not what I had expected at all. I had imagined the *Weinführer* would have been grey-haired and overweight from a lifetime of eating and drinking too indulgently. He was the opposite. When he said 'please' there was some sincerity in his tone, which had put me at my ease, but perhaps he had been a bit too gushing about our "world-famous" village? Trying a bit too hard to win us over on this first meeting. As I sat down again to finish my typing, I kept hitting the wrong keys and making mistakes. I wanted to know what they were talking about and what impression he was making on my father.

Their discussion lasted fifteen minutes and as the door opened, I heard the *Weinführer*'s silky tones once again.

'I feel sure we shall enjoy a happy partnership, Monsieur Lemoine. Please understand that we bow to the superiority of your knowledge and understanding in all aspects of wine production on the Côte d'Or. I look forward to our future meetings. Good morning to you!'

As he marched passed me, he touched the brim of his cap and smiled, opening the door out onto the front steps himself. Together my father and I stood and watched him climb back into his car.

'So, what did you talk about, Papa?' It was obvious that there was some urgency behind this swift, impromptu meeting.

'The Boches are concerned about the harvest: they know the vines have been severely damaged this year, but it hasn't escaped their attention either that many of our menfolk are now stuck in PoW camps, so they recognise there is a labour shortage. I outlined our plans as they stand, and he has asked for a copy of the lists you've been drawing up, Lily, for the grape harvest. Send them to him through the post.'

As he spoke, we saw Herr Futtermann skilfully reverse the car towards the square and steer it towards the main street.

'Apparently he's on a tour of all the Côte d'Or villages with this message,' Papa said. Making his presence felt, I should say. No promises, but he might be able to send in some labour to help out where it is most needed.'

He thought for a moment before adding '*Dis donc:* his words flowed like a bottle of cheap Bordeaux. Watch that one, Lily!'

Chapter Eighteen: Saint Denis

The long, hot weeks before the *vendange* stretched interminably ahead of us. Our town felt to me like an inferno which I longed to get out of, but from which there seemed to be little chance of escape. With ten German soldiers now living on the premises, we were under surveillance morning, noon and night. Josephine and I, Maman and Papa, we had all become like the poor rabbits kept in their hutches at the back of our house, waiting for their moment of release.

It was as though my mother, after years of obedience to the Catholic Church, found it easier than any of the rest of us to be civil and well-behaved towards Major Schiffler and the others. Increasingly, mealtimes in the kitchen seemed intolerable to me. When the men had their supper, my mother, Josephine and I were expected to serve them like waitresses.

Invariably the meal would start with Major Schiffler asking: '*Et du vin*?' His question would never be directed at anyone in particular, but my mother would usually ask me to bring up two or three bottles from the cellar. I would place these on the table with seldom any thanks, I hated feeling their eyes on me, assessing me. As the men consumed their meal and their wine, their talk in German would get louder and louder. None of us knew what they were saying but their glances, their nudges and their raucous laughter gave us a good idea. If any of them stepped over the line of politeness though, Schiffler would slam his fist on the table and order the offender from the room.

The four of us sat down for the family meal only after theirs was finished. At this time of year there was an abundance of vegetables and fruit from our garden, but with more mouths to feed the portions were rationed and any leftovers were carefully guarded. However, my mother's solicitous attention to the Germans infuriated me and on one particular evening I challenged her.

'Do you think we should be caring quite so much for representatives of an army that has imprisoned Auguste?' There was a stunned silence. Josephine, my father and mother looked at me astonished at what I'd said. I pulled back my chair and left the kitchen through the back door.

All I knew was that I resented her more than I could say. She hardly seemed to acknowledge the work that I put in to help my father in the *mairie* or in the Lemoine wine business. In fact, I had come to the conclusion that she knew and understood very little about it. That was what men did and it really didn't have much to do with her.

The kitchen garden was full of orderly rows of vegetables near the house and fruit trees grew near the back wall. The apple trees were laden with ripe fruit which nobody had yet had time to pick. I reached up and plucked a ripe apple from one of the trees and ate it as I left the garden through the back gate and made my way across our neighbour's vineyard, downhill towards the rue des Charrons. I tossed the core into the stream near the road and saw it was running low, but as I watched the apple core be carried away, I remembered the summers of our childhood when Auguste taught me to swim in the deeper stretches of the stream.

I hated the thought of returning to the house, feeling trapped in a round of domestic tasks, so instead I decided to take a long walk up through the vineyards, heading for the viewpoint near the woodland. There was still some time before the evening curfew.

Several vineyards higher up, the slopes in front of me were now overgrown and neglected, their leaves looking brown and shrivelled, grass and weeds choking the roots of the vines. Here and there khaki motorcycles purred their way on an early evening patrol of the *vignobles.* I kept out of view. My way took me past the Lemoine 1938 gateway, the green paint on the gate now peeling and showing the rust beneath. The serried ranks of Lemoine vines would be ready for pruning any day, but the grapes did not look good. Many of the bunches were gnarled and rotten.

I could see the door of the *cabotte,* the dry-stone wall

hut on the far side of the vineyard standing open, and I looked in to check the store of tools: all were neatly lined up, cleaned and ready for use, standing alongside large, empty wooden crates for harvesting the grapes. I pulled the door firmly shut and heard the latch click.

Leaving the tall wall of our vineyard behind me, I carried on up a well-beaten pathway flanked by tall rambling hedges interspersed with fruit trees, stopping briefly to crop and eat a palmful of the ripe blackberries, tasting the burst of sweet juice in my mouth before I summoned the energy for the hottest part of the climb: the stretch of unshaded track that led into the borders of the woodland which capped this part of the Mont des Mélèzes hillside.

Sweat was trickling down my cheeks and my light cotton dress was sticking to me as I climbed up the final stretch of pathway. There was a strong smell of pine and the resinous scent was quite overpowering in this heat. The track finally swung to the left on a bend that opened out into the flat grassy space where the statue of Saint Denis stood. I was expecting to be alone, to have a few moments to take in the view, which miniaturised our village and made the huge problems of the day seem insignificant.

There was someone standing close to the monument and my automatic reaction was one of irritation. I had come this far to get away from people, only to find myself cheated out of a few minutes of solitude by a stranger. Then with a sudden stab of fear I noted the grey uniform of a German officer and as he turned his head towards me, I saw that his cap looked even more ridiculously cluttered with insignia than Major Schiffler's. Beneath the brim, two clear, blue eyes were staring steadily back at me, wary at first then with a glint of humour. As our eyes met, we recognised each other immediately. I felt myself blushing with embarrassment whilst he simply smiled and lifted his cap in a gesture of old-world courtesy.

'Mademoiselle Lemoine! *Bon après-midi!*'

His greeting had a note of warmth and friendliness which took me by surprise, prompting me to reply in a similar tone.

'*Bon après-midi,* Herr Futtermann!' As I stammered out his name, I felt the yawning gulf between us.

'I have received those lists you have typed so neatly, Liliane. Do you mind if I call you that?' He paused, watching me and waiting for my reply. I heard my father's words echoing in my head: 'Be on your guard, Lily.' Then I said

'No, I don't mind. You may call me Lily.' I heard my own voice and thought I sounded very childish.

'You have walked from your house, I presume, Lily?' And he pronounced my name carefully, self-consciously even.

'Yes, I have.' He appeared to listen attentively to my brief reply.

'It is a long way in this extreme heat, I'm afraid.' I thought he was lingering a bit too long on this point. Did he really care as much as he was pretending?

'Mmm.' Was I supposed to give reasons for coming here? After a short pause he continued.

'My good friend Henri Boissart in Beaune advised me to visit this spot, you know. I happened to tell him that I was pining for my native Bavaria: the smell of the pine trees, the deep blue skies above them, and the mountains. He told me Burgundy could never be Bavaria, but it could give me pine trees and it can let me have a view of mountains: what more could a man want?'

He had fixed his eyes on me. He must have noticed my reaction at the mention of the Boissart name. The coincidence was surely uncanny? Of all the *négociants* in Beaune, why did it have to be him? Here in the warmth of a pine-scented summer evening he seemed to be letting his guard drop by making personal disclosures, which showed that he was taking me into his confidence. Surely this was out of bounds?

'Perhaps your father knows him? His cellars are some of the finest in the region and his family one of the oldest. But I think I can tell you know all this already?' I nodded.

He was trying not to be condescending, to avoid sounding pompous and arrogant. Despite his uniform, his trappings of power, his abhorrent connections, I was starting to like him.

At that moment the sun was dazzling me, I cupped my hand over my eyes and tilted my head back to see him clearly. The look in his eyes was softening as he eyed me up and down.

Hesitantly I turned and walked ahead a few paces as if to take in the view. I needed to break away from his intense gaze. I tried to focus my attention on the spire of Saint Vincent, the *mairie* with its mosaic of yellow and green tiles glinting in the sunshine and, mostly masked by other nearby buildings, the rooftop of my own home. How could I escape? For these few seconds I tried hard to concentrate on the clear, deep turquoise colour of the sky and the far-distant mountain range, no more than a blue smudge on the horizon. I wanted to dissolve, to disappear.

As I was turning, I felt him reach out and slowly take hold of my right hand. He had removed his cap with his other hand and his fair, tousled hair glinted in the sunlight. 'I know this is out of order in these times, Lily, but it is not wrong.' And he bent over and kissed me.

Muttering an apology, he strolled back over to his car and opened the door. The sound of the car engine starting up cut through the bird calls and the silence of the place. So I stood on that spot at that moment in time watching Karl Futtermann manoeuvre his black car and the rumble of the engine noise seemed like an earthquake, shaking and threatening the ground where I stood. I felt unsteady, about to faint. Then he accelerated and the tyres stirred up the dust. The car disappeared from view and I heard the sound of the engine fade into the distance. It was getting late and I walked at speed back the way I'd come.

Chapter Nineteen: The Weinführer

'People are calling him "the Scarlet Pimpernel" because he crops up anywhere, and everywhere. I'm not surprised by what you say, Lily.'

It was supper the following day. The four of us eating our soup in stoic silence. For something to talk about, I mentioned my meeting with the *Weinführer.* My mother and Josephine listened. My father spoke first.

'Was he wearing his uniform, Lily?' I nodded, irritated by such an obvious question.

'That's interesting. I'm hearing from several different sources that he sometimes appears in plain clothes, no uniform. Apparently, he turned up one weekday morning for a visit to the *Reine Marguerite* cellars in Beaune, looking like one of us. Well, not quite. Apparently his "plain clothes" are distinctively Bavarian, so they say. He wears one of those green-felted loden jackets which, of course, certainly marks him out from folk round here.' My father continued, 'I'm surprised he doesn't die from the heat, wearing cloth like that at this time of year.'

He carried on scooping up the thin soup Josephine had prepared. 'A bit watery, this, Josephine. Could have done with a bit more flavour.'

Josephine shrugged without replying. I continued the thread of conversation about the *Weinführer.*

'Maybe the jacket was just for the cellars, Papa, they are always cold?' My father nodded and carried on chewing a mouthful of soup and bread. I was about to mention the Henri Boissart connection, but thought better of it. He had shared personal information far too quickly with me. I caught Josephine's eye and knew immediately this piece of gossip would be around the village in no time.

My father continued the topic. 'People are generally liking what they see. The *Weinführer* knows very well how to get on the right side of people. Furthermore, he seems to have all the right connections around here already.'

He paused for a moment to eat a chunk of bread, and to see whether we were all listening carefully.

'I was at a special meeting of Saultmur *vignerons* yesterday,' he continued. 'We were meant to be planning the *vendange*, but you know how it is. Eduard Lacon had all the facts about him. His wife is the sister of Madame Boissart and he told us that the Boissart family were personal friends of the Futtermanns going back a long way. A Beaune-Munich business connection originally, I believe, made after World War I. The *Weinführer's* father forged the connection, coming on trips to sample the wine because he liked this area of Burgundy. He got friendly with Père Boissart, started stocking up on his wines for his cellar in Munich. He began in the wine trade in a very modest way, I understand, but his business has flourished for obvious reasons in the last ten years.'

He paused, took another spoonful of soup and seemed to be reflecting carefully before resuming. 'You know something, Lily? I like all that I am hearing about the man. I've only met him once, but I'm a good judge of character. Based on what I've heard, I'd even go so far as to say he's a decent enough chap.' He looked at me and nodded.

'The only problem with the *Weinführer* is that grey cloth and those badges. The man is both friend and foe. A lethal cocktail, we might say. All we can do, each and every one of us, is to be on our guard. Be careful what you say and whom you say it to.'

I nodded and stood up to gather the soup dishes, carry them over to the sink, careful not to catch anyone's eye.

*

Shortly after this a letter addressed to my father from the *Weinführer* arrived in the office at the *mairie*. Under the impress of the black spread eagle in the letter head were several lines of elegant gothic script I found hard to decipher. As I tried to make sense of it, I thought of his touch, his kiss, and wondered whether from now on he would keep his distance and communicate by letter only.

'You read it, Papa. The *Weinführer* plans to make a tour of the vineyards during the harvest.' I handed over the letter and saw my father frown as he read it, then he said:

'Listen to this, Lily. "*I would like to propose bringing a professional photographer with me to record this year's harvest in pictures.*" Why on earth does he want to do that? What's wrong with just letting us get on with our work? Whatever the reasons, we have no option: send him a reply!' Angrily he passed the letter back to me and carried on with his work.

Day by day the *Weinführer* was asserting his authority over the wine growers of the region and my father naturally resented it. The changes imposed on him by the Germans limited his authority, hurt his pride. He was under the *Weinführer's* boot now and there was little he could do about it. Although he liked the man personally, he detested the authority he had over him.

On behalf of my father I sent a polite and formal reply to the letter, accepting the proposed arrangement, wondering when the photographic tour would take place.

We all knew this was going to be a lean harvest: bad weather had spoilt the grapes, but still they had to be harvested. The usual high spirits at harvest time had deserted us all and in the second week in September, in baking hot sunshine, we made our way to the vineyards seated on a horse-drawn cart driven by my father. Our team consisted of the four of us: my parents, Josephine and I. The cone-shaped wicker baskets and wooden crates for grapes were heaped on the cart and we steadied them to stop them falling off as the horse climbed the steep slope. We were cropping chardonnay grapes in one of the vineyards on the higher slopes where the ground was rockiest. Tricky work, I remember, because we had to separate the rotting grapes from the healthy and then we had to be very careful not to overload the panniers or to crush the newly cropped bunches. I worked alongside my father, Josephine alongside my mother. Each time we filled the panniers, we tipped the contents into the back of the carts.

Major Schiffler had posted German soldiers in the vines and I remember my father's saying 'If they're going to stand in the beating sun watching us all, why doesn't he tell them to get on and help with the harvest! That was supposed to be the plan, at least. What use are they to man or beast standing stiff as posts?'

'Hush, Antoine. He'll hear you,' was my mother's reply, fearing the soldier would hear his words. My father knew he was safe. The soldier could not understand a word of French.

'Thanks to them we're seriously short of manpower: you may be sure there'll be French hands cropping the grapes on the slopes of the Moselle and the Rhine this year.'

The German soldiers were sweating like pigs in the

hot sunshine while we trudged up and down the vines, snipping, snipping and dropping the bunches into the panniers. Ridiculous in their knee-high shining boots, woollen uniforms buttoned high to the neck on sentry duty, while Papa and I worked from the end to the middle of each row, disheartened by the poor condition of the crop. Suddenly we heard a voice.

'Look this way, straight at the camera, Fräulein.'

Glancing up I heard the shutter click, saw a German soldier with a camera. 'I try another, please?' He spoke some German words and gestured leftwards with his arm to the soldier at the end of the neighbouring row, telling him to move across. His aim was a group shot with my father, myself and the soldier on duty, and as he made us look his way, the shutter sounded again. We were taking a few steps back to the row of vines we were cropping, when we heard a different voice calling to all the pickers.

'Good morning to you all. At least the weather has done us proud for the *vendange*. Thank you for letting Otto here do his job. Our men are here to make sure you all have what you need, especially water in this heat.'

It was Herr Futtermann addressing the workers. Today he was in plain clothes, a light grey lounge suit, shirt and tie. He patted Otto, the photographer, on the back as he walked over to speak to us.

'I will see to it personally that you receive copies of these pictures. I will send word to your office when the prints are ready, Monsieur Lemoine: let's say in two to three days.' He looked awkward, almost ridiculous in his city clothes, towering over my father, who had not heard him approach and was bent double as he cut through the stalk of a bunch of grapes at the base of a vine. Straightening up quickly, Papa nodded his assent, pausing in his work to see whether more was expected by Futtermann. He watched carefully as the *Weinführer* addressed me.

'Perhaps, Mademoiselle, you will collect them on your father's behalf? He is a very busy man as you know.'

Painfully conscious of the sweat trickling down my face, the damp patches under my arms, I managed to stammer out my assent.

'Monsieur Lemoine, I will ask you to let me use your daughter's services that morning, if you would be so kind? I will need her help in identifying the subjects in each of our pictures. Their names are on those excellent lists she prepared so carefully, but I need her assistance in matching names to faces. It would have seemed unnecessarily impertinent to interrupt their important work to check for names this morning.'

I could tell that his complicated turn of phrase and his heavy-handed courtesy was beginning to win my father over, despite himself.

'That should be possible, of course, Herr Futtermann.' There was a note of determined resignation as he added: 'We are always at your service, *bien sûr*.'

Shortly after this brief exchange, we stood and watched him turn his back on us and make his way to a neighbouring vineyard. He had made a date with me, that was clear. A private meeting for apparently business reasons. With my father's permission.

'He's a skilful negotiator, that one, Lily. He knows exactly what he wants and how to get it.'

Chapter Twenty: At the Kommandantur

It was sunny and there was a slight wind at my back as I pedalled my bicycle from Saultmur to Beaune that late September morning. It was three months since I had last ridden along the road to work in Henri Boissart's office. In the vineyards on either side I could see people still slowly moving along the vines, bent under the cone panniers, harvesting the last remaining grapes.

As I approached the *route nationale* there was a roadblock ahead of me: a couple of armed German soldiers were standing ready to check people's documents as they passed through. I had mine in my bag: a letter to my father from the *Weinführer's* office stating the date and time of today's meeting along with a *laissez-passer* signed by Herr Beauftragte Karl Futtermann. One of the soldiers took the documents from me and read them carefully before handing them back. Then he nodded to his colleague, and together they waved me through.

After a further short, ten-minute ride to the Hôtel de la Chasse I noticed the driveway was filled with a cluster of army vehicles and recognised the black Mercedes parked at a distance from the rest. The swastika flag was waving from a flagpole high up in the middle of the building where the tricolour should have been. The word KOMMANDANTUR was in capital letters on a large banner hung above the front entrance. I propped my bicycle against the wall and entered through the large swing doors.

At the former reception desk, a uniformed German woman stood watching as I approached. She listened as I told her why I was there. She beckoned me to follow her up a carpeted staircase leading to a suite of rooms on the first floor.

The first room we entered was an administrative office occupied by three uniformed men working at their desks. There was the rapping sound of typewriters and one of the men was speaking in German on the phone.

My guide knocked on an inner set of large double doors and these were opened by Herr Futtermann himself. He was in full uniform today, his collar and epaulettes embroidered with the insignia of his rank.

'Good morning, Mademoiselle Lemoine. Please take a seat.' He gestured to a satin-backed chair. While he spoke curtly in German to the young woman who had led me up the stairs, giving her a set of instructions, I sat down. In front of me was a large table strewn with photographs. The door closed behind my guide and suddenly I was alone with him.

'The photographs have turned out splendidly, and I have them here on my desk. But I can see you have been hurrying; you may need a drink of coffee, or water perhaps?' I declined his offer.

'As I explained to your father, I need your help matching faces to names in these photographs. I'm hoping that you can tell me something about these people whom you must know quite well, I should think?' At this point he sat down on the leather seat behind the table and fixed his eyes on me.

'Yes, of course. Most of them I have known all my life.'

He nodded, offering me the first photograph from the pile. It showed a group of villagers working their way up the vines; they were mostly women. Smartly dressed and standing slightly apart was Madame Flavigny, Charles Santot's aunt. She was wearing a silk headscarf, not the traditional headdress like the others in the picture, and elegant, wide-legged trousers with a light jacket. Clearly, she had not intended to pick the grapes herself. I was able to identify most of the other *vendangeurs* by name.

'What can you tell me, please, about Madame Flavigny?' I hesitated at first. Not exactly sure what he wanted. Then I told him that she was a widow. She was now overseeing the harvesting of the grapes, but generally these days she also managed the significant wine-production business her husband had left her.

'Do they produce quality wines, would you say?'

His probing led me to give the story of this significant

family, their links to the Château de Vougeot and their white and red wines which, so my father believed, were some of the finest in the whole of Burgundy.

'Except for your father's own vintages, surely?'

He threw in this question without expecting me to answer, then he passed me another photograph and asked more questions. This process went on until we had covered many of the lesser and greater inhabitants still active as wine-makers in our small town.

'The people of your town are very skilled and talented, if I may say so. There are few such places in the whole of Burgundy. Do you have any questions to ask me, perhaps?' He had his eyes fixed on me, waiting for what I would say.

'The photographs of the Lemoine family group? Do you have those, please?'

'Would you like to see them?' He paused, waiting for my answer.

'Yes, if possible.'

He brought over three larger prints. The first he handed me was the picture of the three of us: Papa in the foreground, standing in front of me, then behind us the German soldier, upright, hands behind his back, looking on. The second picture showed me in close-up alone, looking up as I was crouching down to clip bunches near to the ground. My hair was untidy. My expression resentful.

'The first, of course, is business: the harvest continues but under a watchful German eye. In the second the camera…'

He looked closely at me, his blue eyes soaking me up. '.... captures you for just a second.'

He handed me a third print of a picture taken, literally, behind my back showing me walking away from the camera, carrying the cane pannier filled with of grapes, my back to the row of vines.

'And now I must let you go, Lily', he said as he stood up and walked round the desk to stand in front of me. 'Go back to your beautiful village and carry on the good work for your father. Just one more question before you leave.'

He paused to take the pictures lying on my lap. As he bent down, I could see the short cut of his blond shining hair, his masculine smell up close to me. I felt my hand shake as I picked up the rest of the photographs and passed them to him.

'The question which remains to be decided is whether your father would kindly host a wine-tasting for myself and one or two of my men? I have it on firm authority that the wines of the Domaine Lemoine are of an even higher order altogether.'

He seemed to break off in mid-sentence as he looked down at me. There was an awkward pause before he added hastily 'I have the utmost confidence in your father and … you, of course.'

His flattery made me want to say something more, but I was too tongue-tied.

'Please, as a token of my gratitude, take this photograph to show your family.' He handed me the one of father and daughter. 'Let us hope the visit to the Lemoine cellars can be arranged as soon as possible.'

Briskly and efficiently he steered me to the door, politely shaking hands as he ushered me out in full view of the staff in the outer office.

*

Two or three days later an envelope arrived from the *Weinführer's* office, addressed to Monsieur Antoine Lemoine. It enclosed two documents, one the *laissez-passer* and the other a work permit, together with an explanatory note: 'M. Lemoine, please find enclosed the requisite documents for Liliane to resume her part-time employment with M. Henri Boissart, Beaune.'

Papa handed me the documents, saying: 'He wastes no time, that one. I'll speak to Henri myself and arrange a date for you to start work for him again. It won't be for a few weeks yet, though. I need your help here in our office and at the *mairie*. It'll be November. When things go a bit quiet.'

Chapter Twenty-One: The Wine-Tasting

The proposed visit from Herr Futtermann to our cellars worried my father acutely. During the week prior to the visit we worked late into the night to ensure new bottles were properly labelled and all our account books up to date.

'If they want to see our accounts, show them the ledger for the past couple of years only. As you know, our records from the twenties and thirties are stowed away in the attic.' He winked at me.

'Leave all their questions to me, Lily. You and Josephine can pour the wine. As the spokesperson for the Domaine Lemoine, I'll give all the details about the *appellation*, the *lieu-dit* – the Germans should love all that. I'll fill them in about the angle of the sun on the vines, the quality of the soil, the *terroir*. I'll teach them a thing or two about our Lemoine wines! You and Josephine are simply there to pour a sample of each wine into their glasses. I'll do all the talking, don't you worry!

His voice echoed around the walls of our dimly lit

cellars. Two upright barrels stood as tables for bottles and glasses. My father was planning to offer six wines, three whites and three reds, all taken from the last decade.

'He will probably want a walk through first, which I shall lead. Your mother says she would prefer to stay upstairs.'

As the church bell struck seven, we heard the slamming of car doors, the rattle of the gates. Papa went to greet the visitors whilst Josephine and I waited inside. I heard a familiar voice:

'Good evening, Monsieur Lemoine. I am delighted to present to you two of my assistants: Herr Kettner and Herr Dortmann. They are here to improve their grasp of the fine wines of the area, as of course am I. We hope we will not take up too much of your time.'

Footsteps sounded across the courtyard and grated on the stone steps into our kitchen. Papa led them quickly over to the cellar door and within moments the three men stood opposite us, in the dim light.

'Delighted to meet you once again, Mademoiselle Lemoine,' the *Weinführer* said, glancing deferentially at my father as he acknowledged me. He also nodded graciously towards Josephine who stood silent and aloof.

'I must thank you for the prompt organisation of this special event.'

His glance made eye contact with each of us, like a skilful leading actor in the scene of a play.

'I have heard much about the Lemoine wines from

my business associates in Beaune. I think I would go as far as to say they have a towering reputation, but as yet I have not had the pleasure of savouring them for myself.'

My father led the party through the cellars, giving them the history of his business as he went. I could tell he was nervous, he limped badly, stumbling as he spoke. As we passed from the first cellar into the second, the *Weinführer* put his hand up to halt the party.

'Just a moment, Monsieur Lemoine. I'm trying to work something out. My good friend Henri Boissart says that one can get easily lost in his cellars. They are in a maze formation under the streets of Beaune and run a far distance from the boundaries of his house and land. And these cellars? Are they the same? How far do they extend, would you say?'

My father was quite nonplussed by the question, I could tell.

'These cellars run below the footprint of the house and do not extend beyond our own boundaries.' His eyes caught mine for an instance, then shifted to the *Weinführer*, who was making us both very nervous with his interrogation.

'Is there another layer of cellars under these, may I ask? I've heard that there are several ancient cellars in Saultmur *à deux étages*, though I have yet to visit one.'

As he finished speaking, he marched over to the door that led, directly, to the secret cellar. He tried the handle, but the door was locked. My father glanced meaningfully in my direction.

'Lily, go and fetch the key to that door, will you? I can show Herr Futtermann our fine collection of *tastevins* which we keep locked away down here. An old Vannet custom, you understand.'

I made a move to return to the kitchen, having no idea where the supposed key would be and wondering how we might escape detection. And why mention *tastevins*?

'No, please. In my short time in the region I have seen many impressive collections of *tastevins* already and need not see another one tonight. Let me apologise for my curiosity. Please, I beg you to continue.'

As my father led the way, with what must have been a profound but noiseless sigh of relief, he spoke about the problems of the two-storey cellars, placing a special emphasis on the fact that the *vignerons* tended not to use them since they were subject to flooding in winter. Eventually he stopped where the bottles and glasses had been set out ready for the wine-tasting.

The *Weinführer*'s questions continued on a more personal level:

'In which year did you take over from your father-in-law, Monsieiur Vannet?' or 'How does a man turn a *vin ordinaire* into a *vin extraordinaire?*' and Papa told the true story of how he had inherited a cellar filled with his father-in-law's inferior '*vin jaune*'. 'It had all been produced in the days before we brought in the AOC designation. Every single barrel of Chardonnay tasted like yellow vinegar. It all had to go. So I summoned a team of local men and they cleared out all the old dusty bottles and emptied the barrels of the Domaine Vallet's *vin jaune* in the stream at the bottom of the hill. My wife was not very happy, I'm afraid!'

He chuckled, remembering my mother's distress.

'We started from scratch and year by year since then we have tried to create wines of the highest quality. Some better than others, as you will see.'

Josephine and I stood at a distance, not making any contribution to the exchange between the two men, waiting to serve the wine. I remember the voices echoing from the damp cellar walls blackened with algae, smelling of musk.

'I think he likes you, Lily,' Josephine whispered the words, smiling broadly.

'Shhhh!' I raised my finger to my mouth. Frowned. 'Who do you mean?' I was not going to let on.

'The *Weinführer.*' She nodded in his direction as she muttered the word.

'Nonsense, Josephine. How can you say that?'

I should have put a stop to the discussion then and there. I was foolish to encourage her with a question.

'The way his eyes lit up when he saw you. The way he looks your way when he's supposed to be speaking to your father. He's got an eye for the ladies, that one!'

The men were coming back towards us now, so we stood ready, each with a bottle to pour.

My father presented the first wine with a short introduction. 'We shall start with our 1932 Pinot Noir: this was a very good year. An excellent harvest and this wine has been one of our most popular.'

I poured a small amount into each of the glasses and handed one to each of them. Herr Futtermann made a great show of plunging his nose into the glass, saying

'It has a very good nose.'

Then he held it up to the faint light and announced 'Yes. A good robe also, if I may say, and as to the flavour…'

He tossed his head back and poured all the wine into his mouth at once. Then followed a swilling and swooshing of the wine around his cheeks before he swallowed it in one gulp.

'That had a wonderful, full-bodied flavour. Some fruity notes, I believe? Mmmm. A most delicious, long aftertaste.'

His eyes settled on me. 'So, what is your opinion of this 1932, Mademoiselle Lemoine? Is it up to your father's best standard, do you believe?'

'I am sure it is.'

'But have you tasted it?'

'Not for some while, I think.'

I could feel my cheeks burning with embarrassment at his questions, at the way he was singling me out and making me conspicuous with his attention.

'Ah, I see.'

We moved on to the next wine, a white Chardonnay,

and my father spoke about the taste and the way he had developed the production of the wine over the past two decades.

'This is the wine we can say has the greatest following from Paris to New York. My daughter can show you our photographs of the rich and the famous who have ordered this wine in recent years.'

As the *Weinführer* sniffed and sipped at his glass, he nodded at me.

'Let me guess, Mademoiselle, who these might be. Could it be our American friends Mr Hemingway or Mr Fitzgerald, perhaps? Or what about that famous *bon viveur* from across the English Channel – Mr Churchill? He's a man well known for his love of fine wines!'

Each time, I was surprised by his persistent questions. I wanted him to leave me alone, in the shadows, but he kept on with his direct inquiries until my father interrupted him by saying:

'Show Herr Futtermann our famous customers, Lily.'

I led him to the noticeboard, to let him see the evidence for himself.

'Ah, the King who abdicated! There can be no question but that this wine must bring solace to one who, like us all, must miss his cherished "sceptered isle", his *Heimat*.' He placed heavy stress on the German word, before throwing his shoulders back as if he were about to address a troop of soldiers.

'So, Monsieur Lemoine and Mademoiselle. I have

to tell you that I am here on official business also. My superiors have firmly requested that I remember their cellars as much as my own here in Burgundy! Of course, Göring you know, is a Bordeaux man. Pour him a glass of Château Lafitte-Rothschild and in no time he becomes a quite different fellow. Truly.'

He looked closely to see my father's reaction and turned his head to catch my eye. His eyes were full of laughter.

'Goebbels has a *penchant* for Burgundy, you may be glad to hear. His wine cellar is graced with the names we all know so well: Romanée-Conti, Échezaux, Leroy-Bèze. To my knowledge, he has yet to savour the unusual notes of the Lemoine Pinot Noir 1932 and I should like to send him several cases of this and also of a variety of your Chardonnays. How should I buy some of this wine? Would you like to prepare the cases now, or would you prefer for me to send you my order and then to call to collect the cases?'

'As you wish, Herr Futtermann.' My father caught my eye and nodded assertively.

'It is always a very great pleasure to visit your little town, so I think I shall say goodnight and thank you for now. Tomorrow I shall send an order to you and perhaps your daughter can kindly let my office know when the order is ready for me to collect?'

'Of course, Herr Futtermann,' consented my father on my behalf.

'This has been a most agreeable experience. Good night. And sincere thanks to our most delightful wine waitresses!' He bowed graciously towards Josephine and me, then turned briskly away, following behind my father who led the way to the gate across the courtyard lined with German army vehicles.

I stood near the kitchen door as the closing gate clanged loudly. In the distance came the sound of car doors slamming, an engine starting up. I watched as my father approached with his uneven steps. He took me by the arm and together we mounted the stone stairs to the front door, leaving Josephine to wash the glasses in the kitchen. Starting with a whistle through his teeth, and speaking in conspiratorial tones, Papa said:

'I thought we were for the chop, Lily, when he tried that door. Of course, I had the key all the time, here on the main key ring,' and he reached into his trouser pocket and took out an assortment of door keys hanging from an old piece of string. 'It's this old Vannet key he needed. This one.' He pointed to the letter V cut into the handle of one of the keys. 'As you know, Lily, all our silver is walled up down there in the cellar. You may not have seen this yet but behind that door are only a few empty bottles on the shelves I put up to hide the new brickwork.' He opened the front door and we went through to the living room where my mother was at work on a piece of embroidery.

'Time for a glass of wine, Jeanne. Our *Weinführer* was quite impressed, wouldn't you say, Lily, with the Lemoine selection he tasted? He says he will be sending through an order in the next few days, even discussed payment details.'

He held out a glass of wine to my mother, then to me. 'Here's to our new customer!' And we all three raised our glasses. 'To the *Weinführer!*' My mother and I echoed his words.

*

Later that same week I visited the small grocer in the town with a list from my mother. As I stood in the queue, waiting my turn to be served, the grocer, Eric Cordier (my friend Marthe's father) called out a question at the top of his voice: 'How's your friend the *Weinführer*, Lily?' Then he winked at the customer he was serving.

I turned on my heels and left the shop.

Chapter Twenty-Two: Wine Business

'"Ten cases: sixty bottles of each wine. The following wines:"' Papa read out the list in the *Weinführer*'s letter, which arrived the day after his visit to our cellars.

'Work it out for me, Lily: he told us to use our current price list. Not that the profit on this order will be significant: the Boches have made sure of that by devaluing the franc against the Reichsmark. None of us will see profits again like before the war. But let's face it, if the *Weinführer* wants to buy our best vintages and he's prepared to pay the price, I have no objection.'

In the half-light of the freezing cold cellar I pulled out each dusty bottle from the rack, marking them off carefully on the wine lists at the end of the rows before ensuring each one was correctly labelled. I remember the pain in my fingertips and hands as the cold touch of the glass numbed them. The dust and algae caught in my throat and lungs as I levered the bottle caps in place and pasted on each of the labels.

My father packed the bottles into the wooden wine

boxes stamped with the Lemoine crest; working swiftly, stacking up the boxes in the ground-level stock room from where they would be dispatched. He took a perverse pride in seeking to impress our latest customer with his wine, commenting wryly when the stack of crates was assembled: 'I just wish I could tell which bottles Goebbels would be drinking, and I would make bloody sure they were spiked with arsenic.'

There was nothing I could do at this time except what I was told. At my father's bidding I contacted the *Weinführer's* office to inform him the order was waiting for checking and dispatch. My hand shook as I held the receiver to my ear and heard the now-familiar voice at the other end of the line.

'I shall organise the delivery of the consignment to the station in time for the late morning train tomorrow. I shall be there to check through the order myself.'

I did not expect to hear the change of tone in his voice, the increased firmness as he said, 'Please bring me the inventory yourself. Do not concern your father with this little task.'

My father was astonished when I repeated the arrangement to him.

'But surely he expects me to go through the order with him? What if he has a query you can't answer? Tell me what he said exactly, Lily?'

'That he considers it a "little task" and thinks you have more important matters to deal with.' This was not quite what he had said. Near enough to persuade Papa not to come with me to do all the talking.

'He's right about that, for sure. I have a million tasks to do, thanks to this bloody war. It goes against my grain, this, but if that's how he wants it, you go, Lily, in my place.'

Next day I cycled to the station with the inventory. I could see in the distance the men emptying our crates from a horse-drawn cart and stacking them on the station platform. The *Weinführer* was already there, directing them. As I drew closer, I dismounted and stood watching the men from a few metres away, uneasy, wondering when I should present him with the inventory. Seeing me he called out a loud greeting.

'A very good morning to you, Mademoiselle.'

His voice was good-humoured and cheerful. As he drew nearer, he looked down at me with a glint of amusement in his eyes.

'Good morning, Herr Futtermann. I have the list of the wines you ordered here.'

I opened the satchel I was carrying and handed over the envelope.

'Please may I take a look?'

I passed the envelope to him, which he promptly tore open and pulled out the document signed by my father.

'Now that you are here, we had better check the wines carefully, to be on the safe side: I see your father has carefully labelled each box. Good man!'

Then he appeared to check each of the stacked boxes,

ensuring that the Lemoine inventory was accurate. I was impatient, wanting him to finish. Wanting to escape.

Eventually he seemed satisfied with his work and returned the paper.

'I trust, young woman, that the contents are true to this list?'

He spoke sternly with a new note of authority in his voice; the soldiers, having finished their task, stood around, watching the scene.

'Because it has come to our attention that our *vigneron* friends are not always honest when they fill up the wine cases. There have been too many examples of wine bottles filled with watered-down cassis. This will not do! Punishment is severe!'

He paused to see how his words affected me. Indignant and on the defensive, I said:

'My father and I completed this order together, Herr Futtermann,' I replied indignantly. 'These bottles are all first-rate wines, I can assure you of that.'

'Of course, of course. I have great respect for your father,' adding in a lower voice, 'and for you also. As I think you know?'

There was a loud rumble on the tracks, and we looked up the line to see a goods train approaching. He gave orders to the men to load the crates into the wagon indicated by the station master. When the operation was complete, he dismissed the men, thanked me and walked briskly to his car. I watched him start the engine and pull away.

Afterwards I climbed on my bicycle and pedalled in the same direction, towards home. When I rounded a slight bend, I was surprised to see the *Weinführer's* car parked at the side of the road ahead of me. What was going on? Panicking, I steered my bicycle to the left, into the middle of the road to cycle past, as if I hadn't seen him. After I had overtaken and pedalled a few metres further along the road, I heard him call my name. Now I had no option but to stop and turn around.

In that brief moment he had climbed out of the car and was walking towards me, saying 'Let me say that I would very much like to give you a special reward for your efforts on my behalf. Please, let me take this.'

Taking the handlebars of my bicycle, he wheeled it across to the verge nearby and placed it on its side.

'Come with me.' With a gesture towards the passenger door he opened it. I climbed in.

Chapter Twenty-Three: A Short Journey

It was one of those autumn days on the Côte d'Or when the leaves on the vines are turning to burnt orange in the midday sunshine. There were a few people at work, trimming out the dead leaves and pruning the vine stock ready for winter. A few braziers were burning the detritus and plumes of smoke made the air hazy in places.

How could I not feel uneasy? A fugitive. I was running away, escaping with Karl Futtermann. Seated on the comfortable leather passenger seat, guiltily seeing men and women toiling in the vines. What if somebody recognised me as the *Weinführer's* car flashed past?

It was as if he understood what I was thinking when he said 'You needn't worry. There won't be anybody where we're heading, up to the *Hautes Côtes.*'

Sure enough, almost immediately he steered the car off to a road on our right and we started to climb up a steep, narrow track.

He broke into my uneasy silence.

'Goebbels should have his bottle of Lemoine Pinot

Noir by tomorrow evening, I should say, if that train is on time!'

He spoke the words with a note of pride in his voice. Then he looked at me, placing his right arm behind my neck, along the back of the car seat, continuing to steer expertly with his left.

'I can tell from your silence that you are not impressed by this news, Lily.'

He looked straight at me, but I found there was nothing for me to say. He allowed us to continue in silence for a further ten minutes or so until he had reached a stretch of open heathland, where he pulled the car off the road and switched off the engine. I felt his hand stroking my shoulder, gently and calmly. I stayed silent. Afraid. Excited.

'Please, Lily. I mean you no harm. I would like you to accept a small token of my appreciation'.

He reached in front of me to take out a gift-wrapped parcel from the glove compartment. Gifts were unheard of at this time. Money was scarce, luxuries superfluous. The wrapping paper around the small item was printed with the name of a Munich pharmacy. With trembling hands I untied the ribbon and slipped off the paper. Inside was a small, red leather case printed with the monogram: LL. I unzipped it and discovered a manicure set, the scissors and the tools embossed with the name of the Essen steel manufacturer.

'This company is a customer of ours. Their goods are

very high-quality indeed. They never wear out. I'm sure this will be in very good hands!'

Taking the case from me, he placed it on the dashboard of the car, then took hold of my left hand as he spoke.

'These are dark days for us all, Lily. Germans, French, Dutch, British. The people of Europe. You don't need me to tell you that.'

He paused, turning his head towards me, testing my reaction. He carried on talking quickly, telling me a few facts about himself. But I couldn't listen to what he was saying. His expression changed when he looked at me carefully as I gave a nod, tried to smile, looked into his eyes. He suggested we should move to the back seat where he deftly squeezed sideways next to me, placing his face close to mine.

'Perhaps you have a boyfriend already? A young Frenchman who writes you love letters from far away?'

I didn't answer. As he kissed me, again and again his bristly stubble scratching my face as he pressed his lips against mine, harder and harder, pushing his tongue into my mouth.

I felt his hands moving up my legs, stroking the inside of my thighs, moving higher. I felt his mouth moving from my lips to my neck. Suddenly, his hands were unbuttoning my dress, feeling my breasts, and he was saying 'Will you let me love you, Lily?'

A question or an order?

Later, back at the house, I tried to wash out the

bloodstain, rubbing it with Josephine's bar of *savon de Marseilles*, then scrubbing and scrubbing at it with the wooden brush on the kitchen draining board. The suds and the water turned a russet colour and I carried on until the water ran colourless and clear down the plughole. In my room I draped the sodden garment over the chair, hoping it would dry before anyone would see it.

Chapter Twenty-Four: The Postcard

'It pains me to say this, Lily. I sincerely wish that he was not our best customer, but the *Weinführer's* business has brought our sales back to close on our best-ever figure since before the war.'

My father was studying his ledgers one evening, bringing them up to date.

'It's good for us, of course. But the people in Saultmur don't like it. Now I know how Rossiteau must have been feeling back in July.'

He was referring to one of his local rivals, Marcel Rossiteau, a *négociant-propriétaire* and, at sixty, the most senior member of one of the older families in our village, whose vineyards and property dated back several centuries. My father and the other smaller winegrowers locally had objected when Rossiteau had been singled out by way of special "invitation" from the *Weinführer* to trade with the Germans.

Months later, there was still a faction of local *vignerons* who vowed never to sell their wine to the Germans and who criticised anyone who did. Some were also tradesmen like Eric Cordier. Whilst they were not raising money by selling their wine, many were trading their wine for food or other services. They were clever and resourceful, making sure they and their families would not starve.

As mayor, my father had a foot in both camps now, and several of his longest-standing friends felt he was compromising his principles to trade with the enemy.

'*Tant pis!* There's no pleasing everyone, Lily. That's all you can say in times like these. If you refuse to trade with the Germans, you have no money coming in, so how can you keep your business going? If, as we are, you sell wine to the *Weinführer*, people accuse you behind your back of collaboration. You just can't win in a small place like this.'

'Maybe we should try to spread the business to the other *vignerons* in the town, Papa, besides Rossiteau and yourself? Encourage them to open their cellars. Let the Germans try their good vintages. At this rate, our stocks here will soon be completely exhausted. Give these others a chance.'

Of course, I had my own reasons for suggesting this course of action. My father's face seemed to brighten. 'Yes. You may be right, Lily. I will talk to the others. Point the *Weinführer* in their direction. Or perhaps you could do that? You know, sweet-talk him a bit. I've noticed he likes to deal with you rather than me when it comes to his orders.'

I could feel myself blushing, wanting to deny what he

was saying. ‘That’s not true, Papa. He knows you’re busy in the *mairie* very often and doesn’t want to hold you up. But I’ll try to speak to him, recommend some other cellars in Saultmur for him to try.’

He patted me fondly on the arm: ‘You’re a good girl. That’s right, speak to him when he gets back.’

He turned his attention to his bookkeeping. I didn’t want to signal my interest. So Karl Futtermann had gone away? For how long?

I asked no questions. Kept my mouth shut. Showed no concern.

*

In November, addressed to me at the *mairie,* I received a postcard of Neuschwanstein castle. It was posted in Munich: I see the postmark here on the envelope: 16.11.40, franked over the red Hitler stamp. As I read my name written in the elaborate copperplate handwriting, I start tugging at the thick card inside. Here is the fantasy castle on one side and on the other, the pressed, furry edelweiss flower taped to the back, with his words beneath: ‘For you, Lily. K.F.’

This brief message short-circuits me back to the dark, secret joy that I could not share with another living soul. Except him.

Chapter Twenty-Five: Winter 1940

'Henri says because it's wintertime you can stay two nights with them, Lily, instead of just the one. Cycle back on Thursday morning in the light. With the *vendange* out of the way and our paperwork under control, I told him I'm happy for you to help him out again.'

Papa sounded unusually cheerful. 'I may have to review the arrangement come the spring, though. We'll see.'

I tried not to show the pleasure I felt at this news. Now in mid-November in Saultmur, food was scarce and a strict system of rationing in place for basic ingredients such as butter, milk and sugar. Things would be better in Beaune. At least, they could hardly be any worse, I reasoned, as I set off by bicycle one Tuesday morning.

M Boissart's office was much the same as I had left it five months earlier. Now, though, there was a large scale map of the Côte d'Or hanging on the wall, with each of the Boissart vineyards and *parcelles* carefully coloured in red.

'A gift from the *Weinführer*, Lily. He got a map-maker

to do it for me in Munich. This is an enlargement of the smaller one we all have round here. It's impressive. Have a look.'

I could see from where I was standing the red blocks of Boissart land represented a huge number of hectares spreading from North to South of the area.

'Things have changed a bit here since your last visit. Have a seat. I'll ask my wife to bring us a pot of coffee.'

He returned a few moments later. 'You may have heard already about the curious coincidence?'

I nodded, guessing he was referring to Karl Futtermann's link with the Boissart family. This was common knowledge by now.

'We're keeping it dark that the *Weinführer* is, in fact, my godson.'

He paused as he made this announcement, watching my reaction. I must have shown surprise because he said 'You look frightened, all of a sudden! No need to be. Understand you may see him quite often, off-duty that is. Don't spread it around though, Lily. People won't like it. It'll be another reason for them to hate the Boissart family! Round here they have been doing that, of course, since the Revolution.'

He chuckled, then his expression changed. 'Before he died his father and I were friends, you see. He used to scratch my back and I his.' I didn't see what he meant. 'He sold cases of Boissart wines in his shop in Munich and I made sure there were ample outlets for his German wines here in France, and in Paris especially.'

Mme Boissart came into the room at this point, carrying a tray of coffee. I stood up to greet her and she hugged me warmly. She looked pale and thin, and as she passed me a cup of coffee, I saw her hand shake.

She said, 'Enjoy this, Lily. We don't have any ground acorns here!' She smiled at me, like a co-conspirator and I thought of the *ersatz* coffee at home made by grinding roasted acorns and chicory. It was as if I was on holiday.

'Karl's like one of our boys, wouldn't you say, Hélène?' She nodded without saying any more and left the room.

'Still don't know where they are, Jacques and André. Missing. Hélène is sick with worry. Karl has offered to try and help trace them, but so far, we have heard nothing. But she will look after you, Lily. Keep you safe from the boisterous German soldiers in the old stable block these days. Now let's see.'

He lost no time in telling me what to do before leaving me on my own to get on with the work.

So, I could expect to see Karl Futtermann on his 'off-duty' moments. The Boissart household was full of possibilities. I knew I was waiting for him to come back. Preparing myself. In the small bedroom, I propped up the postcard of Neuschwanstein Castle next to the manicure set.

*

On Thursday morning, I cycled home to Saultmur, reluctant to leave behind the piles of unfinished paperwork and the creature comforts provided for me by Mme Boissart. I preferred to go straight to work in the office at the *mairie* where there were always letters and documents to type for my father, rather than to set foot in the kitchen at home, where countless domestic chores lay in wait for me.

When I finally returned home late in the afternoon, my mother was strangely animated: 'Lily, we've heard from Auguste! See this.'

She handed me a small buff-coloured postcard, on which I could recognise a few words of his handwriting.

Working hard in Saar steelworks. Thinking of you all. With love, Auguste.

I didn't want to think of him under enemy orders, working in harsh conditions like a slave, but to my mother his words brought comfort. They showed he was still alive, at least. Not missing. Not dead.

Somehow, she found the motivation to campaign on behalf of other prisoners of war like Auguste. She worked tirelessly in conjunction with the Church to maintain a minimum level of communication about those husbands and brothers who had last been seen in 1939. She ensured that the priest spoke out from the pulpit to remind the congregation of the plight of these men. Meanwhile women's groups gathered together to produce food parcels and warm clothes to send to them.

It was over a year since Auguste had been at home,

and I hated the place without him. Somehow, though, the cold of the winter, the shortage of food, the absence of Karl Futtermann; all of these had gradually numbed me. Sometimes I even wondered whether I cared about anyone anymore.

Nevertheless, in mid-December, Auguste was allowed to send us a full-length letter, which I kept with his others, slipped inside the photograph album.

Dear Maman, Papa and Lily,

We have all been allowed one sheet of paper to send our Christmas message home.

It has not been all work here, for a change. We were allowed to attend mass on Sunday at the small village church near this godforsaken camp.

In all my years as an altar boy at Saint Vincent, I never felt quite this power and beauty of the Church. Here the stone building is very small, very simple but what caught my attention as I stepped inside was the crèche near the doorway: the santon figures were, maybe, twenty centimetres high. They were a bit chipped and scratched after many years of use. Unmistakably though, here were Mary, Joseph, the ox and the ass grouped around a little crib (empty, of course, until Midnight Mass on 24th December). The stable was a miniature masterpiece made by a local carpenter: a scale model of a timber-framed barn with cross-beams and large arched double doors, the floor was strewn with real hay!

My only regret is that I couldn't take a photograph of it

to send you!

Immediately I saw it I remembered the crèche in Saint Vincent and the memory gave me some hope in these dark times.

Thinking of you all at Christmas,

All my affection

Auguste

Our joy proved to be short-lived. Barely a week later, a short, official typewritten letter arrived from Germany.

We regret to inform you that your son Auguste Lemoine died in an accident at the Saar steelworks. We have arranged for his body to be buried in the nearby cemetery.'

Chapter Twenty-Six: In Memoriam

A few days after Christmas the bells of Saint Vincent were tolling loudly in the late afternoon. Mourners filed in wearing black, many were the mothers and sisters of friends who, like Auguste himself, were now in POW camps. Every pew was packed with the people of the village who had known him all his life.

There was a figure kneeling in our pew as we approached, head bent. It was Charles Santot. When he stood up and noticed us, his eyes filled with tears and he embraced us all warmly without speaking. He held my hand and gestured for me take my place by him.

My father read aloud Auguste's last-ever letter and the small choir sang a carol. The priest read the account of the Christmas story from one of the gospels, I don't remember which one. Nor did I care. The words were wasted on me in this hour of complete darkness.

As we were filing out, turning to make our way down the aisle, my glance drifted to the back of the church. Standing there, in a long, black overcoat and looking straight at me was Karl Futtermann.

As my parents approached him, he stepped forward and shook their hands, then it was my turn. As I put my hand in his, I looked up. His eyes held mine, then he quickly bowed his head and stepped back. The bells were deafening, and my head was throbbing as I followed my parents through the doors, closely followed by Charles.

'I didn't recognise the stranger in the black coat, Antoine. Who is he?'

'We call him the *Weinführer*. I did not expect him to come to Saint Vincent, today of all days. I don't think it is right that he came here.' This was our family business. Karl Futtermann was an outsider. He did not belong.

In the place de L'Hôtel de Ville, darkness was closing in. Friends and distant relatives stood with shoulders hunched in the freezing cold. They expressed their condolences, embraced us, shook hands, and their faces and their words were intended to give comfort to all of us.

I glided past them all without saying anything. For me now, here in this place, a dream was dying and the cord that had linked Auguste and me to all these people in this small village had snapped. I was alone. Totally. Charles was at my side, my parents a few steps ahead and Josephine behind, but there were worlds separating us. Reluctantly I crossed the courtyard, mounted the stairs and entered the house again.

The dimly lit hallway with its cold blue-patterned floor tiles, lofty ceiling and glass-panelled front doors was cold as a morgue. The candle my mother had lit that morning stood encrusted with wax and with our entry the flame danced erratically, then vanished, leaving a feeble puff of smoke behind.

'What use is this damn thing?'

I reached up and grabbed the plaster figure of an emaciated Christ pinned to the cross, his head drooping to one side with its crown of thorns. The figure was feather-light, and I threw it violently at the floor, where it shattered instantly. My mother drew in her breath sharply, made the sign of the cross and lifted her black-gloved hands to both lips.

'How dare you do such a thing, Lily? You'll be sent to Hell for this!'

She bent over quickly, trying to salvage the broken pieces of the dismembered Christ figure, now covering the floor.

My father looked on, stunned into silence. Pointing to the door of my room, he dismissed me, saying 'Control yourself, Lily!'

Charles, who stood at his side, said nothing.

I hurled open my door and slammed it shut. The loud echo was deafening. Silence fell and I heard hushed voices murmuring outside, then disappearing into the living room. I listened to the sound of the door being closed and was glad to be away from them all.

None of the rituals of the Church, so faithfully followed in this difficult time, were of any use to me now. Auguste had died in a stupid accident. No priest, no prayers, no pomp or ceremony could ever bring him back: the plaster effigy of Christ was a sick joke.

In a mad frenzy, I unlocked the tall doors of the oak wardrobe where all of Auguste's clothes were kept since Josephine had moved into his room. The wardrobe exhaled the stale smell of mothballs; one by one, I unhooked the jackets, piling them on my bed. They were old and worn, patched at the elbows. Three, each one larger than the next, showing how fast he grew in those teenage years. I rummaged through the pockets, feeling the silk lining, surprised to salvage a few random objects: an old handkerchief, a few *centime* coins, a small knife for trimming the foil of a wine bottle, a half-empty pack of Gitanes with a small box of matches. How unlike Auguste to leave a packet unfinished!

I piled these items on my bedside table: museum objects now.

Also in the wardrobe on a shelf was a stack of his white shirts: each one neatly ironed and folded by Josephine. I pulled them all off the shelf, throwing them on my bed, noting how they were worn out at the collar, frayed at the cuff, yellow with sweat stains under the sleeves. He had packed his best shirts to take with him when he left that day. Grabbing the small, hooked pocket-knife I started to slash mindlessly at these shirts, ripping through the fabric. Shredding it until each of them lay in a pile in front of me in tatters.

Then I crumpled into a heap beside them and sobbed. What was the point of anything now?

After a while my fury subsided. I stood up and studied the contents of my room: on my table were Auguste's portable gramophone and pile of records, neatly stacked, and the Leica. I thought of him, pacing round the vineyards and the streets of the village, focusing the lens, clicking the shutter. I took out the album, this album, the one he had given to me for my eighteenth birthday. I looked again at pictures of us, our village, our people, and I knew that world had disappeared forever.

Auguste would never be back to toil again in the Lemoine vineyards, to agonise when the grapes were spoilt by hailstorms or to savour the first tasting of a new Lemoine wine. He would never have the chance to bring in the new machinery, to take on the business when our parents were too old.

And without Auguste, I had no-one I could trust with the secrets of my soul.

Auguste had gone forever, but Karl Futtermann had returned and put in an appearance at Saint Vincent. A strange exchange.

From downstairs in the kitchen the smells of the evening supper, prepared by Josephine and me that morning, wafted up: thin consommé, beef stew thickened with lentils, one small potato each. A slice of stale bread. The thought of this food made me want to be sick. I sat down on my bed, preferring to go hungry than to share the misery of the evening meal here in our house.

On an impulse, I took Auguste's crumpled pack of Gitanes and extracted a cigarette. I had watched him light up so many times, always refusing one myself: the good girl. Now it was my turn to try to imitate the expert way he used to do it, clenching it between his lips at the side of his mouth, the tip pointing downwards as he lit a match. Next, I grabbed the box of matches and pressed open the tiny drawer, picking out one of the red-tipped wooden sticks between my forefinger and thumb and striking it quickly along the side of the box. The flame burst into life, and I leaned forward, just as Auguste used to, lighting the tip of the cigarette, sucking on it to make the tip burn. And I tasted the bitter-sweet taste of tobacco I had smelt so often around him, practising pulling on my first ever cigarette, thinking of the pictures in my magazines of Katharine Hepburn and Carole Lombard posing provocatively for the camera, cigarettes in their hands.

As the smoke billowed around me, I thought about *him*: K.F. Herr Futtermann. The *Weinführer*. So, he called me 'Lily'. What should I call him the next time we meet? Always 'Herr Futtermann' in public? But what about in private? I thought of his first kiss under that clear September sky and the drive in his car through the lanes between the vineyards. What he did to me on the back seat. And what I let him do.

I watched the disappearing cigarette between my fingers, realising there was no ashtray in the room and the cigarette had burnt down, so I stubbed it out in the chamber pot beside the bed. And now came the shame: about smashing my mother's sacred statue, smoking my first cigarette and, worse than either of those sins, thoughts of love. No. Thoughts of sex with a Third Reich officer. There was no Auguste to talk to. No priest I dared confess to. My mother was right. I must be on the road to Hell.

Later in the evening voices in the hall woke me up. I could hear Charles Santot saying to my father 'Just let her sleep, Antoine. Forget it ever happened.'

Of course. There was Charles. Why had I not tried to speak to him? Perhaps he could have helped me? Saved me from the mess I was in? Yet he was so much older.

I can still hear his firm footsteps crossing the courtyard, the clanking of the gate as he pulled it open and the clang as he shut it behind him. Surely, I should have run after him, caught his elbow, told him my sorrows?

But I didn't. The clock in the hall ticked for a few seconds until I heard the sound of my father turning the front-door key in the lock and pushing the metal bolts home before hobbling slowly to join my mother in the silence of the living room.

Chapter Twenty-Seven: After Auguste

There was no time for my father or me to join my mother in her rituals of bereavement: wearing black clothes, lighting candles, saying prayers, attending Mass. Whatever the pain he felt, he never spoke about it. Nor did I.

Early in the January mornings, the two of us tramped up to the Lemoine vineyard to dig out any of the rotten rootstocks and to earth up the healthy ones. I took to wearing one of Auguste's old jackets over a thick jumper, belted tight round me, to keep out the cold. Often, without looking up, my father would issue instructions such as 'Auguste, make sure you check the roots are fully protected against the frost: look at this one.'

Crouching down he would pile soil up over the roots of a vine where rain had washed away the earth at its base. Sometimes he corrected himself, 'Lily, I mean,' and sometimes he forgot he'd even made a mistake. In his mind somewhere, Auguste and I had become interchangeable.

I started to take a perverse pleasure in wearing Auguste's old clothes, even cutting down and altering the trousers to wear for work. At first, they made me feel Auguste was still close to me. They eased my pain deep down. Because of this I took to wearing them at home and in the office at the *mairie*. Much to my mother's despair I stopped wearing my own clothes, the white blouses and plain skirts. The shirt-waister dresses. That girl, the old Lily, had gone.

Even when I worked for the Boissarts, I cycled to Beaune wearing Auguste's old clothes. It disturbed Mme Boissart to see me dressed like this.

'You gave me a shock, Lily! I thought it was André for a moment sat there at the desk! He used to have a tweed jacket like that one. Let me see what I can find for you: you're too pretty for those old things!'

She came back to the office soon after, carrying a pile of silk and linen blouses, a suit, a couple of dresses.

'They will be too big for you, but you're a clever girl. You will know how to cut them down.'

Studying my face carefully, she took my hands and looked at the nails. 'Make-up. Nail varnish. That's what every young woman needs! Leave it to me!'

Back in my room that evening, I discovered she had left a tray of Bourjois cosmetics on the washstand, near the mirror. I tried the red lipstick, the blue eyeshadow and black eyeliner, dabbed my cheeks and nose with face-powder, rubbed in some rouge. Then I looked at my new face, shocked at the sophistication of the red lips.

Soon I adapted the clothes she had passed on to fit me,

keeping them in my room at the Boissarts, wearing them for work in the office. Always, though, I remembered to change back into trousers and tweed jacket for my return to Saultmur. Back there, I chafed at my mother's daily reminders of domestic responsibilities.

'Lily, you need to set the table for dinner.' Or 'Lily, can you please peel the onions and carrots for Josephine?' Or 'Lily, when did you last feed the chickens?'

Her needling questions and her petty demands led me to neglect my duties, avoiding the house as much as I could, making sure that I stayed longer at the *mairie* or spent more time in the *cave* and in my father's office or up in the vineyards. I knew how to make myself scarce.

One January evening as Josephine was serving up supper for us, we looked down at our plates to find a few mean cubes of meat and a suet dumpling floating in a thin, pale brown gravy.

'So, have we run out of carrots or onions, Josephine?' my father asked abruptly. 'What about the potatoes? There were plenty in the larder when I last looked.'

'But Lily did not prepare them, *monsieur*, and today I had no time either,' Josephine replied, exchanging glances with my mother.

She didn't look at me. With a quick, sidelong glance at my mother to see her approval, she fixed her eyes on my father to avoid my glare.

'The vegetables are still in the larder,' she explained.

'I don't think it's fair to give Josephine more kitchen

work than she already has, Antoine', my mother added. 'She minds the kitchen garden for us, she digs up the vegetables, does the baking and much of the cleaning too. With the war effort also, she does not have time for any more tasks.'

As she spoke, she glanced my way, showing her resentment. I couldn't stop myself retorting 'Do you think I'm doing nothing all day? I may not be here in the kitchen or kneeling up at the church, but you tell her, Papa, you tell her what I do with my time!'

I started to raise my voice and could feel a stream of other objections waiting to be spewed out: the concern for Josephine, rather than for me. Her attitudes enraged me. Couldn't she see where her loyalties lay? After all, I was her daughter, her only child now. But I held back these resentments, waiting to hear my father's response.

'Lily, you should not speak to your mother in that way. It is not like you and it is unbecoming,' he said at last, in a steady voice wiping his mouth on the white napkin and throwing it down next to his plate.

He studied me closely, his features stern and serious, before he turned to my mother.

'Look, Jeanne. We can't ask more of Lily. She does what Auguste used to do and more besides. You two have no idea how it is these days. Why? Because you keep out of it. How many times do you attend Mass every week? What about the catechism lessons for the youngsters? All those meetings with other women to knit socks or write letters.'

This was when I first realised that my father resented my mother's nun-like devotion to the Church as much as I did.

'Certainly, in peacetime there would be time for these good causes. But not now! Things have to change in this kitchen too. Lily and I need more help in the vineyards, in the *mairie*, in the *cave* and in my office. Who will give us their help? Shall I tell you? No-one. Hitler and his brutes want more and more of our wine even when they keep our men in POW camps when they are needed here back home. I'm afraid you must split Lily's duties in the house between the two of you and cut back on your service to the Church. Tell the *monseigneur* I said so!'

He stood up, pulling back his chair and turned to walk out without tucking it back under the table. His customary gesture. He left the room without looking at any of us and I quickly followed him upstairs to his study.

He settled himself quickly in his seat behind his desk. I stood in front of him.

'I'm sorry, Papa.' I knew this conflict was my fault, but I also knew that I had to stand my ground, had to get away from the tight, little world of the kitchen. He looked up at me, his expression sad and angry at the same time.

'You need not apologise too much, Lily. Where would I be, where would we all be, if we could not rely on you at this time? Now let's look at the stocks of wine. There is another new order in today from the *Weinführer*.'

I saw a note in his hand and wanted to snatch it from

him to see the familiar handwriting again.

'He sent this by special delivery. Came straight to me here. Now, let's see what we can do for him.'

He handed me the order on the headed notepaper branded with the black spread eagle.

'They must have liked that last consignment. You can see this is much the same choice, mercifully though, a smaller quantity. It says: 'To Be Collected P.M.' We should be able to get this ready for tomorrow, I should say. Let things simmer down in the kitchen first, Lily. Help me down in the *cave*. Don't get on the wrong side of your mother.'

I nodded, unable to show him how glad I was to hear this news. We lost no time in checking off the bottles on our stock lists and packing them into wooden crates. When we had finished, he turned to me and said 'Just give his office a ring in the morning, Lily. Tell them the order's ready, will you?'

Chapter Twenty-Eight: Contented Customers

Following a call to his office next day, the *Weinführer* arrived without warning at the *mairie*. From my desk in the office I saw his car draw up in the square. He was looking directly at me as he approached the entrance along the footpath. In a moment he had stepped into the building and without any salute to the Führer's portrait, he announced his purpose straight away:

'*Bon après-midi*, Lily.' No formal 'Mlle Lemoine' this time.

'I am here to speak to your father, of course, concerning the order of wine. When do you think he will return?'

He had glanced sideways and could see the door to my father's empty office stood open. He appeared distracted, even nonplussed that my father was not here.

'My father is working in the cave today, Herr Futtermann. He has some work to catch up there.'

I felt myself looking down at his shining boots, feeling my cheeks burning red. Then when I looked up at him, his voice softened as he said 'Please give your father this letter on my behalf. I think the contents will interest him, and yourself, greatly. I will arrange the collection of my recent order tomorrow. Perhaps you will bring the inventory to the station, as before?'

The next day was a Tuesday. I explained that I would be working in the Boissart office. 'My father will be happy to check the inventory with you.' He nodded and handed me the envelope addressed to A. Lemoine. Then, wheeling round, he made for the door. I watched him leave the building and stride briskly towards his car. Remote, untouchable.

When I handed the envelope to my father later that day, he said 'Hmm. What's this, I wonder? What do you think he wants now?'

He pulled out a small typewritten note and read the message: 'M. Lemoine, some new customers!' and he extracted a photograph, immediately exclaiming '*Tiens*! This is one for our Rogues' Gallery!' and passed it to me. At a glance I could see three men seated at a restaurant table, their glasses raised. By squinting at it I could just make out the print of the wine-bottle label: Domaine Lemoine et Fils. Chardonnay, 1938. The three men clinking glasses were unmistakeably Hitler, Goebbels and Goering.

'I thought he said the Führer didn't touch wine!'

There was a tightening in the pit of my stomach.

'1938. Ah yes. One of our best years.' He couldn't bring himself to say that this wine, in fact, marked the one and only complete year of his partnership with Auguste. Yes: one of our best years.

I pinned the photograph on the noticeboard alongside all the others.

Chapter Twenty-Nine: Franz

'Just look at these figures, Lily!' This was early February. My father was in his office, standing in front of the huge leather-bound ledger of the Domaine Lemoine, which rested on its own, small oak table in front of the window.

Glancing beyond him I could see the rain streaming down outside and the sheets of water obscuring the view of the German army vehicles parked in our courtyard. He wanted me to see the current list of entries:

'Here is the *Weinführer's* first order last October. After that shocking harvest, remember?'

He was stabbing his finger at the head of the first column, then tracking the long list of wines ordered more recently, since Christmas.

'The '*aigles noirs*' have been coming in thick and fast, I should say, since this one in the first week of January.'

With the frequency of his 'black eagle' orders, Karl Futtermann had won my father's approval, loyalty even.

'You can see a pattern here, Lily. He rates the Lemoine reds more than our Chardonnays, it seems. A man of my own heart, clearly. Let's hope that if we keep giving him what he wants, then he will keep his distance. Keep his nose out of our business.'

Of course, he felt flattered by the *Weinführer's* orders. The reservations he had shared with many other local wine producers about trading with the enemy seemed now to be fading. He justified his own actions by reasoning that since the Germans would not allow him to trade with any other customers, there would be no sales of any kind if he refused to trade with them. No sales would mean no money to keep the business going. He had little choice, he said.

'I'll keep saying this. Whilst he is a Boche he is not a Schiffler. I know whom I prefer to deal with any day of the week. Don't you agree with me on this, Lily?'

I must have nodded my agreement. The two were opposites, no question. Schiffler was a bully. Futtermann was courteous and civilised. Schiffler exploited his power over people and he seemed to revel in seeing them suffer. The village was rife with stories about his acts of cruelty: he carried a whip with him and used it at will to punish any person or animal who got in his way. Everyone was frightened of him.

Papa objected that his cellar stocks of finest wines should be eroded *gratis* by these men, so he had devised what he called a 'wine cocktail' for their use: by diluting *vin ordinaire* with water and cassis cordial. This mixture he decanted into old bottles covered with cellar dust, serving them to Schiffler on a silver tray. He took a wicked delight in quoting the words of high praise the German officer showered on his bogus wine.

'Very fine wine, Lemoine. Which year did you say this is? Very rich and fruity. Beautiful colour too.'

Lucky his trick was never discovered: everyone feared Schiffler's whip.

*

At this time of tension between me and my mother, my father drew Schiffler's attention to the pressures on our household.

'I told him straight: we can't keep this up. We simply don't have the servants to work flat out all the time. The Germans have to share more in the domestic rota here.'

As a result, Franz, the youngest of the soldiers billeted on us, was seconded for "domestic duties" each day to help with the preparation and clearing-up of their meals. In the absence of Auguste, my mother had struck up what appeared to be a kind of mother-son relationship with him.

At supper we heard the snippets of information she had picked up from Franz.

'He's from the Hunsrück, he says. Not far from our borders. A poor family. Too many children. He says he's worried about his mother. She's in poor health. She has a bad heart. Can't afford a doctor.'

I remember sitting and listening to her anecdotes, inwardly fuming. I did not share her sympathy for Franz and wished he had never been imposed on us in the first place. It also sickened me the way she saved scraps of food for him at the end of our meals as if he were a dog.

'If no-one is going to eat this, I will keep it for Franz.' Franz, the charity case. Franz, the Auguste-substitute.

But I never expected what would happen next. None of us did.

My father and I were working in the cellars one February afternoon. It was bitterly cold, and we heard the gate bell ring out suddenly. Someone crossed the courtyard to open the gate and next we heard a woman's voice shouting loudly and repetitively.

'I must speak to Antoine Lemoine! Let him speak to Herr Schiffler on my behalf.' She was agitated, wailing as she cried out. Hysterical.

'*Mon dieu*. What's this?'

My father headed straight for the kitchen door and I followed him. Through the window we could see old Madame Dumont, the baker's wife, standing in front of Herr Schiffler, looking up at him as she spoke. As soon as she saw my father, she rushed over to him, bursting to tell her story.

'Antoine! One of the soldiers here has just stolen my purse! Up in the square, near the *mairie*. I was just putting it back in my bag here, like this,' and she opened her bag holding it so that my father could see it was empty, 'when he rode past on his bicycle and pinched it straight out of my hand, just like that. It had all my money for the week. *Salaud*!'

I saw Papa step aside to speak to Herr Schiffler and they quickly reached agreement. The German blew loudly on a whistle as a signal for the men to muster, and then barked out orders to them. Immediately the ten soldiers crossed our courtyard, lining up at the gate, side by side and saluting their commanding officer. He then ordered them to march to the *mairie.*

Madame Dumont walked next to my father whilst my mother, Josephine and I followed behind them. The noise of the soldiers' boots pounding on the cobblestones grew louder and louder as we approached the centre of the village. Schiffler's order had gone out: all the German soldiers had to line up in front of the *mairie.* There would be an identity parade. It was a frightening sight to see the column of twenty soldiers, one behind the other, like a terrible khaki war machine tailing its way down the main street.

The soldiers stood to attention as Schiffler barked out his commands and we witnessed each man unfasten the band under his chin to loosen his helmet, finally tucking it under the right elbow. They stood stiffly, staring straight ahead of them as Schiffler led Madame Dumont up and down the rows of men. We saw her small figure in a maroon coat disappear between the men standing anxiously, waiting for her to pass. She moved along the line slowly, shaking her head as she passed in front of one man after the other. Then suddenly we saw her stop about thirty paces away from us and heard her call out these words:

'It was this one! This is the thief! It's him, I tell you!'

We heard Schiffler bark a question loudly in German and saw the man reach for something inside the jacket of his uniform.

'But it's Franz!' I heard my mother say, covering her face with her hands. We saw him handing over a small, brown leather purse to Schiffler, who passed it straight away to Madame Dumont.

The next instant there was the crack of a bullet from Schiffler's handgun, aimed at Franz at point-blank range. The young man staggered, blood staining the front of his uniform, falling forwards on his face, arms twitching. Schiffler finished him off with another bullet through his head.

What happened next is a blur in my mind: Madame Dumont clutching her purse in one hand, making the sign of the cross with the other. My father leading my mother away, sobbing. Words in German, then two soldiers stooping down to lift up Franz's body from the ground, gently lowering the body of their young comrade into a small dog cart. And the huge red stain over the cobbles where he had lain. I, like a lost child, wanting to cry for someone to take me home.

Chapter Thirty: Dark Days

Franz's shooting signalled my mother's retreat into silence. His death plunged her again into an even worse state of grief and mourning than she had suffered after Auguste's. She lived out every day frozen in a state of emotional passivity, almost dead to what was happening around her. It seemed irrelevant to her that Schiffler had been removed from his duties. She didn't seem to care what happened any longer. Her fight, her anger, had gone. She became a shadow in the house. A black shadow moving through the rituals of her day, cut off from the rest of us. She haunted the church, kneeling for hours at a time, head bowed in prayer, opting out of all her charitable duties.

Now I understand her, how she needed to avoid the real world, which was too cruel for her, too harsh. Not then, though. I had no patience with her evasions or her piety at that time. Nor had my father.

'One thing is for certain, Lily, Saint Vincent himself will not prune our vines, pick our grapes, process our wines. You and I: that's whom we can rely on these days.

Your mother? In my opinion she's losing her grip. I'm afraid I don't have much time for it.'

We were up in the vineyard on a bright morning in early March. The sound of the bells of Saint Vincent calling the faithful to morning Mass had prompted his words. As he spoke, he pushed his spade into the soil and leaned on it for a moment. He looked weary. His face was pale, unshaven, grimly determined.

We had split the tasks; he was fertilising the roots of the vines, digging in manure. I was completing the pruning of the stocks before the spring growth. It was unprecedented for him to discuss home business when we were working in the vineyard.

'I suppose she will get over it eventually, Papa?' I spoke without conviction. It seemed that the war, Auguste's death, the shooting of Franz, all these events had pushed her over the edge, leaving the two of us to struggle on without her. Shrugging his shoulders, he continued to shovel the dung over the base of the plants.

'The trouble is, Josephine is running around the village telling everybody how we're taking advantage of her, how your mother is leaving all the housework to her these days. Which seems to be true from what I can see. But this puts us in a very bad light, Lily!'

Josephine the gossip. The tell-tale.

'Only the other day,' my father continued, 'Mme Parizot stopped me and said "How is Jeanne, Antoine? I hear she is not herself. Can I do anything?" What can I say? "Yes. Why don't you come and peel the vegetables or cook the supper?" So I try to make light of it.'

He sighed heavily. 'I really don't know what to do.'

I felt the unspoken pressure on me now to offer to take on all the household duties that my mother had abandoned. To help to ease Josephine's load. But I was determined not to turn back. Not to tie myself down again with never-ending kitchen tasks.

'Papa: we need to talk to Josephine, keep a close eye on her. We may need to get someone to help us out. I think Marthe Cordier could do with work.'

My old soul-mate, struggling these days to keep her father's general store open for business even when stocks were badly depleted.

'I hear she is very short of money. This would help her.'

My father nodded in agreement: 'Josephine won't have much to complain about if Marthe will come in. Perhaps it will stop her banging about in the kitchen quite so much!'

He raised his eyes at me in a knowing way: we both knew how Josephine could take out her bad temper on the kitchen dishes. Then he stopped in his tracks, stood up straight and looked at me as he delivered a warning.

'But, Lily, we should be very careful what we say to either of them about matters in the Domaine Lemoine these days, or business up at the *mairie*. Keep our mouths shut. Don't give anything away. Remember.'

*

The house was like a tomb. Cold. Ghost-ridden. Echoing. I hated it. Hated every moment I had to spend there and especially Josephine's evening meals with the four of us sat around the kitchen table. I was looking for an escape.

I took to staying late in the office at the *mairie* after the other staff, even my father, had left. I made sure I read and re-read every notice from the *Kommandantur* in Beaune and lingered over the official letters and notices signed by Karl Futtermann. The notices were generally addressed to all the winegrowing areas of Burgundy to include not only the Côte d'Or but also the Côte de Beaune, Chalon, Mâcon and Beaujolais. Their content fell into two clear categories: requests for names and facts about wine growers, producers and their workers, and orders concerning the upkeep of the vines and the cellars. Whilst my father deeply resented the controlling hand of the *Kommandantur*, here in the *mairie,* it excited me. I took great pains to find the answers to his questions and to send the information carefully tabulated and presented. I took a secret pleasure in typing his name on business letters and again on the envelopes. When he read them, did he think of me immediately? Or was he too busy? Too preoccupied? Why was he biding his time? Hanging fire?

January, February, March: the bitterly cold, harsh months of the year. Still no contact.

In the evenings I resented sitting with my parents as

they listened to Radio Paris, the Nazi-controlled station, which pumped out propaganda broadcasts. I loathed the overplayed signature tune of *La Cucuracha* with its manic, upbeat dance rhythms, then the smooth voice of Pierre Hiegel, the MC, who presented the pro-German classical or popular music choices. Frequently there would be a short break in transmission, with Hitler's voice delivering speeches from Berlin. These gave me my cue to leave and withdraw to my own room.

Alone I switched on the portable gramophone, played one of Auguste's jazz or swing records – music not encouraged by the Nazis – slightly turning up the volume to drown out the stultifying sounds of our house. The hall clock. Voices in the kitchen down below, the clatter of china plates and the chink of cutlery as Josephine set the table for breakfast next morning.

One night I smoked my way through the last few cigarettes I'd rescued from Auguste's jacket pocket. Sitting back on my bed I flicked through the record sleeves, staring at the happy grinning faces of Johnny Hess or Cab Calloway in his clownish, zany poses. Django Reinhardt and Stephane Grappelli at the *Hot Club de France.*

I longed to go to Paris. To travel by train to the Gare du Lyon with the address of a small Left Bank hotel in my handbag. To buy my own packet of Gitanes from a *tabac* on the Boul. Mich. and to sit at a street café, smoking and laughing and drinking. With him. To walk by the Seine, take pictures with the Leica. The Paris of Edith Piaf,

Charles Aznavour, Charles Trenet. Not the Paris of the Third Reich.

But more than ever I wanted to get away. Any escape would do.

Chapter Thirty-One: Summer 1941

I wish I had kept a diary, written down the dates and the times when we had our lovers' trysts, our rendezvous. That first summer of love. First summer of sex. He had me wherever he wanted me. No resistance.

The getaways? I was never short of a cover story in those days. Some lie to get me out of the house.

'Going up to the vines. I'll be back late. After dark maybe.' Three pairs of eyes looked back at me, blankly. No reaction. No reply. Shrug of shoulders. Silence. I always left by the back door, taking the key with me in a pocket.

Odd sequences of time keep coming back, replaying themselves. I wish I could stop them, destroy them here and now. But I can't.

One of these starts at dusk on a late summer evening. I see a young woman – me back then – standing in the shadow of tall shrubs and bushes near the monument. She does not want to stand in the open where someone, perhaps working late in the cool of the day or a soldier on patrol, might see her. She's staring out at the familiar view, looking towards her village beyond the hillside of vines heavy with ripe grapes. Harvest will be soon. Any day now, people are saying. Always the eye is pricked by the sharp point of the church steeple pointing like a finger towards heaven.

Then there is the distant rumble of a car engine breaking the silence of the evening. It is getting louder, louder and louder. She feels nervous. What the hell is she doing here? Waiting for him?

She looks towards the car where it pulls up near the tall trees and she runs over as the car engine stops. She smells the strong smell of pine and damp soil after rain and she sees a tall man – Karl Futtermann – open the car door and step out. He smiles at her, she runs across to him and he catches her in his arms, kisses her. He says 'Lily. *Mein Liebling*. We mustn't stay here. I have a place we can go. It isn't far. Get in.'

He gestures towards the car, she climbs into the passenger seat, asks no questions. She smells the sweet leather smell, familiar to her now. He reverses and drives back a few hundred metres, taking care to turn right onto the single-track road which follows the contour of the hillside close to the woodland ridge. He is avoiding the lower roads, near the village.

Next moment, a short distance down the road, he pushes his foot down on the accelerator and she feels the increased speed of the car in the pit of her stomach. Soon he swings the car right onto the *route nationale*, flat vineyards on both sides of the road, then the open countryside and the darkening night sky.

Eventually we pass through tall stone gateposts, heavy wrought-iron gates standing open. The car wheels crunch on the gravel drive leading up to an austere grey stone building, the shutters firmly closed.

'An old hunting lodge used in peacetime by Burgundian huntsmen. Now it is for the use of German officers fond of hunting game in season and wild boar. Please forgive the plainness of the rooms.'

He opens the large oak front door with a key, and I follow him into a hallway which is pitch black and smells of damp. He switches on the lights. Panelled walls, a broad staircase, hunting trophies surround us on all sides.

We both know why we are here.

He's polite. He leads me into a smoking room filled with stale cigar smoke, which catches in my throat. I cough loudly and the sound echoes in this lofty, empty room. He pats my back, holds out a glass and fills it with wine. I'm coughing too hard, I can't see the label.

'Sip this slowly, Lily. It'll help you.' So I do. The red wine is familiar. It is one of ours, I'm almost sure. He fills a glass for himself.

'Do you recognise it, Lily?' he says, and he swills the liquid round the bowl of the glass, smells it first, then drinks it. All the time he keeps his eyes fixed on me. I nod.

He moves over to sit on a sofa signalling for me to join him. The room is freezing cold, but I feel his body heat and weight pressing against me. Holding me with his arms, he lies on top of me. His breath on my face smells of the wine and when he kisses me, I can taste it. He kisses me with increasing force, pushing his tongue into my mouth, moving it round, then withdrawing it, then repeating it again and again. Wine-soaked kisses.

'You have been in my thoughts all the time, Lily. You must know why I have brought you here tonight?'

Of course.

'Please don't be afraid. I will take precautions, you know? You must come to no harm. We must not allow ourselves to take any more risks. You understand?'

All the time he keeps stroking me, running his hands up my legs, under my skirt. I feel his weight and he comes into me. I want this moment to last, for us to stay together like this, on and on. Afterwards we fall asleep, not for long. He whispers in my ear 'I must take you back, *chérie*.'

Standing up, I find my dress clinging to the back of my thighs.

I hardly remember climbing into the car or the journey in the dark, only waking as he touches me gently on the arm. He pulls up in the shadows of the rue des Charrons and the engine noise stops. We part quickly and I take the path home through the vineyard, opening the back gate into the intense darkness of the garden, letting myself into the empty kitchen with my key. The stale soup smells greet me like ghosts.

No-one to talk to. No-one to tell. This was not the

way love was meant to be round here. Not at all. It broke all the rules. Every girl knew love was about kissing and engagement rings, talk of his and her *parcelles de vignes.* Love meant the preparation of a chest full of embroidered white linen and soon enough, wedding bells and a wedding feast. It was about the bride and groom drinking from a silver *tastevin* with her trying not to spoil her beautiful white dress. Then the bridal night and, in the following twelve months, pregnancy and a baby, a christening.

Next morning at breakfast there would be no questions about my late return the night before. I avoided their looks: Josephine, Papa, Maman. I had nothing to say to them. I ate my portion of dry bread staring into a cup of the black-coloured liquid which passed for coffee. This was a waiting game. Wait for the next time he calls me on the telephone or visits the Boissarts on my working days. We had our lines of communication. We knew how to keep in touch.

'Won't you be too hot today, wearing those clothes?'

My father was frowning across at me. I didn't reply.

'Are you going to be working in the vineyard in Auguste's tweed jacket, Lily?'

I saw what he meant. I had put on these winter clothes this morning without thinking straight. 'No, I won't need it.'

I took off the jacket, hung it on a hook near the door and went out into the courtyard. Papa and I walked side by side without saying anything until we reached the vines.

'So, what did you do here last night, Lily? You were gone a long time.'

I looked at his face where he was frowning, puckering his eyebrows together. We could both see the new spurs of the vines waving untidily in the morning breeze and there were patches of black, shrivelled grapes in some of the bunches. His disappointment remained unspoken. All I could think was how he loved me. He trusted me. He relied upon me. I had let him down. I clutched at a straw.

'I worked up at the *mairie* instead, Papa. With the Boissart work taking my time, I've been getting behind up there.' I couldn't look at him as I said this.

He watched me, studying my features closely; then he nodded, turned away and walked with his heavy limp towards the stone hut to fetch the tools.

He rejoined me, carrying a fork in one hand, secateurs in the other.

'Lily, you can't fool me. I'm your father. Don't forget that. Karl Futtermann is an intelligent, well-educated man. He understands wine-making. He has become a reliable customer of ours, we feel comfortable dealing with him. However, there are too many people around here who believe strongly that we should not be trading with him or any German.'

I remember his steely blue eyes fixed on me as he spoke.

'Futtermann is a uniformed officer of Hitler's Third Reich. If we forget that fact, there will be people in our village who never will. Please remember what I say.'

I started to cry and he put his arm around me. But ultimately, he was powerless to help.

Chapter Thirty-Two: Lili Marlene

Karl. The *Weinführer*. My secret lover. I moved in a dreamy haze through the days, cutting myself off. Maman, Papa, Josephine, the Boissarts: I couldn't give a damn about them any more. Him. I just wanted to be with him. No one else.

'We must be very discrete. Try not to draw attention to ourselves.' He often repeated these words and I allowed them to run through my head again and again when I longed to see him once more without having any idea when that would be. Days, weeks or even months sometimes slipped by. Then he would take me by surprise, suddenly arriving in person when I was sat at my desk, pounding out a letter on the manual typewriter. Tap-tap – tap. Suddenly, there he was, standing in front of me, blond hair shining in the shafts of light from the window. Those blue eyes laughing. And he'd say 'See you at the lamppost at 7.30 p.m.' Then he'd turn on his heels and leave.

This lamppost stood on the edge of the village, near the cemetery. The meeting place gave me a virtuous excuse at home: I was going to lay some flowers for Auguste. I remembered to cut a few roses from the bushes in the kitchen garden before setting out. They were scrambling up the stone wall in a tangled mass of old wood, leaves mottled with brown spots, a few pink blooms past their best. Still among them I found a few near-perfect flowers turning from bud to full bloom. It was a pleasure to find them, to snip them from the tangled stems. The deep pink petals released a sweet, familiar scent sending echoes to me of childhood days spent making *pot pourri* with my mother.

Alongside the garden path leading to the gate I picked a few other summer flowers, cornflowers, marguerites, sprigs of lavender and added them to the posy of roses. With these in my hand I made my way along the road to the cemetery. There I pulled up the catch on the old wooden door, which led to the neat rows of old family memorials. I laid the posy of pink and blue flowers on the ugly brown, ceramic plaque dedicated to Auguste. There were crows squawking loudly in the cedar tree close by. I tried to remember him, my lost brother, but the memories were blocked. His name, the dates of his short life, did not belong here.

The familiar murmur of the car engine interrupted my thoughts. I ran back to the entrance gate, glad to escape the misery of this place, excited to see Karl at the wheel, leaning over to release the catch of the passenger door and let me climb in beside him.

Off we hurtled along the narrow winding lanes between the vineyards. I remember him singing loudly in his strong tenor voice.

Vor der Kaserne,
Vor dem großen Tor …

'Goebbels hates this song you know, Lily. He's tried to ban it. Too anti-war. Too much feeling for the sentry. Not enough love of Hitler in it!'

From verse to verse, his voice grew louder and louder and he would beat out the rhythm on the steering wheel.

'This is the way Goebbels likes it' and he'd deliver the lyrics with a new, militaristic fervour making the soft and mellifluous lyrics sound deliberately hissing and harsh.

Then, as the last verse ended, he fell silent, pressing his foot down on the accelerator, driving the car along twisted, narrow roads at top speed.

Suddenly he screeched to a halt, seeing a farmer up ahead, driving his herd of cattle along the narrow track. The farmer lifted his arm in a kind of salute as he continued down the road whilst Karl stared unsmilingly back at him, drumming his fingers impatiently on the steering wheel. As soon as the farmer had turned off the road, Karl pressed his foot hard down once again and the wheels stirred up clouds of dust on either side of us.

Sometimes he glanced at me, touching my hand. We didn't need to talk, only to watch the vineyards and fields slipping by, gaining an illusion of safety as the car drew a long and twisting line away from Saultmur.

On one occasion he pulled the car off the road, switched off the engine, whispered gentle words in my ear.

'You are my Lili Marlene, *mein Liebling*.' Half in French, half in German, his words worked their charm as I felt his hands touching me, the pressure of his kisses. On the back seat he could help me forget those dark times. I would feel his body on top of mine, the rough texture of his uniform chafing against my skin. I didn't care.

Afterwards we straightened our clothing, climbed back into the front seat. He handed me a small package tied with a bow and said: 'Open it, Lily. It's for you to keep.'

I pulled at the bow, tore open the paper and found a small cardboard box inside, which contained a silver hexagonal powder compact with my initials engraved on the lid: LL.

I twisted open the catch and caught sight of my eyes showing wary astonishment in the tiny mirror. And then he quietly intoned the words:

'Spieglein, Spieglein, an der Wand
Wer ist die Schönste im ganzen Land?

'"Who is the fairest of them all"? Here in Burgundy, I think I know who that is.' He paused and watched my reaction.

'It is beautiful. From Munich?'

No-one had ever given me such a gift before. It was too much like a stolen treasure, to be hidden away.

'But where shall I keep it?'

My words stopped him in his tracks. He knew what

I was saying.

'It is only small, Lily. Your house must have many nooks and crannies. Let it be our secret. Do you like it? The initials, the edelweiss flower?'

I looked again, noticing the flower engraved beneath the letters.

'My friend Hans makes these in his workshop in Munich. He was injured, you know, before the war. He was a great mountain climber in those days. He and I would spend holidays together on climbing expeditions high up in the Alps. But he took too many risks. Had a bad fall. Broke his back, poor man. Paralysed from the waist down so now he's in a wheelchair.'

He paused as he thought about his friend.

'But he has a great sense of humour. When I go to see him, tell him what's happening, he says: "I'm the lucky one around here. I can still do my job whilst you lot dress up in those uniforms, taking and giving orders."'

He stopped in mid-flow again, his expression more serious.

'Mind you, he wasn't quite so cheerful last time I saw him. He'd had an order for a hundred death's head rings, but he'd refused to make them. The fool. He was just too honest!'

His tone was bitter and angry. He stopped talking and left the story unfinished.

'What happened to him?' I asked the obvious question. He looked at me, then looked away.

'I'll tell you some other time, Lily. Hans is alright now. That's the main thing.'

He leaned forward and started up the car engine.

'I must take you back to your village. It is late. After the curfew. You must be very careful.'

He drove back along the same route, dropping me at the lamppost when it was dark, shadowy. I got out of the car, feeling sore when I stood up, pushing the door of the car shut. Trying to make no sound as I turned to walk in the opposite direction.

Bats were darting in jagged lines ahead of me, somewhere there was an owl hooting. I felt the stillness and calm of this time of day. I knew there would be a soldier patrolling along the main streets at this time, so I kept to the back streets and narrow passageways, making my way home unnoticed by the German watch that night. It gave me time to think over what he'd said to me. What we'd done. Put it in some kind of perspective, I suppose. First the manicure set, now the silver compact. Luxuries I could never afford, never dare to mention. Love tokens to make sure I wouldn't forget him when I never knew the next time I would see him: tomorrow, this time next week, in a fortnight?

Within the security of my own room I took out the silver compact, weighing it in my hand, remembering his words. 'Let it be our secret, Lily.' How long could this secret last, I wondered?

Grasping hold of it I fell asleep, surprised to feel the

metal warm in my hand when I woke up next morning. I hid it straight away with the papers in the writing case. Surely no-one would think of looking there.

Chapter Thirty-Three: Chez Boissart

'Don't take any pictures, Lily. It's not safe. For you or for me.' I remember his warning on one occasion when I had brought the Leica along with me. The pictures are still here, in my mind, stuck together with the lies I told to maintain the pretence of honesty.

'M. Boissart is taking me with him to his vineyards up in the Hautes Côtes de Beaune. I will be back late. After supper.' Or another excuse: 'M. Boissart is behind with his documents for the *Syndicat des Vignes*, I will stay very late to help him to complete them. His wife says I can have a bed for another night.' No questions asked. It was understood. My father nodded but appeared not to hear what I said.

It was different, though, with Marthe Cordier, my *amie d'âme* who worked for us full-time since my mother's decline. She knew me well, too well for my own good. As she was clearing up the dishes after breakfast one morning, looking directly at me, she asked 'Do you like the work in M. Boissart's office, Lily? Is he an easy boss?'

I didn't answer, wondering why she was showing this interest all of a sudden. We seldom had time to speak together. In fact, I tried to avoid any situations when she might try to talk to me. For a moment the clattering of plates and cutlery stopped, and she carried on, frowning as she spoke.

'People are saying he's hand in glove with the *Boches*. Is it true?'

She paused, testing my reaction.

'How the hell would I know? I'm just the part-time secretary there. I try not to get involved.'

The arched eyebrows relaxed and she looked at me with more like genuine pity.

'It can't be easy for you these days, Lily. With Auguste gone and your mother the way she is. Always so much work.'

Her soft, kind voice touched a raw nerve and I almost broke down into tears. I wished I could talk to her, as though we were schoolgirls again. But what could I say?

*

Of course, Boissart was up to his neck in *aigle noir* orders. What did people expect? He was the leading *négociant* in Beaune. He didn't have much choice in the matter. I kept the books in order, checking that all entries matched with the cellar lists. He had supplied hundreds of crates of wine to the Germans and the orders were still flooding in.

'You've made a difference to this business, Lily. Your father must be very proud of you, young lady.'

I suppose I shrugged my shoulders. I couldn't tell him how things were at home.

We were nearing the time of the harvest. Early or late September? The cellars were ready for the pressing of the grapes. Vats and barrels had been scrubbed and prepared for the fermentation of new wine to begin. It was just a matter of time before the first day of the *vendanges.*

'The Germans are making unreasonable demands on our stocks, I believe. Last year was a disaster in terms of wine production in this area. When I look at the vines this year, despite our best efforts, I can't see the production will be much better. The Germans have marshalled the workforce, I'll give them that. But they can't do magic, that's for sure. They're draining our stocks at a time of close-to-zero production. What does Antoine say about this?'

He paused to see if I had a reply, but before I could respond, he continued.

'If Futtermann keeps on badgering all of us for hundreds of crates of wine, he will soon bleed our cellars dry. He might be my godson, but I'm afraid one Third Reich officer is much like any other when it comes to getting what he wants.'

He peered at me over the rim of his glasses. I could feel myself blushing.

'I tell you what: why not tell your father to call in to

see me next time he's in Beaune? We can put our heads together a bit like old times!'

I nodded agreement before he left the office, making a mental note not to pass on his message to my father.

Chapter Thirty-Four: Harvest 1941

'Henri Boissart told me yesterday the *Weinführer* won't be troubling us in Saultmur during the *vendange* this year. See this, Lily.'

He passed me the notice. 'It's from the *Kommandantur* in Beaune, giving the dates of when he'll be in Mâcon, Beaujolais and Chablis, but NOT the Côte d'Or. You may need to make a note of them.' I wasn't sure what he meant.

'When did you see Henri, Papa?' I tried to sound neutral, disinterested.

'At a meeting of the *Syndicat* in Beaune, yesterday. We had a brief chat at the end.'

He nodded. 'Your name cropped up, of course.'

I dreaded what he was going to say next.

'He says you have made all the difference to the business at this time, though he seems to be a bit tired of the demands the *Weinführer* is making. Unreasonable was the word he used.'

He was leafing through papers on his desk as he spoke.

'Henri told me the *Weinführer* had asked if he might "use your services" when he takes his staff to the other wine-growing areas. Futtermann thinks you could be an excellent intermediary with the wine-growers, helping to put them at their ease, perhaps, and reassure them that the Germans are trying to support their endeavours.'

He stopped, noticing my look of surprise. I was astonished. Karl had not breathed a word to me himself about this proposal. Suddenly, this changed things. Without consulting me first, he had made our private arrangement public, out in the open. He was letting me step out of the shadows. Papa was watching me carefully, studying my reaction.

'Is this what you want, my girl? You're not here to dance to the *Weinführer's* tune, you realise. It's up to you.'

This was an invitation to travel with Karl, visit vineyards and sample wines. To be his "intermediary". I liked the word.

'Yes,' I said. 'I do want to do this, Papa.'

He nodded, thinking carefully before he said: 'Don't say too much about it to people round here, that's all. When you're not here, let them think you're working for Henri. Simple as that.'

I understood what he was saying.

'Now it's business as usual. We need to set up the rotas, same as last year, and send them to the *Kommandantur.* There is a rumour that some of the German soldiers will actually be drafted in to help with the picking, unlike last year. Remember that, Lily? Schiffler and his men!'

How could I forget? I spooled through the memories from our chance meeting at Saint Denis, all the other meetings for business. For pleasure. The secrecy. The evasion. Was this a turning point?

'No day-dreaming, Lily! We must get these rotas sent out.'

I sat down at my desk, rolled another sheet of paper into the typewriter.

After this, I expected to hear from Karl himself. I expected some explanation, guidance even. Then one morning in Boissart's office, I found an envelope had arrived addressed to me:

'For you, young lady. From a sweetheart, no doubt!' Henri said, handing the envelope to me whilst he continued to tear open and read his own letters.

The handwriting was immediately recognisable: my name and the Beaune address, Karl Futtermann's now-familiar handwriting. The envelope contained a postcard showing a German sentry guarding the door of his barracks, to the left of it the verses of the *Lili Marlene* song. I turned over the card, looking for a message, but it was empty.

'So, what does your letter say, Lili? Go on. Remind me what it's like to be in love!'

He was looking carefully at me, over the rim of his glasses. He could see my confusion.

'There's been some mistake, I think. It's just a postcard

without a message and no signature. It's not interesting. Really.'

I slipped the card back into the envelope and sat down at my desk, began reading the documents in front of me, my cheeks burning and my head pulsing. I could hear the tenor voice singing those words again and again and see those laughing blue eyes looking at me, the strong hand holding mine.

Rummaging through the writing case here in front of me. I want to find that envelope, to read the German song again. But it's not here.

I knew the dates by heart for the Burgundy tour: the *Weinführer* was due in Mâcon in the second week of October. Meanwhile in Saultmur the harvest of grapes was due to start. Despite Henri Boissart's pessimism about the harvest this year due to the harsh weather in the spring and some neglect of the vines, they were in fact laden with ripe grapes.

One morning comes to mind, when, shortly after daybreak, I was sitting next to Marthe Cordier as the wagon driven by my father carried several of us grape-pickers up to the Clos Lemoine for the day's work. The Germans had allowed us to use horsepower for the period of the harvest only. Behind us on the cart was the stack of panniers and baskets to contain the grapes as we picked them.

'It's just like old times, Lily, wouldn't you say?' Marthe observed, as we rattled along, legs dangling from the edge of the cart driven by my father. The hillside was bathed in early morning sunshine, the vines were deep green against the gold and as we drew closer, we could see the bunches of grapes hanging heavily from the main stems.

The horse strained as it crossed the road to head upwards towards the Clos Lemoine, so Marthe and I slipped off the wagon to walk the rest of the way up, leaving Josephine on board with the elderly couple who were helping us that day. On either side of us were tall dry-stone walls covered with ivy, a few straggling hollyhocks still in flower, their stems thick with bulging green seedpods. All around us the neat rows of vines stretched gracefully, their lines following the curves of the hillside. I smiled at Marthe, happy to be on familiar ground with her once more.

Together we collected our conical wicker baskets from the wagon and followed Papa's directions for the picking. We worked silently alongside each other, hearing the birds trilling and jabbering in the trees, feeling the hot sun on our skin and the backs of our necks despite the cotton headdresses we both wore as protection.

If I close my eyes, sitting here at this table now, I can go back there again to the moment when the heavy weight of the basket pulled at my shoulders as I filled it to the brim with ripe grapes. Then came the emptying of the fruit into the large wooden container and that rush of the scent of fresh, ripe juice. With the return to the next row of vines, the sight of Saultmur in the distance, the roof of the *mairie* glinting in the sunshine, the Lemoine home nearby. It is printed on my memory with a longing to go back there one last time. I can see the full, gathered cotton skirts we wore, Marthe's was red that day, mine was pale blue, and as we picked, our hands turned dark red from the grape juice and we had to wipe them on our skirts as we worked, leaving patches of mauve stain on the cloth.

Towards noon when the sun was at its height overhead and the birds fell quiet, we heard someone shouting '*La soupe! La soupe!*' and saw a queue forming on the flat scrubland near the entrance to the *clos*. Marthe and I lined up behind the elderly members of the party and a couple of German soldiers as they, too, waited to take their small bowls of vegetable soup with a crust of dry bread to eat in the shade of a nearby tree.

'I remember us all playing hide and seek in the *cabotte*s here, and Paul Dumas scratching his initials next to yours on one of the walls. Which was it, Lily?'

I thought back to when we were girls again, running through the vineyards with the boys chasing us, wanting to catch us and to kiss whomever they caught. Paul Dumas had been a friend of Auguste.

'Will there be a *bal de vendanges* this year, do you think?'

Marthe interrupted my gloomy thoughts. She was eyeing up one of the German soldiers as he drank his soup and he was smiling back at her.

'If there is, will you dance with the *Weinführer*, Lily?'

She watched me intently, with an unnerving and cheeky expression. She seemed oddly triumphant as if she'd been plotting to use this ammunition for some time. I felt my cheeks burning.

'What do you think, Marthe? There's a war on. Food is rationed. We're not supposed to consume alcohol in public places. How can there be a ball in these times?'

My annoyance abruptly ended our friendly chat. We ate our soup in silence, hoisted the panniers onto our backs again and carried on with the picking. I didn't look in Marthe's direction again.

Chapter Thirty-Five: A Tour of Burgundy

'Pack your case, Lily. We leave early tomorrow morning and should be away for three days and three nights. Meet me outside the *Kommandantur* at 5.30 a.m. Goodbye'. The briefest message was all I had needed: he must have known I would be at my desk in the Boissart office. So it would be easier for me to comply with his last-minute orders there than in Saultmur.

Three days. Three nights. I remember it as if it were here and now.

In my small bedroom in the servants' block I keep the special garments Mme Boissart has given me and now I quickly fold and pack a few for this trip.

Dawn departure from Beaune, my travel bag loaded next to his *valise* in the boot of the car – smaller, a different model. He hands me a map and an itinerary when we are both seated and the engine is running. He pulls away from the small car park of the Hôtel de la Chasse and accelerates down the road, away from the town. Beaune slips behind us and we are out on the open road heading south towards

Mâcon.

Men and women are still working the vines, picking grapes in the chill morning air, throwing the bunches into big wicker panniers. Horse-drawn carts stand ready to carry the grapes to the nearest press and I think of the Lemoine cellars where the new wine is already fermenting. Only my father knows where I am; the others think that I am typing letters and checking the cellar lists for Henri Boissart. Marthe and Josephine – wouldn't they like to know?

Here, seated beside him, I feel invincible. People can say what they like, I don't care. The *Weinführer,* Karl Futtermann, Karl: *he* can protect me. I am safe with him.

As he drives, he speaks to me about the visits in Mâcon, Beaujolais and Chablis scheduled for the next few days. I am only there to make notes. Karl expects to do the talking. Have I understood? Yes. I understand. Do I have any questions? No, I do not. He seems remote. Preoccupied. I have never seen him in this mood before, and until now I have not appreciated the extent of his responsibilities. I assume his silence shows his mind is on the job.

The journey takes us across lush green countryside and grazing lands and eventually, close to Mâcon, we see serried ranks of vines where the harvesters are steadily at work. We soon come to a halt near the tall gates of an ivy-clad château where the vines nestle up close to the old building. Karl switches off the ignition and climbs out of the car, instructing me to stay where I am. He enters alone through the gates and walks the length of a long driveway. In the distance I see him shake hands with someone before they disappear among the vines.

It is warm in the car. I sit waiting, expecting to see him any moment. Eventually it becomes so hot that I have to open the car door and get out. Not long after, Karl reappears on the driveway, walking towards me. I wave, but he does not return the gesture. As he approaches, I can tell he is not pleased. He says 'Get back in the car! Immediately.'

His tone frightens me. He has never spoken to me like this before. Why has he asked me to come with him? He climbs in beside me again and drives off. We pass through several small villages and towns and eventually arrive in front of a small farmhouse where fat white chickens scatter as the car approaches. A farmer in a blue woollen beret comes out of one of the outbuildings and greets him warmly by name. They talk for a while before the farmer returns to his work and Karl opens the boot to remove the cases and then opens the passenger door, offering his hand to help me out.

'Come this way, Lily.' I follow him through the front door into a large, low-ceilinged and beamed living room.

'This is our home for these three days. You'll be safe here, I believe. You must not travel with me. Make yourself comfortable, *chérie*.' He pulls out a chair from the table and gestures for me to sit down. Why can I not travel with him? Is that not why I am here?

'There have been, how shall I put it, "developments" since I suggested to Henri Boissart that you accompany me on this trip. I cannot give you the details, Lily, but understand that there was an incident last week when I discovered the brakes of my car had been tampered with. I had been to Saint Romain and parked the car up near the old castle ruins. My meeting with the *vignerons* took an hour or so, and on the journey back, travelling down the steep, winding roads I discovered the brakes weren't working. The car kept on gaining speed and was almost out of control when, just past the cemetery, I was able to steer it sharply up a bank into a field and stop the engine. When our mechanic checked the car, he found the brake cords had been cut. Of course, the Gestapo have been scouring the area for the culprit. It's very bad for the people up there.'

He stopped, then went on 'There have been other signals, too. I can't go into detail, but it is why we have to be exceedingly careful, Lily. I don't want you to come to any harm.' He is stroking my hair, holding my hand, kissing me.

Why do I not ask any questions? Instead, in that remote farmhouse I allow myself to be cocooned from the real world. For that short dream-like time I am his make-believe wife, spending whole nights with him, waking next morning to see the rays of the sun streaming in through the window, lighting his face. There are breakfasts with the simple ingredients left for us on a tray by the farmer's wife and suppers in the evening that she has made for us and which we eat with a bottle of wine Karl has brought back from the day's visit.

When I was with Karl I persuaded myself, poor fool, that I was safe. Invulnerable.

Chapter Thirty-Six: Winter 1941

'How dare they use this picture without my consent!'

My father was sitting at his desk in the *mairie* with a copy of *La Terre* in one hand and the local newspaper in the other. Ten days or so had passed since the trip.

'These statistics in the local paper are all lies, Lily! We all know that 1940 showed our yields were at a record low and we only have the Germans to thank for that. Of course, volume was up this year, but only because every French man, woman and child who is not behind bars or in a POW camp has made sure of it. Ring your friend the *Weinführer.* I want to have a meeting with him. I demand an apology!'

Throughout Burgundy the yields were up on the previous year by a significant margin. On his fact-finding tour of the region the *Weinführer* had found "irrefutable evidence" of how the Germans had helped to boost wine production in the region. Tables of statistics and photographs of French harvesters working alongside German uniformed soldiers appeared in the local press.

The photograph of Hitler, Goebbels and Göring sharing a bottle of *Lemoine et Fils Pinot Noir, 1938* made the national newspapers.

My father was justifiably outraged by this breach of his confidence. I returned to my desk, lifted the receiver and put a call through to the *Kommandantur*, leaving a message: 'Please could Herr Futtermann speak to *le Maire*, Antoine Lemoine, as a matter of urgency!'

It was hard to see what anyone could do. I tried to get on with my work but felt a sense of rising panic. How would the local wine-growers in Saultmur react to this news and when would we find out?

'What are you going to say to the *Weinführer* when he calls you, Papa?' I saw that he was cutting out the offending articles with a pair of office scissors. His hand was shaking, so I finished the job for him.

'I tell you what I'm going to do. I shall invite him to a meeting here in my office and I shall pass these articles to him and see what he has to say about them. I shall demand to know why I was not asked to give my consent, or at the very least, forewarned that this image would be spread all over the front page of a national newspaper! Whatever his reply, and I would expect him to be very convincing, I have decided what our next step must be.'

As he said this, he stopped and looked at me for a few moments.

'This will not be easy for you, Lily. But from this moment on we must cease any business with the

Weinführer.'

His words struck me like a blow in the stomach. If my father severed our business connection with Karl Futtermann, there would be no rendezvous at the station and clandestine trips in his car, no reason for us to see him in Saultmur. The phone on my desk rang.

'Hello. Can I help you? This is Antoine Lemoine's assistant.'

'Lily.' I knew the voice and caught the note of urgency in the way he spoke my name. 'I know why your father must be very angry. Please tell him that I am coming over to see him now.'

Then he put the receiver down. A short while later, we heard the car engine cut out, the door slam and the rattle of heels on the cobbled stone. Karl appeared in the doorway of the *mairie* and without any ceremony he marched straight into my father's office unannounced, closing the door after him.

I heard the murmur of heated voices and quick exchange of words and my father shouting: 'Do you realise what this means for me and my daughter here in Saultmur? Have you any idea what the people round here are saying?' For a few seconds there was no reply. Then I heard Karl's voice speaking in lowered tones, sounding controlled, reasonable.

A few moments later the door of the office opened, and Karl glanced at me for a second before walking out of the building. My father and I watched him climb into his car and drive off.

'What did the two of you decide, Papa?' I followed him back into the office, closing the door behind me.

'This was not a joint decision, but an instruction, Lily. He agreed that I should let it be known locally that we had "temporarily" ceased trading with the Germans.'

I sank down onto the seat in front of his desk, trying to take in what he was saying.

'People should understand that supplies of our best wines are now so seriously depleted as a result of "popular" demand that we shall be attempting to replenish our cellars and allow our wine to rest for a couple of years.'

I nodded, wondering what this change would really mean for us. For me. Meanwhile, my father continued, the *Weinführer* would be sampling other wines, in Saultmur, Santenay and Auxey-Duresses and he would be looking for wines that would match the quality of the Domaine Lemoine. He would be sending out a public notice to that effect.

This sounded like a reasonable resolution to the conflict. Months earlier I had provided him with a list of the most respected wine growers in Saultmur, though for obvious reasons at the time the *Weinführer* had not acted on it. Now he would have to, and I felt some sense of relief that his business interest would settle elsewhere for a while. Our cellars, as my father suggested, might have some chance of recovery.

Chapter Thirty-Seven: In the Boissart Cellars

'Plenty of work in our cellars in the months ahead.' Boissart was speaking to me in his office. 'We need to update our cellar lists now that the ledgers and filing here are under your careful control, Mademoiselle!' It was mid-December. I had yet to encounter the cold and damp of the Boissart cellars.

'We've got our friend the *Weinführer* coming round later today. He says he wants to hear about the volume of *vin de goutte* here, so I'd like you to check that for me, Lily, and give him the figures when he comes.'

He led me out of the office, along the corridor and into the main courtyard. This was solidly parked with German army vehicles, which he ignored as though they did not exist, leading me towards an immense arched oak door which he opened with a large old key.

'I'm going to tackle him about the nitrogen deliveries he promised us. We're almost out of our stocks here and we need it to ensure proper fermentation happens this time round. He won't like me for reminding him.'

He led me through the main stockroom and down some stairs. It was pitch black until I heard the click of a switch, igniting a string of dim lightbulbs which illuminated the ancient vaulted cellars that lay under the house and even extended under the nearby streets of Beaune.

'I see you have your notepad there, Lily. I think I can leave you to get on with it here?'

He left me and despite the cold I was glad to have a new task to do. I knew that I had been there some hours, making painstaking notes and gathering the information he had asked for when I heard the familiar footfall on the stone staircase. I saw Karl Futtermann coming towards me, stooping to avoid bumping his head on the low vaulted roof of the Boissart cellar. He was in uniform and alone.

'Greetings, Lily. M. Boissart tells me you can give me the latest information I require? Is that so?'

He stepped quickly across the brick floor towards me.

'But I need some other information also, young woman.'

His tone had changed, his voice was softer now. 'When can I meet you again?'

He was standing close to me, looking down at me. He reached out and took hold of my hand.

'Don't be afraid, Lily.'

There was no calling a halt or turning the clock back. Karl Futtermann was a man who got what he wanted and at that time he wanted me. Snow and harsh winds made it bitterly cold and the time for secret drives along remote country roads was over. So he advised me to make more use of the small bedroom in the Boissarts' house.

'We can meet there. If we're discrete, no-one will know.'

How pliant I was to fall in with his plan. It was easy for him to gain access via a side gate which I could ensure was left off the latch, then it was a few strides to the wing of the house where my room was located. But for me it meant that I must be conspicuously absent from home more often, to keep him happy. Three or four days each week in Beaune.

Of course, I let it be known that there was no stopping the cases of wine on order from the Germans or the administrative work for each one of them. By arrangement with Boissart, I extended my working days to Mondays, Tuesdays and Wednesdays and in the evenings I usually worked late. Often my back ached from sitting at the desk for hours at a time typing letters, sorting correspondence, making entries in the huge ledgers. But the working days were followed by the nights with Karl. I knew I wanted him. Wanted this time together. Thought it would have a happy ending, fool that I was.

He spoilt me, making me feel special with extravagant gifts from Paris or Munich: silk underwear and stockings, crêpe de chine blouses, fabric bought on the black market. With the stylish hand-me-downs from Mme Boissart I developed my own wardrobe of tailored clothes, amateur reproductions of those worn by my screen idols at this time. I plucked my eyebrows like Bette Davies. Always appeared *bien soignée*. For him.

Only I dreaded the return to Saultmur and the switch back to the other Lily, the unsophisticated local girl. Before I set off from Beaune on my bicycle, I made sure to change into a simple shirt-waister dress worn clumsily with thick stockings, Auguste's jumpers and jackets on top to keep warm, to cover myself up. But I felt awkward. Out of place. I knew I no longer belonged. As soon as I stepped back into the kitchen, small suitcase in hand, I felt the pairs of eyes drilling into me, Marthe and Josephine looking for tell-tale signs of the other me. A whiff of perfume, perhaps, or lingering touches of mascara on my eyelashes. Traces of eye-liner.

I was a stranger now in my parents' home. There was little work for me to do now that German orders of wine from the Domaine Lemoine had dried up completely.

Chapter Thirty-Eight: January to May 1942

My father needed me to prop him up. Since my mother's decline he had lost momentum. Frequently, unless I alerted him, he would fail to read or act on important documents.

In late January, I was sifting through a pile of unopened letters in the tray on his desk in the *mairie* and noticed one stamped from the regional prefect's office in Dijon. I tore it open and read the contents.

I would like to propose to the wine growers of Beaune a gift in recognition of Maréchal Pétain. This year we shall mark the second anniversary of the Armistice with the Germans and celebrate the stability and continuity of purpose that has marked the Maréchal's period in office.

I showed it to my father immediately. He read the letter, frowning and shaking his head, until at the end he slammed the letter down on the desktop in front of him, pinning it down with the forefinger of his right hand.

'Can you credit it, Lily? Does he really believe what he's saying here? He actually wants the wine growers of Beaune to get together to celebrate the great hero of Verdun. For what? For capitulating to the Germans? For signing over our wine to the *Boches*? Does he really believe there will be wine growers who will support this measure in the whole of Burgundy? I'll speak to Boissart about it.'

He passed me the letter.

'Send a polite reply, Lily. Tell him I'll meet with my fellow *vignerons* shortly.'

I took the letter from him and sat down at my typewriter to do his bidding. Since his outrage over the publication of the photograph he was becoming increasingly resistant and hostile to any new measures. By agreeing to stop trading with the *Weinführer* he had saved face locally, and he had actively helped to encourage others to benefit from German sales.

Times were changing. The Germans were not so dangerous as first feared here on the Côte d'Or, but my father was not going to admit it: give them what they wanted and things weren't so bad, after all. That's the way I saw it at that time. Better still, give the *Weinführer* what he wanted, and I could have *ma vie en rose* there and then. A glass of champagne on special occasions in the restaurant at the Hôtel de la Chasse, a choice of *foie gras* or *pâté de campagne* followed by a fish or meat dish from the *à la carte* menu. One of Boissart's reds to wash it down. *Crème caramel* or *tarte tatin* for dessert and a cup of genuine coffee to follow, with one lump of white, glistening sugar.

Late one April evening, after most tables had been

vacated, we left the dining room, crossing an empty reception area to take the lift up to the first floor. I was following Karl along the corridor to his suite, swaying slightly on my high heels, mind clouded by the alcohol.

He opened the door with a standard hotel key and ushered me in, taking out a small box from the jacket of his lounge suit.

'I'd like to give this to you tonight, *mein Liebling*.'

He took out the ring, slipping it on my finger. The seed diamonds glinted in the light, forming the shape of a diamond edelweiss, its spiky petals grouped around a blue sapphire. I straightened my fingers.

'Please don't look so scared. I commissioned Hans to make it. For you. Promise to be my wife, Lily, when the war is over. We shall have a big wedding, here in Beaune. You will be my beautiful bride. Think of it: there will be a cloudless sky on our wedding day and your father will lead you up the aisle in the basilica and you will see me waiting there for you. We shall say our vows. Then we shall have a magnificent reception in the *Hospices de Beaune*, fine speeches. Promise me. Be mine for ever.'

And I did promise him. For that one night we shared the same vision.

*

I cycled home early next morning. Mist hung over the vineyards and I could see the buds swelling on the vine stems, the tiny fringe of leaves starting to form. I felt a rush of hope for the future, our future. If we could skip over the weeks and months, even years, ahead, I believed that one day we could be together. For ever.

Surely, we could make it work out, somehow?

I parked my bicycle in the shed, entered by the back door. No-one was up yet so I went quietly upstairs to my room. After a short time, there was a knock at the door of my bedroom. It was Marthe.

'Can I please speak to you, Lily?' She looked sheepish. What did she have to say to me?

I beckoned her in, cleared some clothes strewn over a chair to let her sit down. She looked awkward and embarrassed and didn't know how to start.

'We've always been good friends you and I, Lily. You know that. I'm not a tittle-tattler like Josephine. I like a bit of gossip now and then, who doesn't? Especially in these times. But I think you should know what they're saying.'

She stopped and looked at me, working out how to soften the bombshell.

'Marthe, who are "they"?'

'I promised not to give away their names. I don't want to get anyone into trouble.'

She looked warily at me.

'Go on then. Say it. Say what you have heard.' I could hear I was raising my voice, getting near screaming pitch.

Without looking up, and avoiding my eye, she replied 'They're calling you terrible things, Lily. I don't want to repeat it. And Antoine too.'

I had not expected this. Not that day. 'Tell me what they're saying, these people, even if you can't tell me who they are.'

I knew what she was going to say, even before she said it.

'They're calling you "the *Weinführer's* whore", Lily. And they're calling Antoine "the *Weinführer's* pimp." Josephine and I try to shut them up, but there's no stopping them.'

'Get out, will you? Just get out of this room!'

I saw her scuttle to the door and disappear quickly. There was whispering in the hallway outside and on an impulse, I hurled the door open and startled the two of them: Josephine and Marthe.

'You were listening at this door, weren't you, Josephine? Trying to pick up a few more juicy bits of gossip for the village, were you? I hope you weren't disappointed!'

I saw her stupid face turn bright red and she glanced shiftily to one side, avoiding meeting my eye. I retreated back into my room, slamming the door loudly, the echo sounding through the house.

Chapter Thirty-Nine: Le Clos du Maréchal Pétain

In the end, Papa refused to attend the meeting of Beaune winegrowers on the matter of the *clos* for Maréchal Pétain. It was his big stand.

'Has everyone forgotten that Pétain himself has waged a war against wine since he came to power in 1940? He sees it as the root cause of the decadence of the French people! How do they think he will react?'

He was stubborn, refusing to pick up on the mood of the times.

'After all this mighty fuss, who knows? He might even turn it down, hand the keys back to Roger Duchet! I thought Boissart and I saw eye-to-eye on this?'

'Boissart has been talking to the other Beaune *négociants* on the committee of the *Hospices de Beaune*. They are all solidly in favour of the gift to the *maréchal*, so he's not going to stand out of line, Papa.'

I could tell this comment infuriated my father even more.

'You make it sound as though you think he's doing

the right thing, Lily! Just whose side are you on these days, young lady? I think I know the answer to that question.'

He muttered this last remark under his breath, as though I wouldn't hear it. The innuendo was clear.

'Papa, think about it: have we really suffered since the Germans came in 1940? Of course, times have been hard. We've been short of manpower and the work has been never-ending. But compare us to the ordinary people in Chalon, or Lyon or Paris. Look at your ledger: a steady stream of orders since autumn of that year. Regular payments until you yourself called a halt to the business. It may be unpleasant to admit it, but the Germans have not been our worst enemy since they came to the Côte d'Or.'

I was surprised to hear myself coming out with this defence. But it was true. Papa seemed to be blind to the obvious advantages that had come his way.

He looked at me, lost for words for a moment.

'What you say is true, Lily. Not only that, we have practically drained our cellars dry to oblige the *Weinführer* and his obnoxious bosses.'

I wasn't going to contradict him, but he knew what I was thinking, and he added, 'Yes. We both know we do have some reserves left and with the help of *le bon Dieu* maybe we can keep them untouched until this bloody war is over. But it is against everything I stand for to honour the very man who signed over France to Adolf Hitler!'

With that he sat down at his desk in the *mairie* and started reading through the documents I had put on his blotter for signing. There was no point in arguing with him. The honouring of Maréchal Pétain may have been against my father's principles, but he could not stop its going ahead.

When I was next in Boissart's office he told me about the site they had chosen to donate.

'You will know it straight away when you see the stonemasons at work next week, Lily. We decided on a section of Les Theurons. A strip of vines on a slope with a good view over the town of Beaune. The old man can't complain. We've all agreed to do our bit building the wall and setting the gateposts in place. We've even set out a rota for the year ahead for the care of the vines.'

He paused, sensing my embarrassment that his "we" did not include my father.

'You'll have to try to talk Antoine round to come and give us a hand. After all, he has profited more than most from trade with the Germans. He must recognise that as well as anyone. Tell him the *maréchal's* wine is going to be among the best!'

But my father had isolated himself from the other winegrowers by this stage and they stopped inviting him to their meetings. The name Lemoine did not appear on any of the duty lists for the management of the *Clos du Maréchal.* I avoided ever mentioning the subject back home.

Chapter Forty: Nowhere To Hide

Love blurs the way you see things, like looking in a curved mirror. It stops you seeing straight. I knew people knew: Josephine, Marthe, but I thought they didn't matter, idiot that I was. I chose to ignore them, and others like them. What could they do to me? We were discrete, the two of us. We did nobody any harm. What could anyone do to me when Karl, the *Weinführer*, was there to protect me? Or so I thought until that photograph.

It was published in the monthly German news-sheet and delivered to the *mairie* in early June. The print was poor, the image was dark and even slightly blurred, but each person in the line-up at the *Clos du Maréchal Petain* was all too easy to recognise: from left to right, Boissart and the leading members of the *Hospices de Beaune* committee looking on as the stonemason prepared to slip the final stone into place in the new archway. In the group to the right of him there I stood, elegant in my tailor-made suit. Fool. In that moment I'd shifted my gaze upwards to my left, I was smiling up at the *Weinführer*, who had rested his right hand on my shoulder.

What could I do? Caught on camera like this for all to see, I had nowhere to hide.

A few days later, as I sat at my desk in the *mairie*, the German news-sheet arrived in the post with this photograph centred on the front page. I had to speak to him, to Karl, urgently. Desperately, I picked up the telephone and called his office and one of the members of his office staff answered my call.

'Please allow me to speak to Herr Futtermann. This is Lily Lemoine. It is about an order of wine.' I tried to keep the note of panic from my voice.

'Herr Futtermann is not in his office today. Perhaps I can deal with your inquiry?'

I hung up. What could I do?

Meanwhile my father was in his office. There were three local *vignerons* with him. Voices were raised. I could guess what they were discussing. Suddenly the door was flung open. The men filed past my desk without casting a glance my way.

'Lily, come here, will you please?' I stood up from my desk, sick with dread.

'Yes, Papa?'

As he gestured for me to sit down, I saw his face was pale. He looked ill. Unshaven. His collarless shirt was unironed. He was neglecting himself. For a moment he stared at me, struggling to find the words he wanted to say.

'Have you seen this photograph, Lily?' He tapped his

forefinger on the offending image. I nodded.

'Have you any idea what people round here are saying? They are shocked by this! Shocked that the mayor's daughter is not ashamed to flaunt herself at the *Weinführer* in public like this.'

Anger made me want to defend myself, but I knew I'd lost the battle before I started. The despair in his eyes told me everything.

'Of course, I had suspected something was going on for some time between the two of you. And Josephine misses nothing, as you know very well. People don't like it, and they want to kick you out of your job in this office.'

He spoke with controlled anger and I had no idea how to answer him.

'Will you let them do that to me, Papa? After all the work I've done for you and for them?'

Through my tears I saw he avoided looking in my direction as he replied 'You need to know the villagers are holding a meeting here tomorrow, Lily. They want to discuss what should be done and to vote on whether they want me to stay on as mayor.'

In a gesture of despair, he put his head in his hands.

'Now you'd better pack up your things at the desk. You can tell the *Weinführer* he's the one who has made you lose your job at this *mairie*.'

The final kick in the stomach. As I left the room, closing the door behind me, I found it hard to believe this was really happening. I glanced at the telephone on my desk. It stayed silent.

As I left the *mairie* carrying my few belongings in a cardboard box, I was in a trance, numb, unable to believe that my work in this building was at an end. As I stepped out into the square and in the glare of the morning sunshine, I heard a man's voice shouting from an upstairs window.

'*Va-t-en, putain!*'

I stopped in my tracks, back to the church, and looked up. The voice had come from one of the first- or second-storey windows of the old buildings lining the square, facing me. Some were shuttered up, paint flaking off, the owners trying to screen themselves from the fierce heat of the day. Further round the square, I caught sight of the back of a man's head as he moved away from a pair of balcony doors, slightly ajar, immediately above and opposite me. Sick with anger and disgust I ran home fast.

At the gates of the Domaine Lemoine, it was the sight of the German armoured cars and motorcycles in our courtyard that gave me some illusion of safety. The anonymous name caller was the new enemy now.

One of the soldiers was about to leave as I was crossing to the house. Breaking all the unspoken rules Karl and I had between us, I quickly scribbled a note and asked the soldier to deliver it to Herr Futtermann.

'Please tell him the note is urgent. We have tried to telephone his office, but the line appears to be dead.' The note I handed to him simply said 'I must see you tonight.

Meet me before dark. In the woods. Our usual place.'

I knew this was stupid. That I shouldn't have done it. But I had to see him.

Chapter Forty-One: The Attack

We were taking too many risks. We both knew that. It was at the end of a day of baking heat, up in the pine woods near the monument. Here was our "special nest", as he used to call it. A small clearing in the woods, near where he had parked the car that first winter's day. It was dark and cool even in the hottest sun.

Setting off early from the house, I slipped out of the back door when no-one would notice me, making my way up along the familiar pathway past the Lemoine *clos*, up the steep track as far as the monument. Furtive, wanting to keep to the shadows, to avoid prying eyes.

When I reached the clearing, which was just as we had left it last time, I was relieved to lie down, spend a few moments staring upwards at the sky, a patch of deep blue circled by the tops of tall pine trees. No sound apart from the song of a few birds. I closed my eyes, soothed by the combined scent of earth and trees and the sound of wildlife.

I opened my eyes with a start when I heard the

sound of twigs being trampled underfoot very close to the clearing. Immediately afterwards, there was a click of metal, then a terrible report which reverberated in my ears and seemed to leap out of my chest. The sound of a rifle being loaded and fired. Uneven footsteps retreated. Silence. A poacher? Heart thumping, I felt like a hunted animal myself.

Not long after, the distant throb of the familiar car engine cut across the noise of an owl hooting. Headlights lit up the dusk. The car came to a halt and I heard a door slam. I felt a rush of relief hearing Karl's firm tread approaching and I got to my feet, ready to greet him. Straight away he put his arms round me, held me tight.

'*Was ist los*? What's wrong? Why the note? I've told you not to send messages like this, not on any pretext.'

There was irritation in his voice. I told him about the fury of local people, the public meeting due to take place the next day. The insult shouted across the square.

'Oh God, what a mess!'

I saw him push his hand through his hair, a sign of desperation.

'I want to take you away from here, to keep you somewhere safe.' I felt the seconds tick, waiting for the solution he could offer me. He said nothing and held me tight, kissed the top of my head, then put his finger under my chin and looked at me closely as he said 'You have to realise this is just impossible in these times. No.'

I heard the word 'impossible' and started to lose my

nerve. 'But what can I do? What will they do to me? To us?'

For a moment he turned away, lost for words, unable to come up with a plan.

'Simple. You must show them they have got it wrong. I will stay away from you either here or at Boissart's. People have too much to worry about with a war on. They will soon forget the rumours about us and move on.'

How easy it was for him. Safe and secure in his office at the Hôtel de la Chasse. No-one could get at him. But here, in the village, I knew that no-one ever forgot anything. I was a lamb for the slaughter. Karl was not going to help me. I was completely alone. Completely exposed.

'When we meet again, Lily, it will have to be a long way from here. I will come up with a plan, don't worry.' And he started to stroke me, to caress me, but I felt completely frozen inside. I pushed his hands away from me.

'Something's still the matter, Lily?' I told him about the gunshot I had heard earlier. The strange footsteps.

'You're nervous. Just imagining things. Don't worry. No spies except the birds.'

As he said this, he sat down on the ground, pulling me to lie next to him, both of us staring up at the purpling sky.

'Did you know that in Bavaria some people call edelweiss flowers "little stars"? Why? Because when you see them growing high up in the mountains they look like bright, tiny white stars growing near the rocks, but as soon as you pick them, they turn cream, then yellow, then brown. One day we will go for a long walk in the Bavarian mountains, Lily. I will take you and show you where the edelweiss grows.'

He was looking straight into my eyes, but I looked away. He'd talked about the edelweiss before. Given me the ring. What did any of it mean?

'Forget your dreams, Karl. Can't you see I'm in a nightmare and I can't tell how it's going to end?' I heard my voice sounding harsh and desperate.

'What are you saying, Lily?' He had propped himself up on his elbow, he sounded uncertain.

'I'm saying that this has to end. Our meetings. There is no future for us while the war is on. We both know that. Have you any idea the names people are calling me or my father?' And I reported to him Marthe's story.

He sat silently listening, looking at me as I did the talking. There was a long pause afterwards. Neither of us spoke. Finally, he said 'I know this is a difficult time for you. And your father. For us both. But listen. I want to take you away with me. To Paris.'

He reached out and held my hand, but I pulled it away.

'This is a ludicrous suggestion! I'm sorry.' I could feel the tears welling up, knowing that this had to be the end of the whole affair. It could not continue. There was no future.

'Nothing's impossible. You know that.' He spoke with

his usual tone of confidence.

Standing up, he straightened his uniform and pulled me to my feet with his free hand.

'I won't let you go, Lily. I will have my way.'

As we were leaving, walking along the moonlit pathway towards the car, we heard a gunshot and a voice that I thought I recognised, shouting into the darkness, echoing into the night.

'*Salaud! Putain! Tuez les Allemands!*'

We ran for the car and got in. Karl started the engine, reversed and accelerated towards the downward track. At that moment another bullet hit the back of the vehicle. Then another. The loud clash of metal was deafening and the car veered across the road. I glanced over my shoulder, trying to see the gunman but he had disappeared in the bushes.

Karl braked to stop the car lurching into the ditch. The back tyre was punctured. He drove forward slowly, saying nothing.

Chapter Forty-Two: Afterwards

Who had fired the gun?

It was common knowledge that there was a powerful cell of resistance workers in the Morvan, brave men and women who were risking their lives to defend their belief in a free France. Closer to home I had heard rumours that a few villagers were supporting escaped POWs in hideaways in the hillsides nearby. It must have been one of them, some desperate vigilante, patrolling the woodland, trained to kill any uniformed Nazi on sight.

These days I never asked anyone any questions. I didn't want to know. I wanted to keep quiet. Keep safe. To lie low. To keep my secrets to myself.

But who had fired the gun?

I kept telling myself that had to be it. The last time we would ever meet. Someone was out to get us, to get him, and I was terrified. He wasn't worth the risk. Not any more. I could get by without him. I didn't need him. I was strong enough.

The next day Papa avoided attending the public

meeting in the village, sending his apologies and giving no explanation. He stayed in his office at home with the door closed. He knew the people well enough to let them boil with rage against him, to talk behind his back, but he had his loyal supporters too. Who else could have done what he'd done in these times? Who would be willing to take on the job after Antoine Lemoine?

I quickly discovered that my detractors were not limited to Saultmur. Though I tried to continue working for the Boissarts, one morning Henri entered the office looking shame-faced and avoiding my eye:

'Lily, I must tell you to clear your things from your room here and leave this office. We have had letters of complaint. Threats shouted in the street. Messages daubed on our walls. You cannot continue to work here. I can only give you one piece of advice: keep away from the *Weinführer*. He's a *Boche*, remember that. He can use sweet words, that one, but he cannot change his uniform!' He stood and held the door open for me. I said nothing as I left the room.

The silk blouses and dresses, fine linen suits, the stockings, make-up and silver compact, the small ring box: all this finery was waiting for me in the small bedroom like a reproach. In a frenzy I snatched the clothes from their hangers and tried to cram them into the small travelling bag I had used for our trip to Mâcon. It was hopeless. In the end I packed only a blouse, suit and stockings with the smaller items and left the room. Something clattered to the floor: the manicure set from Essen with my initials, LL. I did not stop to pick it up.

I lose track of time. Then and now. Days are slipping past and the past is getting more slippery. More treacherous. I must keep going. To the end.

I remember nothing about the grape-picking that year, only being terrified of the public taunts and insults whispered or shouted wherever my back was turned: '*Charogne, dégueulasse*'. I kept away, stayed down in the cellar, learning to prefer darkness to light. Normally my father took charge of the cellar jobs with a boy from the village to help him. This year he left them all to me, with no help. I knew what to do and didn't need telling. How to wash and scrub the baskets and boxes used by the pickers for their grapes; how to make sure the huge wooden press and its heavy metal crusher had been thoroughly cleaned. It was man's work. But it stopped me thinking and I was glad of that.

Day by day I noticed the skin on the tips of my fingers turn raw and chapped, the fingernails broken and spoilt.

I stopped eating meals with the rest of them, to avoid either listening or speaking, and lived off whatever I could find on the pantry shelves: stale bread, cold boiled potatoes, meat leftovers. I lost weight, my clothes felt loose and baggy. I became a kind of spectre in our home, and no-one seemed to care. I hated people I had known all my life, especially the sneaks. Josephine and Marthe. My betrayers.

Weeks went by and I heard nothing from Karl. Not a single word. He was untouchable. Safe. Protected. And me? The opposite. I thought of the edelweiss flower, the white petals turning brown. Withering slowly. Dying.

One October morning as I collected the post from the box at the gate, I saw the familiar handwriting on an envelope addressed to me. Instinctively I wanted to tear it to shreds. How dare he write to me? What more was there to say? I pushed the letter into the pocket of my skirt and walked back into the house. Alone in my room, I tore it open and found a printed stocklist of the Lemoine wines inside. I flicked through it and a letter slipped out. It had been typed neatly on the *Kommandantur* typewriter, then folded with a tight crease before it was inserted into the envelope.

Kommandantur,
Hôtel de la Chasse
Beaune.
20th October 1942

Dearest Lily,

What is there for me to say to you? I mean it from the bottom of my heart that I love you. That I want you.

These are dangerous times. You know that – we both know that – only too well. But I believe we must try to meet in better circumstances. After that we may need to part until this bloody war is over. We shall see.

I beg you to find a way to make a trip to Paris where

I will have several important meetings in early November.

Please send me word to let me know if I can expect you? Take care, my dearest Lily.

Karl F.

In my anger after first reading his letter, I screwed it up and threw it in the wastepaper bin. Then I relented. Took it out, tried to smooth out the creases as I re-read it before penning a letter telling him how much I had been missing him, too. How much I hated it now at home and how home was even more of a prison since the ending of my work in Beaune: I agreed to join him in Paris.

I have no recollection of how we settled on the dates and times for my trip, I have no more letters from him after this one. In Saultmur, I was already *persona non grata*, nothing I could do or say could alter people's view of me. Somehow out of desperation came the belief that Karl would have a plan for us, Karl would have the answer.

Chapter Forty-Three: Paris

I have his letter in front of me now, crumpled, but with the neat fold across the centre. And as I read his words an iceberg in me melts and I want to go to him, to be with him in Paris. To have those last days together.

I knew at the time there would be consequences, but I was past caring. I had to get out of the cold, dark cellar of the Domaine Lemoine. Only for a couple of days. That's all. Would anyone notice? Who would care? On my bedside table, I left a lie scribbled in pencil: 'Chez Boissart'. Before daybreak on a cold November morning, I wheeled my bicycle through the back gate and across the vineyard, finally setting off to Beaune along the rue des Charrons.

Karl had arranged the necessary travel passes for me, my papers were all in order. The German guards at the station and on the train checked them silently, returning them to me without a query. Nevertheless, I was furtive and anxious as I stepped down from the train at the Gare du Lyon. The jaunty hat and tan-coloured suit I had chosen to wear suggested a brash confidence I did not feel.

The hat was one of those wartime constructions made from cardboard and covered clumsily with the papery fabric that was all the rage. I suppose I'd hoped we would have one of those clichéd reunions just like the films: eyes meeting across the crowded platform, the instant embrace.

The platform was packed with people, civilians, German soldiers and officers. I searched the faces, thinking I'd see him, but I couldn't catch sight of him. The crowds emptied towards the exit gate and gradually I was left almost alone, except for the station staff and occasional porters. Where was he? What should I do? He was never late.

I started to have second thoughts: why not catch the next train back to Beaune? Return to my role as a celibate recluse, down in my father's cellars. Then I heard his brisk footsteps, saw him smiling and waving in my direction. I walked towards him, felt his arms around me and his kiss on my lips. I was safe.

'Bad timing. I still can't work this city out. You're brave to have come to Paris, Lily, but I knew you would.'

A car was waiting for us outside the station where people were milling around under umbrellas or sheltering from the pouring rain.

'Here comes your tour of Hitler's Paris.'

Through the blurry car windows I looked up at the Eiffel Tower hung with the swastika flag, and huge red Nazi banners lining the Champs Elysées. Flags, banners and even bunting brandishing the swastika were everywhere:

in the Place de la Concorde, at the entrance to the Tuileries gardens, over the stalls of street vendors and waving from the high walls of the Louvre.

'No-one can mistake who is in charge here these days! What do you say to all this, Lily?'

Karl threw the question at me without expecting a reply. It looked as if the whole of Paris was celebrating the German takeover.

Soon the car came to a halt outside the Hôtel Madison on the Boulevard Saint Michel. Karl spoke to the driver in German as he held the passenger door open for us. We entered the hotel through a heavy rotating door. On the other side was a small lobby where, behind the desk, was a stooped and elderly woman dressed in black and wearing a pair of round spectacles. I noticed her turn to unhook a room key from the shelves behind her. Ignoring me, she looked unsmilingly at Karl.

'Is your wife staying for a few days also, Monsieur? She must sign the hotel register in that case.'

Officiously she presented the open book to Karl. Quickly he turned back a page and stabbed at his signature.

'That will not be necessary. I have signed for us both here, thank you.'

He shut the book abruptly and returned it to her, arrogantly guiding me past her desk to the small lift.

'This is my favourite hotel in all Paris. It is all the more special because you won't find any of my colleagues here. They're booked into the Crillon or the George V. Even the

Ritz. Here we will feel the real Paris, you and I, without them.'

He led me into the lift, which took us up to the third floor, then I followed him along carpeted corridors with windows overlooking a neat courtyard below, up several short flights of stairs and finally to the door of our room.

'I chose this room for the view: see for yourself.' He ushered me across to a pair of tall French windows, which I opened and stepped out onto a small balcony. We could see the Eiffel Tower standing like a small chess piece in the far distance, its lines softened against a background of grey clouds. Closer to hand we were looking at a narrow street lined with tall town houses with garret rooms set in slate rooftops. The street below us was deserted except for the street-lamps standing sentry-like. Paris seemed oddly silent, as if holding its breath.

The cold wind made me shiver, so I retreated back into the beautiful room. Our room. Dark wood furniture gleamed with polish. The glazed cotton curtains shone in the bright daylight. A scent of pot pourri hung in the air issuing from tiny dried rosebuds heaped in a cut-glass chalice which stood on the dressing table. His silver monogrammed brushes were set out by its side, seeming to belong in this world where I was the complete stranger. I felt gauche and awkward. Out of my depth.

Suddenly I caught sight of myself in the mirror. It was like seeing a self-portrait in a gallery, unexpectedly: my thin face in an oval frame, eyes wary, heavily defined by thick eyeliner, cheeks powdered and rouged. Unsmiling lips heavily glossed. That demented hat.

Karl appeared behind my shoulder, pulled me away from my own reflection, and snatching the ridiculous hat from my head, he threw it on the bed.

'Take that off, please. And this!'

He gradually made me shed the layers of winter clothing, the coat, suit jacket, thin cardigan, 'And these!' and in broad daylight he unbuttoned my blouse, pulled me towards the bed.

'We must warm each other, Lily!'

The crisp white sheets were cold to the touch. I felt the mattress rock with his weight. In a moment he held me in his arms, but I no longer felt warmed by his touch and turned away. Around us the room was full of shadows. We both fell into a loveless sleep, and I woke first. Turning over I saw his head resting on the pillow next to mine, eyes closed, still asleep.

'Do I love you?' I asked myself the question, knowing the answer. When he opened his eyes he said:

'Lily, *mein Liebling*.' He spoke my name and used the German endearment with his special tenderness, insisting there and then that I was his. His loved one.

'Tonight let me be your guide, Lily. Let's stroll along the Boul'Mich and see a few landmarks before we return here for supper. But why do you frown? You want to stay here? In this bed with your German lover?'

I was hardly listening to him. The sound of the bells

ringing in the Eglise de Saint Germain des Prés sounded the hour. Five o'clock.

'How can you and I make time stand still? Is that what you're thinking about? My Lily. My Lili Marlene.'

He started to hum the tune softly, adding the words, trying to make me sing along with him. By closing my eyes I could see the two of us side by side, driving along the narrow lanes between the vines. But I could not sing with him.

Soon we left the hotel. The pavements were carpeted thickly with autumn leaves, which bunched around our ankles. Karl led me through the Latin Quarter on an anti-clockwise route.

'First the Jardins de Luxembourg, one of my favourite gardens in the whole of this city. But you will miss their ultimate splendour: the brilliant hibiscus trees, which burn with colour in the summertime, reminding us of the Mediterranean.'

At this time the shrubs lined the sandy pathways, looking shrunken and plain. We stopped for a drink on the Boulevard St Michel, and he continued his tourist patter to entertain me.

'Now you're sitting where Hemingway and Scott Fitzgerald drank their nights away. Did you know that Hemingway supposedly downed quantities of Puligny-Montrachet with his oysters?'

We chinked glasses and sipped a glass of house red from the Pays d'Oc.

'I thought wine was banned in public bars these days', I said.

He smiled ironically at my question.

'Nothing's banned, Lily, if you know where to get it and you can pay.'

He took a sip from his glass and pronounced with authority, 'Hemingway would have spat this out. I'm telling you, Lily, far too much tannin in it. People in the south of this country need to learn a few lessons from you Burgundians!'

I suppose I must have nodded in agreement to humour him. The alcohol was starting to go to my head. I glanced at the other clientele, seeing tables of German soldiers with their girlfriends. Here, this was not a crime. Here in Paris, lovers did not have to hide.

Karl paid the bill and we walked hand in hand along the streets.

'That's part of the Sorbonne over there, and I can point out two excellent bookshops close by: over there, Didier's. And there, Bude's'

As he presented these landmarks to me, it jolted my memory of Sophie. Sophie Edelman and her postcards from Paris. Her student days.

I must have them here, in this case. Yes. This stack of letters and postcards written in her tiny, neat handwriting. I gave up replying to her messages, containing chatter about boyfriend problems. There were two of them, I seem to remember, both students. That was it. They both adored her, but she only loved one of them. His name was Jean, I think. He had a Polish surname I've forgotten. She wrote fluently, amusingly, about her feelings. About her celibate love affair. How could I ever have told her that I had a lover in the Wehrmacht?

We'd lost touch, she and I. I received her last postcard early in 1941.

'Are you listening to me, Lily?'

Now we were crossing the river with Notre Dame looming huge and dark in front of us, its silent presence dwarfing us both. Putting the cathedral behind us, we walked on, hand in hand, along the riverbank where the leafless trees were skeletal, their branches jagged and angular, tossed by the icy wind.

From the Pont Neuf, we took the steps down to the Vert Gallant, 'a special place only for lovers' he said, the shafts of light from the street-lamps dancing on the restless surface of the water, and looking up river, the receding loops of bridges.

There in the darkness, he held my left hand up, checking to see I was still wearing the ring, the diamond edelweiss. His ring. It was too dark for him to see my rough hands and chapped fingers.

'Remember, won't you, Lily? This edelweiss will never grow old. It will always stay white and it will always shine for you, even in the darkest times.'

He kissed the ring on my finger, then he kissed me with the Seine rushing past and the distant noise of cars and the horns of the barges.

As he let go of my hand, I felt the ring spin round towards my palm, the band too big now for my skinny finger. I had to hold it in place with my thumb to stop it from falling off and rolling into the river.

When I take it from its box to look at it here, I see the tiny seed diamonds shining. If I take off my wedding ring and try to slip it on my ring finger now, it's a struggle. My joints are swollen with arthritis, it takes some pushing to ease the ring over them. It just about fits. I try to straighten out my fingers, but it's painful. I see it in all its flickering glamour, unchanged after all the years. Never worn since those Paris days. And I need it here and now to shed some light on what happened.

Chapter Forty-Three: Next Day

Next morning, Karl presented me with a Paris street map marked with crosses.

'Look, follow this route to the Eiffel Tower. Take your time. Have a look in some of the bookshops. Try the patisseries at this bakery. Get a feel for the city in daylight, Lily. Later, cross at this bridge and make your way to the Louvre in the afternoon.'

I followed his finger along the lines of the streets, trying to register the names correctly.

'Arno Breker's exhibition is finished, but some of his work is still there. You should have a look. I will meet you near the ticket office at 3.00 p.m.'

And I remember him taking out his wallet and handing me a wad of notes to cover my expenses for the day. No-one had ever given me so much money before; when I tried to fit the cash into my purse, the clasp would not close.

I studied the map more closely before setting out, and realised on my way to the Eiffel Tower, I could easily take a detour along the street where the Edelman family lived in their apartment on the avenue Elisée-Reclus. In fact, it should be simple to walk directly to the house from this part of the Quartier Luxembourg.

On the map it looked a short distance, but as I walked onwards every street seemed longer than the previous one, and I remember the weariness and surprise when I eventually looked up and saw the street name ahead of me, two and a half hours after setting off. It was easy to recognise the apartment block: a fine, period, greystone building with tall windows on each floor and elegant wrought-iron balconies. In the early days Sophie had sent me a postcard of the street, marking her bedroom window with a label in her handwriting.

There was a set of bells for each apartment, marked with the owner's name. Next to 43b, the Edelmans' flat, the name tag had been removed. I pressed the buzzer several times, embarrassed by what I would say when Sophie or her parents appeared at the door.

After a while, I heard footsteps coming down the stairs and bolts drawn behind the door. A fashionably dressed woman opened it, I explained who I was and that I wanted to speak to Sophie if she was at home.

'She no longer lives here. I cannot help you, I'm afraid,' she replied in a strong German accent, but before she closed the door I asked when the family had left the apartment.

'In July this year, I believe.' Stepping backwards she

closed the door in my face.

So why had the entire family moved away so recently? Surely the news would have reached our village somehow. I thought of Mme Bèze-Conti vanishing altogether when the Yellow Star order was introduced. What was the story? Josephine had told it to me at the time. She had refused to follow the order, to be branded. 'I shall not wear that bloody badge, even if it kills me!' So she took a few things, saddled her horse in the stable and cantered off in the direction of the woodland late one night. That was the last we saw of her. That's all any of us knew. Perhaps the entire family were now hiding out together? If Josephine had been right, perhaps the family were now in some remote country house in the Morvan? It was impossible for me to find out.

My first reaction was to speak to Karl. That's what I should do. See if he could use his authority to find out. Pull some strings even. That's what it was about nowadays. String-pulling. As I carried on walking in the direction of the Eiffel Tower, stretching above me in the near distance, flying the Nazi flag, I realised something I'd been too naïve, too isolated to see before. No. This invisible string was tying us all together. Me to Karl. Papa and Boissart also. There was no cutting through it, no unravelling it. As I approached the huge, latticed metal structure it seemed to me like an elaborate and gigantic cage, a trap ready to snap us all up inside its metal frame. At any moment.

The grey November day stretched emptily ahead

of me. It was cold. I was disorientated, a country girl in the great metropolis. The spirit of adventure failed me. I wanted to go home. But where was 'home' these days? With Karl in the hotel room? In my parents' house? Homeless. I felt homeless. Nowhere to go and belonging nowhere.

I continued to walk through the Champs de Mars towards the river and the Pont d'Iéna. The swirling brown water curled away ahead of me. With one easy jump it could carry me off in its currents. I could disappear in its icy depths. So simple. So easy. A rush of exhilarating air, a cold splash of water. Then nothing. People could forget about me. I would escape this trap.

As I was leaning over the parapet, gazing downwards, I thought I heard someone calling my name.

'Lily? Lily Lemoine?'

The voice sounded surprised, shocked even. I stood up, and hurrying towards me, I was astonished to see Charles Santot, wearing a trilby hat and a long, dark winter coat.

'I don't believe it! What brings you to Paris, young woman? Or is that question none of my damned business?' Embracing me warmly, he continued 'I saw you from a distance. Recognised you straight away. But why these tears? Here, have a handkerchief. Dry those eyes!'

I took hold of the white square he offered me to wipe my eyes and blow my nose, overwhelmed by this lucky meeting.

'Come with me. You need a hot drink to warm you

up. There's a café nearby.'

He linked his arm through mine, guiding me to the other side of the river, to a café near the Trocadero.

'Now, tell me what a lovely young woman like you is doing wandering this lonely city all by herself on a cold November day?' He looked at me piercingly whilst handing me a menu card.

'Please go ahead and order food. You look like a starving refugee, Lily! Hasn't Antoine been feeding you lately?'

I studied the list of dishes in front of me and knew I had no appetite, nevertheless ordered a *croque monsieur* when the waitress came to our table. Playing for time.

'I'm here for a wine competition. Until tomorrow.' I lied, trying to avoid his fierce gaze, turning my attention to my gloves, slipping them off. Then, realising he would see the ring, I quickly covered the fingers of my left hand with the other hand.

'How come I know nothing about this? How come your father did not let me know of your visit? *Il est fou!*'

Shrugging my shoulders, I avoided giving any straight answers and realised it was easier to ask him a few questions.

'This morning I was trying to see an old friend. You may not remember her, Charles. Sophie Edelman?'

He nodded. 'Not sure I remember her but seem to recall the name. She is the niece of Mme Bèze-Conti, I believe?' It was my turn to nod and carry on.

'I was surprised to find she and her family had moved out of Paris. In July, it seems. I visited their flat and found they had left. Germans had moved in.'

I looked at him. His expression suddenly changed.

'*Tiens!* That is not good news, Lily. July, you say? Surely you know what happened here in Paris in July at the Vel'd'Hiver?' I shook my head. How could I tell him that I had become a cellar hand at the Domaine Lemoine, news from outside had passed me by? Dreading his reply, I asked him to tell me the bad news. Lowering his voice, he leaned forward.

'Fifteen thousand Jewish men, women and children were rounded up and herded into the velodrome, very close to where we are now.' He looked at me without speaking for a while, gesturing to his right in the direction of the popular cycle stadium.

'All of them have been deported, saving a very few. In cattle trucks from the Gare de L'Est and from Drancy. They will never return.'

He looked at me, speaking that last sentence in the merest whisper, leaning even further across the table so that his face was nearly touching mine. His shoulders were hunched, his elbows rested on the table. His features tense. What could I say? I lifted a hand to cover my mouth – the wrong hand – I saw his eyes take in the ring and he looked suddenly angry. Then he flung his arms to his side in an act of desperation.

'France is living through a nightmare, Lily. None of

us can know how it will end.'

The waitress brought our order to the table. Neither of us had any appetite. We sat staring at our plates without lifting knives and forks.

'You must know, Lily, the Germans are merciless bastards. Hitler is a maniac who will stop at nothing to achieve his ends. The deportation of the Jews is just one of his vicious schemes, and the worst of it is, in Occupied France he and his henchmen are seeing to it that, in our small ways, each and every one of us is helping him to achieve his goals. We're all caught up in it. It's sick, but it's true! Here am I with my engineering company and an order book filled with German orders. What would happen if I said no? The Gestapo would come down on me like a ton of bricks. I'd be tortured. Imprisoned. Deported even. My solution? To give them what they ask for. Not as efficiently as they would like. Only a fraction of their orders are ever completed. But I cooperate. I don't resist because I don't want trouble. Look at the Domaine Lemoine: brisk business with the *Weinführe*r for the last couple of years. Antoine's finest wines on the tables of the most evil men in Europe! Then he decides to have no more to do with the *Weinführer*, a bit too late if you ask me!'

As he paused, I thought for a moment he was going to turn on me. To talk about my friendship with the *Weinführer*, but it went unmentioned. Unspoken.

'You wait and see. We shall all have to pay for this trade with the enemy. You. Me. Antoine. The whole damn lot of us.'

I could feel his anger but said nothing.

'My dear, when are you leaving this godforsaken city? Will you allow me to take you out to a proper restaurant this evening, perhaps?'

I wanted to say yes. To tell him the truth and let him help me. But I couldn't. I shook my head, gave an excuse. I checked my watch. Time was moving on. It was already 2.00 p.m. I had to say *au revoir*.

I can see him now, waving and smiling to me, standing among the pavement tables and chairs outside our café as we went our separate ways: he back to his office, I to my German lover.

Charles, why did you let me go back to him?

Chapter Forty-Four: The Parting

'We shall all have to pay for this trade with the enemy.'

Charles's words were churning through my head as I followed the embankment footpath towards the Louvre. If only I had had the courage to go straight back to the hotel, pack my bags and take the next train to Beaune. To free myself of the *Weinführer*. I couldn't do it. Not then. Not there.

He and I met as planned in the foyer of the Louvre and he led me through empty galleries, his voice echoing loudly whenever he spoke as he steered me to see the outsize sculptures of Arno Breker.

Alongside the huge heads of Albert Speer and Hitler, Karl stopped and in a very hushed tone of voice he asked: 'So what do you think of these likenesses then, Lily? Do they stir you with awe and wonder? Here we stand, you and I, face to face with Europe's most powerful man. Should we salute him, do you think?'

I was too much of a coward to say what I thought: that the outsize scale of these heads seemed to pulverise me, making me feel nauseous and faint. I caught sight of a wooden bench along the wall of the gallery and moved quickly over to sit down, resting my head in my hands. Karl followed me, showing his concern:

'Ah, Lily. This is too much for you. We will return to the hotel where you can rest for a while. We can take a taxi.'

Relieved that he could not expect me to say much, I followed him back towards the entrance and from there into a taxi, my head throbbing as I tried to take in the scene through the rain-drenched window of the cab.

*

Back in the security of our hotel room, Karl insisted that I rest whilst he shaved and changed his shirt ready for the evening event. I watched him casually at first as he lathered his face using the soap and water on the washstand. Looking closely in the mirror he took the long-handled razor and dragged it skilfully through the stubble on his cheeks, wiping it to clear the blade of soap suds before he moved on to a new section. Finally, he lifted his chin, moving the blade backwards towards his throat.

As he finished off drying his face, he spoke quietly; so quietly that I could hardly make out what he was saying:

'Tonight, Lily, you and I will be sharing a table with Third Reich officers from the administration here in Paris. Each and every one of them is a fervent admirer of Hitler.

They will want us to express full-hearted admiration for Arno Breker's work. To raise a toast to Hitler.'

He paused to see my reaction. I nodded, said 'Of course, Karl.' And he continued: 'You will hear me say that I think it is stupendous, the work of a brilliant genius.' Then his tone changed; he continued in a whisper.

'Rest assured the Gestapo would arrest me on the spot if they heard what I am telling you here: Hitler is a megalomaniac. There is no stopping him, as France knows to her cost.'

He came over to the bed and took my hand. 'I can't tell you the details, Lily, but meetings here in Paris have revealed the full extent of his plans, his evil solutions.'

He spoke with complete authority. I looked at his solemn expression and turned away.

'In other words, you're telling me all we can do is to keep lying? Keep on saying things you don't mean, keep pretending. That may work for you, Karl, but not for me anymore.'

*

That evening, Karl took me to see Charles Trenet at the Gaîté Parisienne. He introduced me to uniformed German officers with their wives and girlfriends. We behaved, he and I. Almost the perfect couple. With his arm around me we listened to Trenet singing about love, about Paris, about '*La Douce France*'. Each time we clapped, the hard surface of the diamond edelweiss scratched my right hand, biting into the palm. Trenet sang his new song, *Que reste-t-il ?* Its nostalgic lament for lost youth left me unmoved, but Karl looked at me with tears in his eyes.

After the show ended and the applause died down, Karl stood up and said goodbye to his colleagues and their wives. I remained at a distance, unable to understand the words they were saying as they joked and laughed, one gesturing towards me with a wink at Karl.

I knew I hated this. Hated them. Hated him. I loathed being pushed around, felt disgusted by my own part in this ugly sham.

We walked together along the rue de la Gaîté to catch a taxi. There was silence between us, the only sound the echoing of our footsteps along the cobbled street.

*

Karl's silver shaving set was glinting on the washstand when I woke early next morning. What if I picked up his razor and dragged it across his throat? The perfect murder. I could dress quickly, leave the hotel by the back entrance, make my way on foot to the station. By the time his body was discovered, I would be on the train back to Beaune.

But I was too much of a coward. I couldn't do it. Not then, in that room on that morning. Another day out there in the future. The right moment would come.

My bag was already packed, my clothes for the

journey draped on a chair. I dressed in front of the mirror, smoothing out the creases in my clothes, leaning close to apply face powder, lipstick and make-up. I had no feelings for the man still asleep in bed.

Disturbed by my movements, Karl soon woke and crossed the room. Taking my face between his hands, making me look into his eyes, he said 'You are a wonderful and brave young woman, Lily. I mean everything I have said to you. Understand that as lovers we have to part. It is too dangerous. I want this bloody war to end soon so that we can be together, for ever. Trust me.'

I remained mute, numbed as I stepped back from him.

'Here, use this for the taxi.' He pulled out another wad of cash from the wallet in his jacket pocket and I took the money from him, slipping the notes loosely into my handbag. I didn't look at him again as I picked up my bag and left the room.

'Goodbye Karl.'

*

In the train on the return journey, I slipped the ring from my finger and placed it back in its box. Snapping the lid shut, I pushed the box to the bottom of my handbag. It was my greatest treasure, my diamond edelweiss, but it was dangerous. Like a stick of dynamite. Like a gun.

Chapter Forty-Five: Endings

On a cold morning in December weeks later I returned early to the house from the *clos Lemoine* where my father and I had been burning the old vinestocks and dead wood. The smoky smell had made me feel sick. Faint. I knew what was wrong, but I couldn't admit it. Not to myself. Not yet.

I entered the house through the back way, heading straight up to my room. I noticed a light on and when I entered, there was Josephine bent over the case, these papers and letters strewn over the bed, the ring box open in her hand.

'Get out of here! What the hell do you think you're doing?' I snatched the box from her hand.

'Who gave it to you, Lily?' I can still hear her demanding an answer, still remember the dank smell of cooking and sweat which hung around her clothes.

'What damned business is it of yours? What right have you to enter my room and disturb my possessions?' As I spoke, I tried to bunch all the papers together and stow them back in the case. Some were caught in the lid which infuriated me even more.

'Was it a German?' She was like a dog with a bone. She wasn't going to let go.

I refused to speak. My head was aching. I was about to be sick.

'Was it the *Weinführer*?' The German word was spoken with a sneer in her voice. 'Well, you should know this. Have you heard the latest? He's got a girlfriend in Santenay. Camille Prideau, she's blonde, looks a bit like you. Fatter, though. My friend Sylvie says she saw them together in his car the other night. Ask your father. He knows M. Prideau. He can tell you the full story.' She was leaning forward as she spat the words at me.

'You're a liar! Why should I care what you say to me?' Barely had I got the words out, when I had to grab the bowl on my washstand and be sick. I saw her watching, taking in every move I made.

'Get out, I tell you! Don't ever come back in here!' I grabbed her by her arm, digging my nails in hard, wanting to draw blood as I pushed her onto the landing.

*

The anonymous notes started after that: 'Lily Lemoine, Nazi traitor', or 'Was it only wine you sold to the *Weinführer?*' Then there was the graffiti: a heart painted in red on our gatepost with a swastika in the centre and the initials LL and KF on either side. When I walked across the place de

L'Hotel de Ville on my way to Saint Vincent I heard a male voice shout: '*Charogne! Putain!*' Walking through the vineyards, I would hear more insults hurled at my back by cowards hiding behind the stone walls where I could not see them.

I was trapped. There was only one way out.

I sent Karl a letter to his office in Beaune proposing to meet him one last time.

*

A dream returns, unprompted, even now after so many years, which started that night: I'm in Paris by myself. It's raining and I have no raincoat, no umbrella, so I shelter under the stripy awning of a bookshop. Ramshackle wooden bookshelves standing outside with copies of student textbooks, second hand. Inside it's very cramped, packed with people, all soaking wet with the rain. I try to push through to a back room, but I find more and more people stampeding towards me. They're like cattle: they smell of sweat, of stale skin, of blood. I feel sick, light-headed and I'm afraid I'm going to pass out. But then, suddenly in this sea of faces, distant at first but coming towards me and smiling, is Karl. He sees me and raises his hand high about his head to wave to me, he smiles a wide, good-natured smile, he comes close, he puts his arms round me and he holds me tight and I feel well again. Then the dream ends.

When I woke at dawn on that January morning in 1943, it was still pitch-black in my room. I felt what I had to do in the pit of my stomach, not in my head. Get up. Get dressed in the shirt-waister with the rosebuds. Make no sound. Find the chamber pot in the bedside table. Be sick, feel better. Feel worse. Don't think about yourself. Don't think about him. The gun. Christ. The gun. Groping around behind the chamber pot reeking of vomit, I felt the cold, hard metal handle. Fumbling, I picked it up. Careful. It's loaded. The pocket of the flimsy cotton dress can't hold the weight.

Holding the handle of the gun in one hand I opened the catch of my leather handbag. It fitted like a glove, but there was a grating noise against metal. The silver powder compact last used in Paris was still inside and as if from the silent corners of the room I heard these words and his voice chanting '*Spieglein, Spieglein, an der Wand / Wer ist die Schönste im ganzen Land?*'

Quickly I slipped out the compact and threw it onto the bed and left the room, closing the door very quietly behind me.

I made my way downstairs to the kitchen and out through the back door. As I headed towards the garden gate, I could see a few rays of light defining the trees and plants in the garden but up ahead, the hillside still appeared as a solid block of darkness. It was misty and icy cold. I broke into a run. Crossing the rue des Charrons, I heard the stream rushing and continued across the road and up the hill. Pausing at the thorny blackberry bush, I could see ahead of me the outlines of the vines, trimmed and harnessed to the wires. No time to think. Just do it.

Do what? Click open the handbag catch, hold the gun. Keep walking. Catch your breath. Put your finger on the trigger.

Turning left along the path, I stumbled on the uneven ground, but hurried on. I wanted to be there first, at the dry stone wall of the Lemoine vineyard. I pushed open the old door standing ajar and continued to walk steadily through the vines towards the *cabotte*, standing small and squat ahead of me, its entrance like the open mouth of a monster's head.

Approaching I could just make out a figure on the left-hand side, in the shadows, standing sideways but moving to face me as he heard my footsteps. Karl! He had got there first. I swallowed hard. He spotted me, raised his hand, waved and stepped forward to meet me. His gold hair was glinting now in the wan light as he opened his arms wide and held me. Held me tight for the very last time, with all his strength.

Only a dull crack sounded, the loud bang muffled by the thick felt of his loden coat. First one, then two, more squeezes of the trigger and he collapsed forward onto me, the complete weight of his body pushing me against the wall. He murmured into my ear those German words that I hear again now: '*Doch Lili, mein Liebling, ich liebe dich!*'

'But Lily, my darling, I love you!'

Bang! One more shot through the side of his head, putting an end to the nervous twitching, the sound echoing round the walls of the little *cabotte* and bouncing out into the hillside beyond as the sun rose in a red sky.

Blood trickled down the side of his face and formed a stream flooding his hair: gold turned to red, the streams started clotting, turning dark red then black on his dear cheek.

It was fully light when I walked back through the rows of vines sticking up from the ground like skeletal hands. My dress was drenched with blood and reeking with the sweet, sickly odour. I ran fast, downhill, hurling the gun into the stream and hearing the splash, but without stopping until I reached our back gate. No-one up yet: get washed, get changed. Then what?

Back in my room, I threw myself on my bed. All I could see in my mind's eye was the body of Karl Futtermann lying where he had fallen, the crows squawking overhead.

How much time was there left before they came for me?

*

The rattle of the catch on my door shattered the silence.

'Lily, Lily, have you forgotten? What are you doing?' It was my father.

Forgotten what?

'The market, in Beaune.'

Get up, shoes on. Straighten dress. Wedge bloody dress behind wardrobe. Stuff things lying on the bed into small case. Tell him. Tell Papa. He'll know best.

'Come on now, Lily!' He was standing outside my door, wearing his overcoat and scarf. Ready to leave. Dear Papa. As soon as he saw my face, his expression changed.

'We must speak, Papa. Please!' He turned and led me into the dining room and pulled out a chair, gestured to me to sit down.

'Whatever is it? Tell me, what's going on?'

As he sat on the chair next to mine, I tried to tell him the whole story. But it didn't seem to make sense. I couldn't find a starting point. So I started at the end and worked backwards. Told him that Karl Futtermann was lying dead up in the vineyards, his body hidden in a stone hut. Then I told him it was me that shot him, shot him with the Browning handgun Auguste had taught me how to use when we were children.

'But why? He loved you, Lily.' Almost the exact same words. His words. Words he could never utter again.

And I couldn't answer the question why. Not then. Not now.

Soon I felt my father's warm hand on my shoulder, and through the silence heard the ticking of the hall clock. Eventually he cleared his voice, and I looked up to see the tears welling up in his eyes.

'You know what this will mean, Lily.' He paused. 'Your mother and I will face the authorities. But you?

You must take your papers and leave on your bicycle. The Germans won't stop you. You will not arouse suspicion. Be sure to pedal fast up the lanes to the woodland above Beaune. Then hide the bicycle somehow and make your way towards Dijon on foot.'

He was standing, looking down at me. He took hold of my arm tightly, pulling me up on my feet. Then he said 'Now leave and never come back'.

So I did what Papa told me, turned my back on him and left the room. Put on my coat, collected my case and the money Karl had given to me in Paris. Then I crossed the hall, turned the handle of the front door, walked down the staircase. Taking my bicycle by the handlebars, I wheeled it across the courtyard towards the open gates.

Part Three

Vera

Chapter Forty-Six: The Notebooks

Back in Bonn I spent weeks and weeks transcribing my mother's words into legible text, sometimes altering her expression to make the meaning clearer. Whilst initially my impulse had been to turn my back on my mother's past, gradually an obsessive drive to find out more, to make the missing pieces of the jigsaw fit together, overcame my reluctance. The contents of the writing case were strewn over the floor of the lounge, the notebooks were by the typewriter in the study and by my bed were the typewritten and hole-punched sections in a ring binder.

My mother: 'the dark horse', 'the weird woman', 'the strange lady'. I kept poring over two photographs from the album picked out from the rest. Two opposites, one blonde, the other dark-haired, one a popular village girl, the other unsmiling, wary, old before her time: Elizabeth Walters, my mother.

Towards the end of the notebook her handwriting turned into illegible scribble. Sometimes in English and other times in French, she managed to communicate what had happened to her. I'm summarising here the gist of what she wrote.

For several days and nights, she made her way along the forest tracks in the Hautes Côtes across the limestone ridge between Beaune and Dijon. She was a runaway, frightened that she would get caught and shot by the Germans if they found her. She had no food or drink but what she could scavenge to keep herself from starving: '*the kicking force inside me made me keep going, gave me a tiny glint of hope in this pitch-black nightmare.*'

Her record becomes incoherent at the point where, weak and half-starving, she started to miscarry. It says: '*Somewhere in the remote countryside near Dijon, blood was trickling down my legs, I felt a terrible wrenching pain.*'

She does not give the details of how she was rescued, but the next thing she knew was when she woke on a settle in a stranger's kitchen, weakened by the loss of blood. Her notes are especially hard to read at this point, the details stomach-churning. I don't see the point of including them here.

After some months with the care and attention of the farmer's wife she recovered her health and strength and the will to move on. She organised transport on a wagon carrying livestock from the farm to a market in Bourg-en-Bresse. From there, through another contact, she hitched a lift with a farmer travelling in the direction of Switzerland.

During this time, she created a new identity for herself. The people at the farm undoubtedly had connections with the resistance movement. They issued her with false travel documents, which I found in the lid of her writing case, where she was named "Elisabeth Lemont" – the name we always understood to be her maiden name.

Details are less clear of how she eventually tracked down and gained admission to a Croix Rouge camp in Switzerland – I am surprised that as a French national with legitimate travel passes, the authorities did not turn her away. Somehow, she argued her way in. She tells how she worked there as a secretary until the war ended, checking in and dealing first-hand with the displaced people arriving from all parts of war-torn Europe.

Quite how or why she found work for herself in London at this time is never explained, but she briefly refers to a journey she made northwards through France to Calais using French francs she had saved.

She was searching for a safe house to hide for the rest of her days and she found it when she met and married Sid Walters, my father. Although she never went back, did exactly what her father had told her, her final sentences show how much she ached to return.

I want to stand at the green gates, paint blistered over rusty wrought iron and look across the courtyard grown knee-high with weeds. I want to see again the old woody roses scrambling up the walls, and the straggling remains of hollyhocks self-seeded near the staircase, flowers replaced with bulging seed pods.

I'd like to rattle the gates and ring the bell, see if anyone still lives there who could open up and let me cross the cobbles one more time. Then I'd mount the crumbling steps of the double staircase to the front door and feel a rush of cold air as I step into the blue-tiled hallway.

Setting down my case I would recognise the familiar odour of wine-scented musk from the cellars below and I would know I had, at last, returned home.

The handwriting and sense flowed smoothly in this section as if, suddenly, some cloud in her head had lifted as this memory of the place came back to her. She made me want to find this place for myself.

*

My boss, Robin Cornish, called me in and said:

'What's up, V? You're not yourself since you came back to work. I'm watching you in meetings, sitting there thinking. No notes. No questions. It's not like you. Your mind's a hundred miles away. Take more time off. Your Dad passed away last year, now your Mum. You must have a hell of a lot to sort out: your parents' house, all their rubbish?' I nodded. 'There's a lot of adjusting to do. Don't underestimate it.'

The phone on his desk started to ring. 'Sorry, V,' he said and picked up the receiver, spinning round on his chair to stare out at the Bonn skyline as he listened to the voice on the other end of the line. I left the room.

I guessed what he wasn't actually telling me: that I wasn't filing enough stories, that for once I didn't seem to care what was happening out there. Robin was right. I couldn't afford to take my finger off the pulse at work. It would be better to book a full month off. To give myself time to sort things out.

The version of events in the notebooks was troubling on many levels. How was it that my mother had not considered the terrible consequences of her own actions as she wrote her account? Surely in the weeks and months after the killing she must have realised that once the *Weinführer's* body had been discovered, her father and all the members of his family would be prime suspects? The Germans almost certainly would have hit back with ugly reprisal killings.

My first step was to contact a colleague, John Hibbert, in the Paris office, to see if he could help me trace a public record of the *Weinführer's* death. I told him I was trying to find the documentary evidence of a killing near Beaune of a German official, early 1943.

His reply was to the point. 'If you want this kind of information, I'd say you need to go in person to the public record office or municipal library in either Beaune or Dijon. You'll need to present a good case for wanting to get your claws on this stuff. The French are as tight as a duck's arse when it comes to divulging this kind of information. *Bon courage*, V!'

Chapter Forty-Seven: Beaune

It was late afternoon when a taxi dropped me at the Hôtel de la Chasse in Beaune. The building – an old coaching inn – stood at the crossroads that led into the centre of town in one direction and out towards the villages in another. The yellow rendered walls were ivy-clad and had a nineteenth-century addition of a lofty stone porch supported by two chunky columns, on top of which were perched two outsize stone fruit bowls, the work of a stonemason with a sense of humour.

No-one was behind the desk at reception, so I rang the shiny bell, relieved to stand where a cold blast of air-conditioning allowed me to cool down. The *ping* brought a well-built young woman from behind a swing door. She quickly checked my booking, asked me to enter details on a registration form and handed me the key to my room. She took me across the lobby and summoned the lift. With a rattle it arrived, one of the old-fashioned kind with a telescopic metal door, which had to be tugged firmly to the side to allow the hotel guests to step in.

As soon as I clamped the lift door shut and pressed button 2 for the second floor, I was beginning to tread in Lily Lemoine's footsteps. This was where she had spent nights with the *Weinführer* in the latter part of 1942, when, as she put it, they had 'started to take risks.' She must have stepped into the lobby through the same doors and been met by the gaze of one of the staff. Had Karl Futtermann left word at the desk to allow *Fräulein Lemoine* to make her way to his room, or did he usually wait for her in the lobby, sat in a club chair, watching out for her?

My room was spacious and dominated by a large double bed with a good-sized TV set on the wall opposite. I made a mental note to resist any inclination to seize the remote control and check on the news. A wide picture window gave a panoramic view across Beaune and after putting down my case and taking a chilled bottle of water from the mini-bar, I stood and sipped the contents whilst looking out. I was high enough to be able to see across to the rampart walls of the old town and to look down on the rooftops of the town houses lining the narrow streets. A town walk before supper: pick up a map at the desk.

It was a relief to have exchanged the claustrophobic West German capital city for Burgundy's wine capital. To turn my back for a while on Bonn and all its government and corporate buildings, to shelve for once my role as watchdog on Germany's economic and cultural life.

Glad instead to have this room with its large bed and starched white sheets to myself. No Hermann with his marital problems and his business worries and his hypocrisy. 'I need you in my life, V', he would murmur in his impeccable English as he climbed into bed beside me in another hotel room in a new city we both happened to be in, for work reasons, at the same time. But I'm not sure I need you, Hermann, I thought. No, I wouldn't call him tonight.

*

Covering the wall of a building on the opposite side of the road to the hotel was a painted mural advertisement for the *Domaine Patriarche Père et Fils, 'les plus grandes caves de la Bourgogne'* with an arrow pointing along the street towards the address in the rue du Collège. I decided to follow the direction of the arrow before returning to the hotel for supper, making my way up onto the rampart walkway to get a better view across the town.

There was the thrill of the old for me, discovering the ancient towers and bastions along the perimeter wall of the old town, and catching a glimpse of the magnificent, coloured-tile roof of the *Hospices.*

As I continued the rampart walk, I noted a roll call of other *appellations*: Bouchard Père et Fils, Reine Pédauque. I was looking out for lines of topiary, perhaps a sign for the Domaine Boissart, but I didn't find the place and made a mental note to make a few enquiries on that point if I had time.

As I zig-zagged my way round I remembered how the old town of Beaune was literally underpinned by miles upon miles of cellars dating back to the Middle Ages, each one containing vintage wine stocks. No surprise that every year it continues to host a world-famous auction of wine produced by the most prized vineyards left in trust to the charitable foundation of the *Hospices*. No surprise, either, that these same cellars must have been the key attraction in Burgundy for the German occupying forces in 1940.

*

Back at the hotel, I started to ask myself what I wanted to get out of this trip. I had arranged it in a rush, without thinking through the details. I had acted on an impulse to find out more: but to find out what exactly? The journey from the airport in Lyon to Burgundy had shown me landscapes changing from the grey concrete industrial sites in the suburbs of the city to green hillsides dense with vineyards and topped with woodlands. Small towns or villages set elegantly into the curves of the hills. Everywhere I looked, these new places were bathed in sunshine and here was I, at the height of a golden summer, searching for a darker Burgundy.

Three nights booked in the hotel and only two and a half days for sleuthing. First there was the question of Saultmur, the village or small town. I had enlarged the sketch map in my mother's notebook and planned a visit the next morning after picking up a hired car.

Next was the question of the killing. John Hibbert was surely right to have warned me. I doubted that I would find anyone in these parts who would thank me for stirring up the past. I needed to get access to archive material. To see the story in black and white. This would be tricky without good reason, so I decided to pose as a freelance journalist researching Burgundy wines of the war years. It would give me a way in and leave Lily Lemoine's story out of it.

The dining room was quite busy when I sat down at a table for two, set with a white tablecloth, starched and folded serviettes. The young waiter presented me with the menu, and I glanced first at the wine list at the back and decided to order a *pichet* of local *pinot noir* to go with traditional Burgundian food: six *escargots* followed by *coq au vin*. I'm no wine buff, I don't go in for gushing wine rhetoric, but the dense flavour of each sip of the glass made me think of it sitting in an oak cask in a local *vigneron's* dark cellar, maturing year by year until he deemed it *magnifique, superbe,* ready to drink.

I could hear snatches of conversation, about the food and vintages 'A Saultmur or Pommard, Melanie?' a well-fed American was asking his wife at the table next to mine.

'I'll give the Saultmur a miss after today, Herbie. It's too heady for me. Something a little lighter, maybe?' I gathered from the following conversation that they had spent the day on a special fine-wine tour of the cellars along the *grand cru* and *premier cru* wine route from Nuits

Saint Georges to Auxey-Duresses. He had placed an order for cases of his favourite wines to be shipped out to the US.

'We can drink a bottle or two at Thanksgiving when the kids come home.' He selflessly proposed this gesture, and I remembered to translate 'Thanksgiving' to 'Christmas' and thought that I might buy one or two bottles for home consumption.

The ritual of the meal, the heady effects of the wine and the filling food made me want to retreat to my room. I was struggling to hold on to the purpose of my visit. I stepped once more into the lift and pressed button 2, relieved to put my mission on hold until the next day.

Chapter Forty-Eight: The Village

It was a ten-minute walk along the rue du Faubourg Bretonnière to collect the hired car, a Renault 5, the next morning. I had a tourist map of the area from the hotel and also Lily's album and the photocopied sketch map.

It was a quiet road out of Beaune and I drove slowly to take in the landscape. Ahead of me and to right and left were the walled vineyards of the *Côtes de Beaune.* As I followed the signpost to Pommard I passed a series of imposing gateways to significant *clos* on the right, and quite soon the square church tower came into view. I drove past small terraced houses on the main street, a patisserie and one or two small restaurants, then followed the road out of the village towards Monthélie. At this point I slowed the car as the road narrowed, noticing that it was flanked on both sides by old dry-stone walls thickly grown over with moss and ivy. Surely little had changed since the days when Lily Lemoine had cycled this way to and from work at the *Domaine Boissart?*

As the car rounded another bend, the hillside sloped

away ahead, and I saw it: the church spire of Saint Vincent! Trees and hedges temporarily obscured the view but as I drove on, I caught sight of the church again with its pointed and beaded spire near the *mairie*, a tall, narrow building with gabled windows in its yellow and green-striped roof, glinting now in the hot morning sun. *Saultmur* – the road sign came into view as soon as I took the left-hand fork in the road. My mother had never used this world-famous place name once in my hearing. Only in her notebooks had she shown it to me for the first time. I'd come here now to let the place speak for itself, to bridge a gap of forty years.

A series of imposing châteaux and *maisons de maître* lined the road on the way towards the village centre. I passed a school, one or two hotels and small terraced houses, and as I pulled up on the place de l'Hôtel de Ville and switched off the engine, I heard the loud bells of Saint Vincent solemnly strike the midday hour: a double beat which lasted several seconds, then faded. There was no-one about. It was lunchtime and it seemed as if even the buildings were taking a siesta.

The place de l'Hôtel de Ville was just as my mother had described it. The church flanking the triangle of tree-lined gravel and the *mairie* at right angles opposite, a few hundred yards away. The mosaic patterning of its roof even more dazzling seen close up: zig-zagging lines of yellow, brown and green tiles, broken by occasional gabled windows and turrets. A mediaeval fortress when it was built and now the local government building, it stood tall and square, flying the tricolour from a flagpole over the central doorway. Even the swooping and darting of swallows nesting in the crevices of the building put me in mind of Auguste's photo taken in late summer 1938: *plus ça change, plus c'est la même chose.*

There was a small plaque on the tall railings in front of the *mairie* proving that by 1966 the French had learned how to laugh at the years of German occupation. The director Gerard Oury had shot the film *La Grande Vadrouille* here in the streets of Saultmur; he used this building as the *Kommandantur* in the film. The plaque stirred a distant memory in my mind of going to see the film in the Woolwich Odeon as a teenager. One Saturday we had decided to go to the matinée. Everyone was raving about it. 'Aren't you coming, Liz? Get your coat and bag then,' my father had said to my mother. She shook her head: 'No. There's too much on here, Sid. You two go ahead without me.'

When we came back home after the film, laughing again at the pompous lines of Terry Thomas as 'Big Moustache' and the hilarious parody of goose-stepping German soldiers, my mother refused to share the joke or answer our questions. 'How would you translate *vadrouille*, Mum? 'The Great Stroll' sounds a bit odd to me.'

She'd replied: 'I don't know that word, Vera.' Not to be put off, I pushed it further, asking her point blank: 'So what was it really like under the Germans, Mum? Give us some idea.' She stood up and left the room and Dad stepped in, as he always did on these occasions: 'Leave your mother alone. Let her sort the supper out.'

I got the message, allowed a dangerous moment to pass. No confrontation. No explanation. Silence.

*

The hot midday sun drove me to a table under the awning of a café on the rue de Lattre de Tassigny for a long, cold drink. Service was slow, but I was in no particular hurry.

The road name was not on my mother's map. It was another war reference: General de Lattre de Tassigny led the Allied army up through Provence in August 1944 to the Occupied Zone, liberating towns and villages as they went. As I sat here now, feeling the hot, settled peace of the town, I tried to picture the scene in this village and this street on the day of Liberation and after. Surely there was also grief and bitterness mingled with the relief and joy?

I left some francs next to my glass in payment and strolled off to take a look in the church of Saint Vincent. Glad to feel the rush of cool, musty air as I stepped inside, I was surprised how bright, airy and spacious it looked as sunlight streamed in through the tall windows. It struck me how solid and safe the building felt. This was where the Lemoine family had attended Mass every Sunday and on special feast days, where Jeanne came to polish the brasses and change the flower decorations. This was where the community gathered after Auguste's death. What about when Lily Lemoine disappeared? Had anyone remembered her in their prayers?

Leaving the church, I turned right and walked along its northern side, amused by the four stone gargoyles staring down open-mouthed at passers-by. I followed the rue de l'Eglise towards a stretch of grass where the war memorial stood at the far end, as noted on the sketch map. There was still a poppy wreath leaning against the base of the memorial, left from the 8 May celebrations I guessed, and as I stepped closer I could read the inscription at the base of the monument: '*A la gloire de Dieu et en souvenir durable des soldats saultmuriens*.' As I read the roll call of names for each of the World Wars, and noted the name *A. Lemoine* entered twice, the name of Antoine's brother, the original Auguste Lemoine, who had been killed in action in WWI and, in a separate list, the name of his son, Lily's brother Auguste. Loss and more loss.

I continued a circuit walk back towards the place de l'Hôtel de Ville along the narrow streets of *vigneron* houses, thinking about the Lemoine family losses. Antoine lost his brother, his son and even his daughter. What, finally, had happened to him? My walk was taking me closer and closer to my mother's family home, but despite the sketch map in front of me none of the road names seemed to match hers, none of the gateways or houses matched the photograph in her album.

Eventually I made my way along the road behind the

mairie. Ahead was the narrow sloping street which led back to the place de L'Hotel de Ville. I glanced up at the blue road sign fixed to the high wall on my left and the words stopped me in my tracks.

rue Antoine Lemoine (maire) – 1888-1943.

Chapter Forty-Nine: Investigation

Antoine's death aged 55 could have been from any number of causes: a heart attack from overwork perhaps. Or even suicide? One couldn't rule out these possibilities. There was a line of inquiry to follow. I needed more facts, eye-witnesses if at all possible, documentary evidence even. Where would I find all that in this sleepy old village?

The obvious first stop had to be the *mairie* itself. As luck would have it, the two-hour lunch break was at an end and I could see someone unbolting the entrance door as I paused by the tall, black iron gates in front of the building. I crossed the gravel yard and opened the door, stepping into a small reception area. The assistant had obviously not yet returned from lunch, but I could see on my left double doors into a larger office where several local government employees were working behind a counter.

I waited in a short queue, glad to think through the information I wanted to extract here. Eventually I stood face-to-face with a woman in her middle years, brown hair trimmed in a man's haircut and wearing heavy tortoiseshell glasses. She looked firm, unyielding. I started by claiming that I was a journalist researching a shortlist of wine producers from the thirties and forties. I showed her my NUJ card to give some proof of my identity. In particular I explained that I knew Antoine Lemoine had been a long-standing mayor in this period, also producer of several significant vintages. Perhaps there was some archive material I might be allowed to look at relating to his role as mayor and *vigneron*?

She nodded whilst I spoke and certainly appeared to be listening intently. I thought I saw some glimmer of recognition when I mentioned the Lemoine name. However, her first words in reply crushed any hopes I might have had of gaining access to archive material that day.

'Unfortunately, we do not keep records from that time in this office. All the archive material from this *mairie* was moved to Beaune during the sixties. I will ask my colleague whom you need to contact for further information.'

There followed a lengthy dialogue with another administrative assistant and some meaningful glances in my direction. I heard Antoine Lemoine's name mentioned, some mutual nodding of heads. Finally, she returned and handed me a slip of paper with the name of her counterpart in the Hôtel de Ville in Beaune, together with the contact number. I thanked her for her time, and we parted on good terms. As I left the building, I felt my hackles rise: surely among the books and files in this place there was some volume containing the dates and short biographies of former mayors who had served here?

Stepping out into the dazzling afternoon sunshine, I was quite uncertain what to do next, or where to go. The street sign had told me more than the employees of the *mairie* despite their air of bureaucratic self-importance. I suppose I had a contact in Beaune to follow up, but I didn't want to tangle yet with an even larger bureaucracy.

There had to be more leads. A few metres from where I was standing was the local Tourist Information Office. The door was open, so I made my way across the square and stepped into the small office, where I was greeted hospitably by a young man, dressed formally in shirt and tie and sitting on a high stool behind the counter. I picked up a street map before introducing myself to him, repeating more or less word for word the story I had just used in the *mairie*. When I showed him my NUJ card it sparked a completely different reaction this time. In stilted English he said: 'This is wonderful Miss, er, Walters. There is so much for you to see in our village and wine-tastings for you to try out. Our history is everywhere you look and we 'ave a leaflet 'ere all about the filming of '*La Grande Vadrouille*', this I think you will find very interesting. Many of our *vignerons* open their *caves* to visitors and please take this list to see who they are. They are also numbered carefully on the map you have there. They know the history of their own *domaines*, how do you say, like the back of their hands. You can speak to them.'

Yes. He was probably right about that. Chat to a few of the *vignerons*, the older the better. Surely, they would have some stories they could tell me, some snippets of information about the Domaine Lemoine?

Meanwhile he continued to talk very quickly, presenting me now with another glossy leaflet, urging me to book into one of the small hotels or *chambres d'hôte* in the area.

I took the leaflet and thanked him for his help. He had not responded to my opening question about the Domaine Lemoine and did not seem to have taken in my interest in this particular family name. Perhaps my own efforts at using the French language had fallen on deaf ears? I was still no further forward on my quest.

I supposed I had at least obtained a map that I could use to track down some of the landmarks mentioned in my mother's notebook. I found a bench to sit down whilst I unfolded the map and began planning a longer walk. I could see where the cemetery was marked near the edge of the village and a lane from there leading into the vineyards I had noted on my drive from Beaune.

The cemetery was a small and well-ordered site in the shadow of huge horse-chestnut trees in the nearby parkland. It was completely deserted and silent except for the birds. Ever since my mother and I had visited Highgate Cemetery together when I was still at school (I can't remember the pretext: history? English Literature?) I have made it my business to be a collector of graveyards.

WWI cemetery at Ypres, Père Lachaise in Paris and most recently and controversially the Bitburg cemetery in Germany, where over 2,000 German troops were buried along with 49 of Hitler's *Schützstaffeln*.

I wandered up and down the rows of graves, impressed by the huge, dignified marble memorials dedicated to particular families, several of their names made famous by their wine. Here was the evidence of a rooted community, generations upon generations of the same families remaining in this one place, dynastic alliances ensuring that the *patrimoine* remained in safe hands. So where were the Lemoines buried, and the Vannet family members?

The cemetery was L-shaped, there was some chronological order to it, and I noticed how the older graves were simpler, the stone inscriptions worn and effaced by the elements, and by moss and lichen. In this section I found the Vannet family memorial: it was a large tablet of cream-coloured stone with a listing of four generations of the family. The final couple named, with their dates, being Jeanne's parents. For sure, this inscription must have been commissioned by her. I now felt I was getting closer to the Lemoines, by implication at least.

On the far wall I noticed a large white-marble memorial engraved with vine leaves and bunches of grapes. It was glinting like silver in the bright July sunshine and the large lettering of the inscription was easy to read from where I was standing:

Antoine Lemoine (1888-1943) et Jeanne Lemoine

(1892-1943), qui furent tués par les allemands le 15 mars 1943. A leur mémoire.

Here in the glare of the sunlight of a beautiful July day came the confirmation. The ugly truth was staring me in the face: Antoine and Jeanne, shot by the Germans on 15th March 1943, had paid the ultimate price for Lily's assassination of the *Weinführer.*

Chapter Fifty: Dilemma

I stood rooted to the spot, reading and re-reading the words, trying to take hold of the significance of this savage event. Soon I wrenched myself away, finding some kind of comfort in the tokens of love relatives had left on nearby graves; small posies or larger bouquets of flowers wilting and fading in the hot summer sun. Near the exit was a standing pipe and several metal watering cans. Local people could tend the graves of their loved ones as part of the ritual of comfort which soothes grief.

On the spur of the moment I decided to return to the village to buy flowers for the Lemoine memorials. Two bouquets. I had noticed the florist near the *tabac* on the square. I took a different route back, passing the Château de Cîteaux on my left and some beautiful *maisons de maître* on my right, their small courtyard gardens colourful with pots of geraniums. Under the blue sky, in the warmth of the summer day and with the stunning beauty of the vineyards and gardens all around, I was trying to distance myself from the horrors of history, but it wasn't working.

Again and again, I was asking myself the question: so why did she leave? Why did she turn her back? Surely, she should have stayed put, taken the consequences of her own actions?

With a bunch of chrysanthemums in hand I returned to the cemetery and laid it near the Lemoine memorial, the bright yellow colour reflecting in the opaque marble. I remembered my mother's story of laying flowers for Auguste on a summer evening before driving away with her German lover singing *Lily Marlene* at the top of his voice. Death and love. Love and death. The cause and the effect of the peculiar legacy that had brought me to this place.

Afterwards I drove the car up through the vineyards to the monument of Saint Denis, parking it under the pine trees bordering the woodland area. The place was loud with bird song and the hum of bees pollinating the flowers and shrubs. I stood by the cream stone figure of the small saint, looking towards Saultmur. There it was, encircled by the vineyards planted by monks in the Middle Ages and tended in an unbroken line since then by the people of the area. Two world wars and the will power of an evil dictator had neither changed nor broken the patterns of the wine year. On that note why couldn't I leave now, and never go back?

*

The Hôtel de Ville in Beaune was already closed by the time I reached it, but instead I discovered the offices of *Le Bien Public,* the local Beaune newspaper, were a short walk from my hotel. It was nearing the end of the afternoon when I approached the young girl at the reception desk with my well-used spurious reason for wanting to delve into their archives: I was a British journalist writing an article for *Decanter* magazine on Burgundy vintage wines. Could I see the back copies of the newspaper between, say, 1935 and 1945? Here was my NUJ card.

She led me to an area at the back of the room where the shelves were filled with leather hard-bound copies of the newspaper, neatly organised in date order. Together we browsed the dates embossed prominently on the spines, only to find that the earliest date was 1950. For the years before this, it was a case of visiting the archive kept in the municipal library in Dijon.

Although it was late in the afternoon, there was still time to arrange a visit the next day. A call to the library should do the trick. Soon I was put through to an officious-sounding librarian in Dijon, who seemed to take smug pleasure in informing me that 'any inquiries to use our archive research facilities must be made in writing setting out your field of interest and the chronology you are following.' I was not used to this tedious red tape. I was much too impatient. I demanded to know if I bought the letter by hand to the library the next day, would they allow me to access the material. 'This might be possible, depending, of course, on the documents you need to locate.' Yes. I understood this and emphasised that I would be arriving at opening time the next day.

Despite my own impatience I had to admit that I'd covered plenty of ground in one day, so I sat down at a table at the place Carnot and was oddly grateful for the slow service. What was the hurry? Time to think. Put things in order.

The waiter brought the bottle of beer and a glass on a small oval tray and placed them in front of me, along with the bill. As I sipped the cool drink, I churned over the story of the death of Antoine and Jeanne Lemoine. The road name. The memorial in the cemetery. Wasn't it enough to know that their lives had ended in this cruel time? Just leave it at that. What else did I want to know? After all, this was not for some TV or radio report or a *Panorama* documentary. Why did I need to keep sorting through the rubble of the past, my mother's past, trying to make some kind of sense of it? Hermann had once told me he thought I should have been an archaeologist: 'You could have spent your days sifting through dust, V, and sometimes you would find some treasure. In your job you keep on sifting through so much dust, then what do you find? A few pebbles to fling at other people.' It struck me this time there was only one person I was flinging pebbles at: myself.

The next morning, I drove to Dijon and located the library in the mediaeval part of the city, ancient capital of the dukes of Burgundy. I had managed to persuade the receptionist at the hotel to let me use her electric typewriter to drum out the letter of introduction that I had brought along with me.

After a long wait at the tall, oak counter in the reading room of the library, the archivist I had spoken to emerged from his office. He was older than I had expected him to be and walked with a pronounced stoop. Taking the letter from me, he invited me to follow him into his small office, which was a picture of neatness and order. It took him some time to read my letter, but eventually he said 'I think we will have some material of interest to you. On microfiche, of course. You do realise that *Le Bien Public* ceased publication during the period of the Occupation?' I looked at him in stunned disbelief for a moment. Why had I come all this way if I had realised that?

'Do you have any public notices from that period, perhaps?' I saw him looking at me over the rim of his glasses. He was trying to weigh me up, or was he trying to test my tenacity? Whether he could throw me off the scent if he made things just too difficult for me?

'Very few, in fact. Any material published under the Germans is now in our war years' archives in Paris. I'm told the catalogue is still requiring completion. A big task.' He nodded. 'May I advise you to take a look at what we have in the months leading up to June 1940 and in the period following the Liberation? Some of it may be of interest. I will ask my assistant to bring the relevant microfiches to you and show you how the machines work.'

I thanked him and left his office, taking a place at the large reading table in the high-ceilinged room filled on all sides with tall bookcases. After what seemed an eternity, an assistant carrying two brown cardboard boxes came and led me into a small cubicle where there were four microfiche readers. He gave me a brief introduction, switched on the screen and then left me alone to work my way through the material. Hours later, I had found nothing of interest to my story. The visit had been a complete waste of time, but nevertheless I left contact details with the assistant in case anything relevant should surface in the future.

Back at the Hôtel de la Chasse, I raided the mini-bar for snacks and a glass or two of wine. Then I spent the rest of the evening stretched out on the bed watching a ragbag of British television programmes dubbed into French. I intended to leave on the earliest train the next morning and return to Bonn as soon as I could.

Chapter Fifty-Two: End Notes

As a journalist I had covered stories in war zones and trouble spots around the world, seen first-hand public buildings and private houses reduced to a pile of stones in one bomb blast. As the weeks went by after I returned to Bonn, I felt my memories of my mother were like those buildings: smashed, crushed, destroyed.

I found it difficult to concentrate. Only one news story could hold my attention at the moment, one that only I had an interest in. My mother's actions had caused her father and mother to lose their lives. She had got away. Nevertheless, in Saultmur, they had been faithfully commemorated, as had her brother Auguste. It looked as if the name of Lily Lemoine, however, had been erased from public memory. Almost as if she had never existed. The question facing me was what to do next? How to put the matter behind me and move on? In ten days' time I was due to return to work. I was dreading it.

Meanwhile the sale of my mother's house was moving ahead: the estate agent had called me to tell me there was keen interest and to ask my views on "gazumping". I told him I didn't really have any and the main aim was to sell the house as quickly as possible to whoever could meet the asking price. The next day he rang me to say a young couple were keen to buy it and were standing by ready to pay a deposit. I agreed that we should proceed with the sale without delay.

It was a relief to know the house and everything in it would soon be off my hands. It simplified matters, making me start to consider my own future. I had always resisted buying property, preferring to be a rolling stone, renting a flat here or bedsit there, refusing to put down roots. Perhaps it was time to change. To look at buying a flat in London, perhaps negotiating a career move back to the UK. I had plenty of options. For God's sake, I thought, at my age I ought to be fixing my sights on my own future instead of churning over my mother's past.

Some days later, and much to my surprise, a letter arrived from the library in Dijon, informing me that their archivist had uncovered a box of documents relating to 1944. Would I like to arrange to see them? I telephoned immediately and arranged a visit to the library later that week.

The lately discovered box contained documents and local newspapers dated from September 1944. In no time, I discovered a special monthly edition of the *Bien Public* newspaper containing obituaries and news stories from the years of the German Occupation. Flicking through a late October copy, I stumbled with a mixture of relief and trepidation on the obituary of Antoine Lemoine, my grandfather, containing the details of his career, his family history and the story of his assassination of Karl Futtermann in January 1943.

Next to a photograph of Antoine and Jeanne Lemoine, the paper had published a thumbnail portrait photograph showing a German officer in full cap and uniform decorated with the brash insignia of his rank. I stared at the face in front of me for several minutes, studying the confident, serious gaze of this man. My mother's lover. His face was well-rounded, fleshy even, with the look of the *bon viveur*, the gourmet and fine-wine expert. His sharp, humorous eyes were looking into mine: *'Doch Lily, mein Liebling, ich liebe dich.'* How could she have killed him?

The obituary contained a substantial news report of the case.

Karl Futtermann was found murdered in a vineyard near Saultmur in January 1943. He had been missing for one full day. His Mercedes-Benz car was discovered abandoned near the Saint Denis monument. After combing the nearby woods, the search party of German soldiers scoured the vineyards close to the village of Saultmur. They found Futtermann's body in a cabotte situated in a premier cru clos. In a stream a short distance away they discovered the murder weapon, a small Browning handgun. Antoine and Jeanne Lemoine, the owners of the clos, were detained for questioning.

I spooled through the rest of the article, which concluded:

Antoine Lemoine, mayor of Saultmur, and his wife Jeanne, along with other members of their household and workforce were all were put to death by firing squad at 10.00 a.m. on 15th March 1943. The event took place in the square, in front of the mairie.

The German military authorities had found them guilty of conspiracy to murder and carrying out the assassination of Karl Futtermann, whose body was found in the Lemoine clos. Le Bien Public *understands that Antoine Lemoine had, in fact, admitted to the crime himself hoping, in vain, thereby to prevent any further killings.*

Antoine Lemoine is remembered by his community as a devoted public servant and a brilliant innovator and wine producer. The ending of his life still sends shock waves through the village he loved.

Chapter Fifty-Three: The Final Visit

The brilliant morning sunshine temporarily blinded me as I left the municipal library in Dijon. Driving back towards Beaune, I replayed in my mind the scene of the German shooting of Antoine, Jeanne and their servants. In my mind's eye I saw the *mairie* with the zig-zag pattern of the roof tiles towering above the ghastly grouping below. At ground level I imagined the backs of a crowd of villagers in front of the *mairie*: an elderly man with a young child perched high on his shoulders, a woman with her face cupped in her hand, an old lady, hair tied back in a bun, brandishing her fist in front of her. Finally, after the crack of bullets from the firing squad, the bodies of Antoine and Jeanne, Josephine and Marthe and others besides, lying covered in blood, on the cobbled street of the square.

If I had one last task remaining it was to find anyone who could still remember that day. One more journey back to Saultmur.

The white vans of the *vignerons* dotted the hillside on my right as I drove through the chain of villages: Chenôve,

Gevrey Chambertin, Nuits Saint Georges. Another day for the workers in the vines, trimming and tying the stems. Checking the bunches of grapes. Removing any blight. I drove on, looking forward to skirting Beaune and following the bends in the road towards the tall retaining wall after the Volnay turning, the now-familiar, knotted steeple and the tall, thin *mairie* building alongside it with its roof of yellow and green stripes. The mixture of châteaux and barn conversions, terraced houses and *maisons de maître* sculpted into the bowl of the emerald green hillside sloping down from the Hautes Côtes.

One last visit.

I had arranged with the Tourist Information Office a one-night stop in the village. When I arrived, I discovered an astonishing location: a *vigneron's* house three storeys high, at least, with steeply-raked roof turreted and decorated with coloured tiles in the local style. I stopped the car at the set of lofty metal gates and had to tug at a rusty old bell-pull to announce my arrival. I heard footsteps and saw the gates opened by the owner, Madame Tricot. I guessed she was about fifty, dyed brown hair cropped neatly and carefully styled. She wore face powder and make-up which emphasised her bright and good-humoured brown eyes. She gestured to me to park the car near the others on the gravel drive.

We shook hands as I took my case from the car and followed her into the hallway of the house. She talked non-stop, blending commands with snippets of information.

'This has been the Tricot family home for over a hundred years, but it is too big for us. Far too big. My sister lived with us in that part there,' she said, gesturing to a small stable block on the left hand side, 'that was after her husband died. Now it's just Henri and I: our children have grown up, married and moved on. There are too many empty rooms.'

Inside, the house had a faded grandeur about it: high ceilings and rooms and a hallway furnished with large, heavy pieces of antique furniture and fittings. Madame Tricot led me up a broad staircase from the hall and into the first bedroom we came to.

'Put your case down here.' She gestured to a luggage stand near a large pedestal sink. 'Have a look from this window.'

I stepped over to a tall double-casement window that had a view sweeping across the hillside towards Auxey Duresses and Monthélie. Close to the house were rows of vines, each row planted at the head with a pink rose bush, and there was a man in blue overalls clipping at the wild stems with a pair of secateurs. I could hear the high-pitched sound of many birds calling and chattering and I noticed swallows circling and swooping towards the eaves here at the back of the house.

'May I offer you some coffee, perhaps? Bread and cheese also?' I admitted I was starving and agreed to join her downstairs.

The slow pace of this place was throwing me off my

course, turning me into a passive listener. I felt I should introduce myself. Make more of an impact.

Downstairs in the stately dining room, served with a small cup of coffee and a plate of bread and cheese, I asked my first question.

'I'm gathering information about vintage Burgundy wines for an article for a wine magazine, Madame Tricot. Have you ever heard of the wines produced by the Domaine Lemoine? I understand they were famous before the war? Somewhere I've read that even the Prince of Wales at the time enjoyed ordering cases of it?'

'You won't find anyone round here who hasn't heard of the Lemoine wines. Some of us still have a few cases of it in our cellars to this day.'

I had not expected this kind of instant familiarity. 'Can you tell me how this happened? That the cases of Lemoine wine were dispersed throughout the village?' I was trying to pick my way carefully towards the heart of the matter.

She frowned and shook her head. 'It was wartime when it happened. During the German Occupation. I was only a child, about eight years of age. My parents were hard-working people. My father worked in the mustard factory and, like everyone, we kept livestock and grew a few crops to feed the family. Our house in those days was just on the rue des Ecoles, near the place de l'Hôtel de Ville there.'

I nodded to encourage her to carry on.

'My father used to help out in the Lemoine vineyards during the *vendanges;* all our family did, in fact. To earn a few francs. Money was short in those days and during the war we got by with *le troc,* you know, exchanging goods for goods instead of money. Antoine Lemoine paid my father in cases of wine rather than money during the harvests in those years. And he trusted him. He was the mayor. Some people didn't, though. They turned against him in those war years. Called him a collaborator. My father never did. He stood by him to the end. That's why he and a handful of others in the town were given many cases the night the Lemoine cellars were emptied.'

Her tone of voice had changed. She stopped smiling.

'How did that come about, the emptying of the Lemoine cellars?'

'It's a very long story and we don't like telling it round here. It never does anyone any good. What happened was really terrible. Someone assassinated a German officer in one of the Lemoine *clos.* It was January 1943. Tensions were high. The German military were ferocious and pinned the blame on Antoine Lemoine and his wife. When he knew the authorities were on to him, Antoine called on about five friends he could trust, my father was one of them, to help him empty his cellars in the dead of the night. Otherwise the Germans would have had it all. As you can imagine, there are very few cases left now and that wine fetches a huge price at auction.'

'So what happened to the Lemoine couple?'

'I was only a child at the time, as I told you. This may not be accurate, but it's what I know. They were both interrogated about the murder and arrested shortly afterwards. My father always said that the Germans were reluctant to touch Antoine because he was a good man, popular with everyone. Some of the locals had taken against him during the Occupation for doing well out of the Germans. But what could he do? His wine was good. If they wanted it, they could have it. Simple as that.'

'What finally happened?'

'There were two public executions in March 43, Antoine and Jeanne went in front of the firing squad outside the *mairie*. Others were put to death up in the pine woods. I don't know who they were. It was a terrible time.'

'I'm sorry.' The words sounded completely inept. What could I say? I needed to move her on, to get away from those dark times. Back to the wine.

'On a lighter note, have you ever tried one of the Lemoine wines yourself?' She smiled and nodded at the question.

'My father used to open a bottle and share it with his memories on the anniversary of Antoine's execution. When we remember, we do the same. His Pinot Noir keeps very well. Sometimes old wine turns to vinegar, especially Chardonnays, but not this. If you want to know anything else, you should really go round and speak to old Monsieur Santot.'

When I heard that name I thought what an incredible

piece of luck. I hadn't expected anyone closely involved in my mother's story still to be alive. I feigned ignorance.

' Did he personally know the Lemoines?'

'Yes. He was an old family friend. He lives in the rue des Plantes, and of course he's very elderly. You'll need to raise your voice a bit because he's hard of hearing. But he's still all there.'

A few minutes later I stood at the gates to Charles Santot's house, Lily's album bulky in my shoulder bag. I pressed the buzzer on the gatepost. There was a distant sound of a shrill ringing, but no-one came. Stuck out on a limb at the front of the building was a pencil-shaped tower with double doors at its base – an odd gothic structure, some sort of replacement for the double stairway more usual in these houses. I could see the top of a tall cedar tree in the back garden and heard the loud chatter of birds. Somewhere there was the sound of an engine rumbling.

I pressed the buzzer a second time. Silence. I felt an irresistible urge to call out: 'Is anybody there?' As I was turning away, I heard the lock being turned in the front door of the tower and saw the handle swivelling round. An elderly gentleman, small in height, stepped out. He was dressed smartly in jacket and trousers and wore a white t-shirt. He reminded me of Picasso: youthful even in his eighties.

'Monsieur Santot?' I called to him, a bit too loudly, through the bars of the gate. He looked carefully at me with his sharp brown eyes and I noticed he was almost completely bald. Then he pulled back the latch on the big gates and opened them to let me through.

We shook hands. 'Madame Tricot has advised me to speak to you if I may.'

I gave him the spiel about being a journalist and writing an article for *Decanter*; even to me, it was starting to ring false. He asked me in and I followed him up a spiral staircase and into a remarkable circular room with book-lined walls, smelling strongly of tobacco.

'Please sit down, Mademoiselle Walters. Fire away.' He settled himself in a leather club chair and lit a pipe, watching me fixedly all the time with those bright eyes. I felt tongue-tied. Phoney. Maybe it was time to put my cards on the table? To cut a long story short?

'I'm tracing the history of a few Burgundy vintages. In particular I'm interested in the wines of the Domaine Lemoine, which were fashionable, I believe, before the war? Mme Tricot has told me the reasons for this and advised me that you are the real specialist in the matter.'

He appeared to be quite distracted by his pipe, pressing the tobacco down firmly with the yellow tip of his left index finger, then drawing on it, making loud noises with his mouth.

'I suppose I know more than most in this place: I go back a long way, you could say! When I was a young engineer in my twenties I helped Antoine Lemoine modernise his business and we became firm friends. If it's the wine you're interested in, young woman, follow me!'

He led me back down the spiral staircase which drilled beneath ground level to a huge wine cellar ranked, it seemed, in date order, starting at 1930. He led me round a labyrinth of racks, eventually returning to our starting point.

'No-one around here has a wine cellar like this, I may say! Latest technology installed to modulate the temperatures very precisely. Perfect lighting also. No barrels here. Only bottles and thousands of them! I was an awkward bugger, you see. Refused to follow my father and become a wine-grower: that's what Antoine did. No. Me? I wanted to be an engineer, an inventor. Spent my career in Paris but kept this place on. Burgundy's my home but Paris is my love, I suppose we could say.' He looked at me knowingly, and chuckled.

'What would you like to try, mademoiselle? Rosé, rouge, blanc? Antoine made all three, but it was his red that made the grade. Want to try some?'

Strolling over to his 1930s stack, he pulled out a dusty bottle. Using his jacket sleeve, he cleared away the dust and then levered the base of the bottle towards me so that I could read the label: *Antoine Lemoine et Fils – 1938*. He deftly slipped the bottle back into its slot and led me back towards our starting point.

'On second thoughts I'll find a more recent vintage for you to try, mademoiselle.' Saying this he picked a bottle from an open wooden crate near the stairs. 'Produced using grapes from the *clos Lemoine* under a *Rossiteau* label.' Taking hold of the neck of the bottle he cut open the foil with the tip of the corkscrew and then masterfully extracted the cork. With an elegant gesture he held the mouth of the bottle under his nose.

'Mmm. No putridity. Can be a problem with wines old or new. Here. You try!'

He pushed the bottle under my nose. I laughed, trying to catch the odour, but could only detect the scent of caulk mixed with wine.

'Now I put two glasses ready. So.' He placed two tasting glasses next to the open bottle. 'We return upstairs for a few more questions while we allow the wine to breathe a bit.'

*

'So, young woman. Another question while we wait, maybe?' We were back upstairs, M. Santot had relit his pipe and settled in his chair.

'What do you think made the Lemoine wines so special at the time?'

'I think we are talking about his wines in the mid-thirties. Antoine knew his *terroir* like no other at the time. He limped. He had to move slowly. He missed nothing when he tended the vines or directed the harvesting of the grapes. Then in the cellar he was experimental: he listened to new ideas, tried them out, sometimes took them on board and sometimes rejected them. One of his tricks: keeping some of the wines in their lees for longer than a year. Two years sometimes. Too long, some would say. Then no filtration. He broke the rules. It worked!' He gestured enthusiastically with his pipe. His eyes sparkled.

'1938 was a very good year for Lemoine wine, nevertheless. I had my doubts about the new *clos* for the *pinot noir* grapes he made so much fuss over. Not a patch on his other *parcelles* if the truth be told. Cost a sheer fortune and debateable whether he ever got it back. I kept my mouth shut, of course. He wanted his Lemoine arch. He got it. And the *cabotte* with it. Yes. But they brought him bad luck. No question.' He drew on his pipe, seemed lost for words for a time.

'After 1938 I would say things started to go downhill: the call-up, the Occupation and then the tragic death of Auguste, his only beloved son. You've heard all that from Mme Tricot I expect?'

I nodded.

'Let's see about that wine. Not nearly long enough but at my age you can't sit around waiting for things!'

He got up stiffly this time, taking the stairs more carefully on the way down. Once in the cellar again, he half-filled each glass and handed one to me. As I sipped, I saw him watch me carefully, testing me out.

'Well. What do you say about that?' He stood, still swirling the wine around his glass, then tossing it into his mouth, and savouring it for a few moments before spitting it out in the stainless steel bucket on the counter.

'A very elegant wine, I would say. I can taste some notes of hazelnut and fruitiness. Delicious.' But I knew he had caught me out.

'Let me fill your glass one more time, like this.' And he filled the glass to the brim. 'This time you must carry it back upstairs and I will ask *you* some questions.' He spoke with a tone of firmness he hadn't used before. Even anger.

*

'I am old, Miss Walters.' He started in English then moved on to French. 'But I am not stupid. You have come here to ask me some questions. You say you are researching vintage wines for *Decanter* wine magazine? So, I would expect you to have some knowledge already concerning the tasting and the commenting on wine. Just now you showed me you have almost none: you made no effort to swill the wine around your glass, even to smell it. Then you just gulped it down without giving all sides of your palate the chance to taste it. After that you came out with the kind of comment you probably found in Robert Parker. And you thought you could take me in? You, *mademoiselle,* are no connoisseur of fine wines. So, who, may I ask, are you?'

Disarmed so suddenly, I didn't know what to say. There was only one way out: to tell him the truth. As a first step I took out the photograph album and showed him the picture of himself with the gramophone and Auguste.

'*Tiens! Mon dieu!* Where did you get this album?

These photographs?' He took it from me and started to skip through the pages.

'Yes, 1938-40. Auguste took most of these with his Leica – a very good camera, which I advised him to buy. Excellent lens. German, of course. Yes, I recognise all these old faces. In the cemetery now. No-one left here except me. So how did Lily's album come into your hands, may I ask?'

It took me several minutes to relate to him the circumstances of my mother's death and the discovery of the album and notebooks and other items. I pulled out the transcript I had made and handed it to him to look through.

'I see it is all in English and mine is very poor. I would need a translation.' He handed it back to me, after which he appeared lost in thought and barely seemed to be listening to what I was telling him. When I had finished speaking, he said 'You are just like your mother, same lovely eyes, and a similar voice. But you are older than her at that time. Different hairstyle; not quite so pretty if you don't mind my saying!' He paused.

'She was the love of my life, you know. I said to her father that night, after Auguste's coming of age: "Antoine. Let me marry Lily. I will make her happy. I am rich and she can have a splendid flat in Paris and a house here in Saultmur. She will want for nothing." But he was stubborn; he said: "Charles, you old devil! Think of your age! Let her find a young man for a husband. If she marries you, she'll be a widow for half her life!" He was wrong. Very wrong. What did she go and do soon after that? She fell in love with the wrong man, at the wrong time in the wrong place. That is my humble opinion. Only met him once, the *Weinführer.* Like all Third Reich officers he had a very high opinion of himself, I should say. But apart from his uniform he was, I believe, a decent fellow. Good looking, athletic even. People liked him because he played fair. Seemed to understand them, you see. He had a difficult role. Very tall, blond of course, and you could see when he looked at her that she meant the world to him. At that moment anyway! *Amor vincit omnia.*' He paused, shook his head. Eyes misty with tears. We sat in silence for a while. He seemed to be burrowing into the recesses of his memory, to a painful place.

'The last time I saw her was completely by chance. In Paris, would you believe! November 1942. Caught sight of her on the Pont d'Iéna, peering over the parapet looking as if she might jump! I called to her and she turned to look my way. When I came up close, I was shocked. Her eyebrows were plucked. Thick face powder and rouge. Bright red lips. Smart suit but so, so thin. Like a skeleton. I took her straight to a restaurant, tried to feed her up a bit and that's when I noticed her poor hands. Fingers chapped and worn. The nails broken, unkempt. Knuckles red and chafed. She tried to hide it from me, but I don't miss a trick: the engagement ring. A ridiculous, showy thing, sparkling so much you couldn't keep your eyes off it!' The spell-binding diamond edelweiss. Who could miss it?

'I wasn't born yesterday. Guessed immediately what she was here for: a secret assignation. What a joke! It turns out everyone knew where she was and with whom. You can't have secrets in a village like this. Impossible!'

He seemed to gaze into the distance as if calling up those days physically. Several minutes went by before he spoke again.

'When she got back the knives were out for her in no uncertain terms. She was trapped in a situation she could not get out of, so she acted irrationally, out of sheer desperation.' He said no more and several minutes passed before he stood up and crossed the room to a cabinet from which he took a set of very old keys.

'Come with me,' he said, leading me down the spiral staircase and then out onto the courtyard: the sunlight was blinding after the dim interior and it was very hot. M. Santot walked over to the gate and opened it to let me through.

'Let me explain something. After my parents died, I was away working in Paris so I made sure Antoine had my spare set of keys to keep an eye on this house. Storms and floods: you have to be alert to those in these parts. When we could see the war coming, he gave me his spare set too: these.' And he rattled them to make his point. 'After Auguste's death during the war, he said to me one day: "I'll never leave this bloody place, Charles, but if you outlast me, you better look after it. And the vines. You sort it all out when the time comes. I know you will see to it that Lily gets her share." Being Antoine, he did that job properly. Saw the *notaire*, same as mine in the rue de Lorraine in Beaune, made a proper will, which of course is still kept there.'

We were reaching the crossroads at the end of the rue des Plantes. The road to our right climbed gently up towards the vineyards, but we continued straight ahead of us along the rue des Charrons.

'I tried to trace her, Lily, you know. After the war and the madness of the Liberation was over. I hired a private detective who charged me a fortune. All he found out was that she had worked for the *Croix Rouge* in Switzerland, then the trail went dead after that.' He turned and looked at me. 'It was as if she had vanished. She was recorded as a missing person by the *notaire* and that is when the Lemoine vines, and house came into my possession. Of course, I have hung on to them, done what Antoine asked me to do. Round here there was no difficulty parcelling out the vines, but the house has been another matter. You must understand that.'

The road curved gently ahead and, keeping the vineyards on our right, we carried on walking. I could see the clearing near the crest of the hill with the statue of Saint Denis and the dark green woodland of the Mont des Mélèzes behind. The hillside was densely planted with vines, each one carefully trimmed and tied to the taut wire frames. Dotted through the walled *clos* were the dry-stone wall huts. Here was the beginning and the ending of my mother's story, which she had never dared to tell. She had tried to be another person in another place when all the time this was where her roots were, where she truly belonged.

We had reached a junction, the point at which the rue de Genevrières climbed steeply towards the centre of the village with the spire of Saint Vincent and the *mairie* clearly visible up ahead. Monsieur Santot stopped in his tracks.

'That hill is too steep for this old man and I must say "*au revoir*". Just one more thing that you should know: I made every effort to forget Lily, but never succeeded. I believed, if she was still alive, that she would want to come back. You can leave this place, you know, but it will never leave you. That is why I've hung onto the Lemoine property all these years, waiting for her to return. Of course, I could have sold it many times over. No shortage of offers.'

Taking out the keys without ceremony, he handed them to me with instructions of where to find the house. Then we parted.

The keys were heavy in my hand as I made my way up the hill. I thought of the evening of Auguste's twenty-first birthday, when he and Lily ran up this road in the pouring rain on that May evening, Antoine limping behind them. Turning right at the top of the street, I saw the sign of the Domaine Lemoine on the tall gate post. The paint on the gates was cracked and flaking, the RV monogram still visible. I slipped the key into the lock and turned it anti-clockwise; with a twist of the handle and a slight push, I felt the catch slide open.

About the Author

Ann Kronbergs lives with her husband in Suffolk, but at the time of writing *Diamond Edelweiss* she was working as a teacher in Brussels, spending several weeks each year in a village in Burgundy world famous for its Chardonnay wines and its remarkable hidden histories.

Since returning to the UK she has written and researched articles and reviews for magazines and literary journals.

About the Book

In imagining Lily Lemoine I drew upon the life story of my Latvian mother-in-law who worked as a stenographer during World War II when her office building in Daugavpils, Latvia, was requisitioned by the Wehrmacht as their operational Headquarters in the town. One of the German officers, later taken prisoner by the Red Army, fell in love with her and, during their short affair, he gave her a series of precious gifts, including an engagement ring in the form of an asymmetric edelweiss flower formed by tiny seed diamonds grouped around a sapphire stone. This glittering item gave me the germ for this story.

Saultmur is a fictional village as are the characters who live there, but I'm hoping readers, familiar or unfamiliar with the Côte d'Or in Burgundy, will get a feel for an actual place, gradually discovering the contours of the landscape and a part of its history.

About the Cover

Stefan Proudfoot of *Spiffing Covers* designed the cover, including the image of the German officer by kind permission of Dan Gilberti from his collection of World War II Burgundy photographs.

Acknowledgements

Thanks: firstly to Ziggi, editor-in-chief, historical consultant, literary adviser all rolled into one; to Sue who was there from the start to the finish, always with wisdom and encouragement; to the judges of *Good Housekeeping* magazine's First Novel competition 2012 who Highly Commended the first 5,000 words and made me think it was worth keeping going; to members of the Brussels Writers Circle for their insights on work in progress; to Alison for rambles through the Burgundian vineyards with our dogs, the late and great Oscar and Lily; to Laura and colleagues at the British School of Brussels who gave the story air time; to Kathy for her invaluable enthusiasm and editorial input; to Frances for her intelligent reflections and Jo for her searching feedback; to Julian who reminded me that a story can't live in a vacuum and must have an audience to survive. Finally, love and thanks to Klara, Bruno and Jenny Kronbergs, my IT, Social Media and Marketing dream team who have helped my #lockdown novel move out into the world.

www.cabottepress.co.uk

Printed in Great Britain
by Amazon

43227032R00220